Read

Merry* *quietly raised herself to look down on Gage, asleep, then lowered her head to kiss his parted lips.

Having to lie so close to him in the plane's cabin, she felt the heat of his breath, felt his heartbeat under her palm. With one last glance at the sleeping man, she admitted that if things had been different, if the world had been normal when they'd met, there could be more between them.

She stopped that foolishness in its tracks. No, not with him. There could never be anything other than friendship, no matter what she felt. Once they were rescued, he'd leave Wolf Lake and she'd stay. Simple. And this would merely be a memory.

But for now, they were here, together, and she'd hold on to him until it was time for her to let go.

Dear Reader,

The popular wisdom is "You can't go home again."
Sometimes your heart takes you where your heart needs
to be. In *Flying Home,* Gage Carson, the youngest of the
Carson brothers of Wolf Lake, thinks he's going home
for a short visit to help his family, but doesn't know the
trip is going to be the most important one of his life.

Merry Brenner needs to get back to Wolf Lake, and even
though she returned to the town alone, it's home–and
the only way to get there this time is on Gage's company
plane. Gage and Merry are unaware that an unseen
detour looms in their path, which they'll have to take
before they are finally home…in Wolf Lake and in their
hearts….

I hope you enjoy their journey where they find out you
can not only go home, but you can find a love that will
make "going home" complete and perfect.

Best wishes,

Mary Anne Wilson

HARLEQUIN HEARTWARMING

Mary Anne Wilson

Flying Home

HARLEQUIN® HEARTWARMING™

Recycling programs
for this product may
not exist in your area.

ISBN-13: 978-0-373-36682-8

FLYING HOME

Printed in U.S.A.

www.Harlequin.com

MARY ANNE WILSON

is a Canadian transplanted to Southern California, where she lives with her husband, three children and an assortment of animals. She knew she wanted to write romances when she found herself rewriting the great stories in literature, such as *A Tale of Two Cities*, to give them happy endings. Over her long career she's published more than thirty romances, had her books on bestseller lists, been nominated for Reviewer's Choice Awards and received a career nomination in romantic suspense.

Books by Mary Anne Wilson

HARLEQUIN HEARTWARMING

HARLEQUIN AMERICAN ROMANCE

The Carsons of Wolf Lake

For Linda Wisdom,
BFF who was there at the beginning
and stuck around for the ride!
Thanks for everything.

CHAPTER ONE

HOME.

All Merry Brenner wanted to do was get home, but with a sinking heart, she realized that wasn't going to happen any time soon. In skinny jeans, suede boots, an oversized red sweater, and her hands full with her meager luggage and purse, she stood off to one side of the crowded customer service desk at the airport.

Even though she'd flown all over the world with her mother and stepfather, who was an officer in the Air Force, she hated flying. She was a white knuckle flier at best, and after the rough unscheduled landing in Pueblo, Colorado, due to a "situation," she was totally on edge.

Right now, she should be collecting her baggage at the carrousel in Santa Fe, New Mexico, where she thought she'd end her trip. Instead here she was, staring at the four at-tendants at the long counter giving every displaced passenger the same company line. "We do apologize for this inconvenience." No mention of cars sitting in long term parking lots that were not going to be picked up, or loved ones waiting for them on the other end.

"Unfortunately, due to mechanical problems with your original plane, we have had to downsize to a smaller carrier." That really meant, "You're out of luck, unless you're one of the chosen few who'd managed to finagle a seat on that alternate carrier." Followed by what the company probably thought was a generous offer. "Of course, you can be put on standby for the other flights out to Santa Fe."

There were two, and both had filled up immediately by displaced passengers. "Or there is a flight departing for Santa Fe…" Her hopes had risen when she'd heard that. "…at eight-fifty-two tomorrow with a five hour stopover in Denver." Just where she didn't want to be. "Arrival time in Santa Fe at seven-thirty tomorrow evening."

Merry had put her name on all the lists, but still refused to accept the fact that there was no feasible way to get out of here tonight. Turning away in a huff, she didn't bother to stick around to listen to their very generous offer of, "Admittance to the flight lounge that has WiFi, along with a complimentary voucher for a meal at the only restaurant in the terminal, and a coupon for fifty percent off your next flight anywhere in the contiguous states."

She lugged her things toward a row of hard plastic chairs that overlooked the runways, and dropped everything at her feet. Then she sank down into the nearest chair and forced herself to stay calm.

All she had to do was get to Wolf Lake, New Mexico, a small town where tourists migrated to in the summer. In the winter it was a stop off for skiers before they headed farther north to the popular resorts higher in the mountains.

It was her home. It was where she'd moved six months ago, coming back after twenty years to settle there, to start a new job. Landing that position at The Family Center, to aid in the development of children who needed the help and guidance of a trained psychologist, had seemed like a dream come true for her. Because the truth was, she'd wanted to return to Wolf Lake from the moment her mother and stepfather had spirited her off to the first of many military posts they would relocate to over the years. Now she was back, or *had* been back, until she'd gone out of town for that three-day child development seminar in Chicago.

Swiping an errant strand of auburn hair off her cheek, she stared straight ahead on the concourse, barely noticing the people milling about in search of their flights. She was sitting still, but her mind was going a mile a minute trying to think of any way to get out of Pueblo and on her way back home. She'd already checked the car rentals, which had none available, and even asked at the charter counter, but immediately gave up that idea when she heard what it would cost. It was far beyond *anything* she could manage on the modest salary she earned from The Family Center.

The kids. She shook her head. They'd never understand that she'd broken her promise. Never. She'd told them she was going away to a conference for a few days, and that had been a bit upsetting for most of them. However, for Erin, a six-year-old girl, who was so small she could have passed for four years old, it had hit hardest. The child had stared at her intently, then thrown her arms around Merry's legs and hugged Merry so tightly that it was almost painful.

Erin was alone in the world, her mother

dead, her father serving a life term in prison.
The girl with a wild mass of brilliant red curls,
and pale, freckled skin, seldom talked. And
she hadn't uttered a word then, just moaned
softly until Merry had settled her down. The
promise she'd made to all the children, she
made again to Erin privately. "Three days and
nights, then I promise I'll be back before you
have to leave with Mrs. Harper."

Maybe the child heard the honest intent of
those words and trusted her, or maybe she just
gave up. But either way, that promise would
mean nothing now, not unless Merry could
make good on it. The urgency in her to get
home grew stronger and drove her to her feet..
Her kids, including Erin, didn't understand
excuses. She couldn't afford to let them down.
Her kids had special needs in varying degrees,
but their foremost need was being able to de-
pend on people close to them.

Merri looked around, frustrated, but still
not giving up. She was proactive, as one of
her college professors had pointed out without exactly saying that was a good thing. But
she thought it was, so on impulse, canvased
the other passengers stuck in the terminal in
an attempt to see if she could secure one of
their seats if they weren't in a hurry. But, once

again, she hit a brick wall. It seemed everyone diverted here wanted to get out as soon as possible. She looked around the main terminal, at the throngs of passengers going in and out of the souvenir and snack shops, checking out kiosks and generally killing time until the boarding call for their flights came over the PA system.

Merry was part of that same crowd, but unfortunately, she was not going to get any announcement in her favor anytime soon. Pacing restlessly around the concourse, she wound up back at the service desk for the airline again. Thankfully, most of the other passengers had been dealt with, and there were only a handful of people near the counters now.

"One more time," she muttered to herself as she headed to the end of a line fronted by an anxious-looking young man, followed by an elderly couple. The young man abruptly pushed away from the counter, calling back over his shoulder, "Thanks for nothing," as he stomped off. The couple moved to the desk, leaving Merry alone in the line. The gentleman spoke quietly to the agent, his tone polite, but his words indistinguishable. The elderly lady suddenly raised her voice to say, "But we have to get a flight out of here now!" Her voice took on a soft, plaintive whine as she turned toward the man beside her. "Ashford, tell this lady we have to get back to Los Angeles."

The gentleman nodded, dropping an arm around his companion's shoulders, and he spoke to the agent again in a louder voice. "Madam, this is not acceptable. We have opera tickets that are impossible to procure, and now you're telling me that there will be two empty seats in the hall this evening! Unacceptable, totally unacceptable." He narrowed his eyes at her. "Who is your supervisor?"

"Andrew Davison," the agent said, and directed them to his office before adding, "I hope Mr. Davison can do something to help you."

With a shake of his head, the gentleman walked off with his lady, and the path was finally clear for Merry to get to the desk. Hi," she said, hating the tightness in her voice as she forced a jittery smile at the agent whose name tag read *Alice Z.* "I need to get home, and arriving there tomorrow evening isn't an option."

April Z, a stunningly attractive blonde, looked a bit frayed from dealing with all those displaced passengers, but that polite smile remained. "I'm so sorry, but there are no open seats on the flights out to Los Angeles right now."

Merry stopped her. "I'm trying to get to Santa Fe. My original plane was going to go on to L.A., but I was getting off in Santa Fe."

"Oh," the woman said, but that information didn't change her demeanor one bit. "I can put you on standby for a flight to Santa Fe if you like? Or do you have a medical emergency, family crisis, or any other compelling reason that you have to be on a flight now?"

Alice Z. looked at her expectantly, but Merry knew that no one would think that her reason for needing to get home would be compelling to anyone except her. "Um…no, nothing like that."

With what looked like real disappointment, the pretty blonde turned to the nearest computer screen, tapped it with a slender finger, then said, "Your last name?"

"Brenner."

"Ah, yes, here you are. I can get you out on a flight out in the morning."

"I already heard that. It goes to Denver first, then a five hour layover before it gets to Santa Fe tomorrow evening."

"Then apparently you know what I know," the agent said with a sigh.

"I just have to get home," she reiterated desperately. "There has to be some way to do that and get there by tonight. It isn't that far."

April Z. turned back to the computer screen, taking several moments scrolling the information, then reached behind her for a swivel chair and dropped down in it before turning back in Merry's direction. "I usually love my job," she muttered, "but right about now..."

As her words trailed off, Merry found herself in the position of showing a degree of sympathy. "I know. You've done your best."

The woman spread her hands. "This airport is not huge, and we just do not have the kind of resources that the other main airports have." She hesitated. "Believe me, if I had any way to get you on an alternative flight or get you a rental car, I would. Or arrange a charter, even."

"Charters are out of the question," Merry said quickly.

"It's pretty important you get home, isn't it?"

"I'm supposed to be home today, by the evening at the latest. I know that's the same song and dance that you're hearing from all the passengers, but I've got a promise I need to fulfill to my kids."

She saw April's eyes soften slightly. "You have children?"

"Oh, no, at least, not my own. I'm a child psychologist and I'm on a grant at The Family Center in a small reservation town northeast of Santa Fe called Wolf Lake."

"I've heard of it," April said with a nod.

"The children I work with are challenged by their limitations and by their lives. I had to be at a seminar the past few days, but when I left, I promised them I would be back today before they went home." She picked up her bags and released a heavy sigh. "I never thought about this happening, but I'll figure this out, some-way. Thanks for trying."

"Sure, and good luck," April Z. said, then called after her, "If I find anything at all, I'll page you, okay?"

"Thanks," she replied as she headed away from the counter. She felt exhausted, not to mention disgruntled that even though she'd given it her best shot, it hadn't made a differ-ence. Worse yet, she didn't know what to do now, except call Dr. Moses Blackstar, who was her supervisor at the Center, and fill him in on what was going on.

Merry headed off to find a place to sit and make the call, then settled for a seat by a side window and dropped down in the thinly padded chair. Setting her luggage at her feet, she sank back and glanced out the windows as a sleek, smaller jet climbed out of sight into the gray, cloudy sky.

She almost chuckled at a crazy image that came to her of her standing on the runway, thumb out, trying to hitch a ride on one of those private jets. They had to seat eight or ten, and surely one of them would have an empty seat and be heading to the Santa Fe area. Then the humor died as she fumbled around in her purse to find her cell phone.

She called Dr. Blackstar's number, but it was a dead end. The doctor was in an emergency surgery and his assistant was gone for the day. She left a message, briefly explaining about her delay and that she was still trying to get back. Then she called an associate at the center—Marsala O'Brian, a twenty-two-year-old intern working under the grant, too.

The girl picked up on the second ring. "Merry, are you back?"

"No, I'm not." She described her situation,

then added, "I'm trying as hard as I can to find out how to make it back there today, but so far I've hit nothing but brick walls."

"What a mess, but it's good that they landed safely, isn't it? I mean, those planes are huge and—" She bit off her words. "Forget I said that. You're okay and that's what's important."

"But I promised the kids," she said softly.

"And you'll be back, just a bit later than you said. I can explain it to them, and tomorrow you can explain it to them yourself."

That made sense, but that didn't mean she was going to sit back and wait for tomorrow. "Thanks, Marsala. But don't say anything to them until I know for sure if I can't get back. I'll call you as soon as I know, okay?"

"Yes. I'll wait until six, when they're being picked up. That's just two hours. Can you get here by then?"

"Maybe not, but just wait until I call you back."

"You got it."

"One more thing? Could you tell Erin one on one, not with the boys around? Can you do that for me?"

"Of course I can. I'll do it first."

"I owe you big time," she said, then ended the call and stood.

It was two in the afternoon, and something had to happen soon if she had any chance of getting back by this evening. She grabbed her bags and purse, then decided to make one last trek to the car rental counter at the far end of the terminal. There was still hope.

As she strode along the concourse, ignoring the gift shops and boutiques on her way, she glanced out the windows overlooking the runway. She saw another small jet taking off, glittering silver in the streaks of sunlight that cut through the gathering grayness of high clouds. She paused to watch the elegant carrier until it was out of sight, thinking that if she only had money, she could charter a plane like that. Well, maybe not like that one, but a plane that could get her home in time.

"That would take a miracle," she breathed at the same time a man cut across the walkway directly in front of her.

She managed to sidestep any impact, but he never even noticed her, he was so intent on the call he was taking on the cell phone pressed to his ear. There was no three piece business suit on his six-foot-plus frame, but instead, he gave more of an impression of an impatient cowboy, in snug jeans, a sheared wool trimmed denim jacket and scuffed boots that were as well worn as the rest of his getup. A baseball cap was the only thing not determinedly Western about the man.

She watched him stop halfway between where she stood on the walkway and the desk for charter flights over by the windows. He tugged sharply at the dark cap worn over slightly shaggy, midnight-black hair, framing an angular clean shaven face. When someone bumped her from behind, trying to get past her, Merry moved to her right, and off the walkway to get out of the way. The maneuver brought her closer to the man she'd been watching. In fact, she was near enough to hear most of his end of the conversation.

"I'll check with him as soon as I can." He listened, glanced around, his dark eyes sliding right past Merry, before he exhaled. "I told you, I'm waiting for clearance." Pausing, his attention apparently on the tiled floors underfoot now. "Nothing serious. A glitch. You know how it goes." He checked the watch on his wrist. "Soon. They said it was almost done. Should be up in half an hour at the most."

While he was speaking, Merry saw a security guard approach the man, then hesitate before he reached out to tap the stranger on the shoulder. At first the man kept talking.

"You, too. I'll call when I get a chance." The guard tapped his shoulder again, and the man turned to him, but still spoke into the phone as he held up a forefinger to acknowledge the guard. "Let me know if I can help. I have to go," he said, finishing the call. "What is it?" he asked. The guard straightened a bit before speaking.

"Are you Mr. Gage Carson?" He nodded and the guard looked relieved. "They sent me to let you know the work's done on your ride, and you've been cleared to take off in the next half hour."

Merry didn't hear the rest of the conversation between the two men as she stared at Gage Carson. A miracle? She couldn't believe the luck or Fate or serendipity or whatever was at work here.

Gage Carson. The man, dressed like a roughhewn working cowboy, was the adult version of a young teenager she'd known over twenty years ago in Wolf Lake. Well, she hadn't actually *known* him, but she'd seen him enough around town with his two brothers, and she knew of him. Everyone knew the Carsons, and she remembered him all too well.

Now he was within ten feet of her, talking

to the guard about his "ride" and "taking off soon." To make this a true miracle, he had to be going to Wolf Lake. She knew there was an airstrip on the Carson ranch.

The guard nodded at something Gage had said before striding off into the growing crowd from a flight disembarking farther down the concourse. But her full attention was on the man who could just be her own personal savior. All she had to do was figure out the best way to talk him into helping her get back to Wolf Lake.

Suddenly, Gage Carson turned, startling her as he seemed to look right at her. But before she could raise a hand and introduce herself, his gaze skimmed right past her as if she didn't exist. Abruptly, he made for the nearest desk for the charter businesses near the windows.

It wouldn't be farfetched, if the man, who led one of the largest construction and architectural corporations in the country, owned one of those sleek corporate jets. Or at least, chartered one of them. Chartering made things a bit more complicated, but it was still doable. She could play on the old hometown connection and snag a ride if the plane was his, and offer to make payments to share the cost of the charter once they got back. One way or another, if he was going to Wolf Lake, she was going too.

She watched him speaking to a woman agent, so attractive that Merry wondered if beautiful women were the only type that the airport employed. The two talked, leaning toward each other across the desk, and although she could only see Gage's back, she didn't miss the dazzling smile on the woman's face as he spoke to her. She was nodding, touching his arm to make a point, and then lifted her hand to break the connection and motion to the row of specialty shops on the far side of the walkway.

Merry's stomach was in a knot as Gage retraced his steps, coming toward her, then going right past her without looking up. She had to make this happen. She'd do her best to reason with him, and even beg if she had to. She glanced back to the counter, saw the attendant was alone at the desk and boldly crossed to her. Merry made herself smile, knowing it was a mere shadow of the version the woman had offered Gage moments ago. "Can I ask you something?"

The woman looked up and nodded. "Why, of course, that's why I'm here."

Merry motioned behind her. "Was that Gage Carson?"

Obviously the wrong way to start the conversation. Privacy had to be one thing a moneyed business, like a luxury jet charter, offered its clientele without any question. The woman's expression changed from warm to cautious. "Is there a problem?"

"Oh, no," Merry said quickly. "I just hadn't heard anything about him being back…in Wolf Lake. You see, our hometown's so small, everyone knows everything about everybody and no one mentioned he had made a visit."

"Maybe he hasn't made it there yet," the woman offered, confirming to Merry that he was heading there.

Perfect. "Maybe not," she conceded, trying to control her growing excitement. "I just never expected to see him here, either. You know, on a charter. After all, the word is he's got tons of money. But maybe it makes more sense to lease instead of buy. I don't know anything about big business."

The woman seemed a bit put off by Merry's confession. "I wouldn't know, but most men in his position have a company plane. He's no different."

His own plane! She felt like screaming,

"Yes," and pumping her fist, but instead she shrugged. "Of course."

"You're friends with Mr. Carson?" the woman asked, the smile all but gone now.

"I knew him since we were kids," she said, deliberately slanting the truth toward the idea that they'd been close. Merry left without another word and carried her bags across to the store that Gage had entered.

She stepped in, and spotted him in a rear display area, looking at snow globes. He lifted one, shook it, put it back, and repeated those actions as he worked his way through about a dozen or so ornaments. She took a breath, tried to still her hammering heart, then headed toward the man.

CHAPTER TWO

"A SNOW GLOBE INSPECTOR?" Merry asked, going for the silly approach as she got within a few feet of Gage Carson. She'd save the serious begging for later, when she worked up the nerve to ask him for a ride on his plane.

The man turned at the sound of her voice, and she met the darkest brown eyes she'd ever looked into. They were narrowed on her, either from puzzlement or annoyance. She wasn't quite sure. "Are you speaking to me?"

"I'm sorry, I saw you checking out all the snow globes and I had images of…" She shook her head, stopping mid-sentence, knowing that hokey line had run its course. "I've always loved snow globes." That was the truth.

He surprised her by not dismissing her abruptly. "So does my mother, and I need a peace offering of sorts for when I see her. I missed Christmas with the family." He glanced at the globe in his hand, and then put it back on the shelf. "The thing is, none of these seem right."

"What does she like—angels, Norman Rockwell scenes, Winnie the Pooh?" She glanced at the American flags encased in three of the globes. "Something patriotic?"

He chuckled roughly at that and shook his head. "No, none of those seems quite right…" Merry scanned the globes and saw a smaller one sitting in a corner and reached for it. "Well, then, how about this?" She held it up to Gage after she shook it so the artificial snow was swirling around a solitary man in buckskins who stood with his head thrown back, and one hand raised to point to something he seemed to be yelling to. Then she saw the shadow on the glass, the smoky silhouette that was barely there, the suggestion of a wolf.

Gage looked at it critically, then slowly took it from her hand and studied it. "Great," he said as he twirled it in his strong fingers. Then his dark eyes met hers again. "Thank you…" He raised an inquiring eyebrow at her in a question.

"Brenner," she said. "Merry Brenner."

He twirled the globe again. "Well, Merry, she'll love this," he murmured. Merry had seen Gage's mother, Lark Carson, a long time ago—a tiny woman with flowing black hair, a ready smile and a real pride in her Indian heritage. As the daughter of the man whose family had given his family name, Wolf, to the town, she could imagine her being particular about the general presentation of the Native spirit, even in a snow globe. And to have a wolf suggested in it would be specific to her. "It will really suit her," she agreed.

He glanced at her quizzically. "How would you know that?"

She blinked, realizing what she'd said. She couldn't take it back, so she pushed on. "You are Gage Carson, aren't you?"

He was obviously surprised. "How do you know me?" he asked, as his gaze flicked over her.

"From Wolf Lake," she said, letting him digest that and ask his own follow up question.

And he did. "You're from town?"

"I was, a long time ago, but then I came back for work. I remember the stories about your grandpa helping form Wolf Lake."

He looked puzzled. "I really don't remember any Brenners in town."

"You wouldn't," she started to say, ready to tell him her birth name, but she didn't get the

chance before the guard he'd spoken to earlier, came rushing up to him.

"Sir, Mr. Carson? It's all ready. Just pick up
the papers, and head on out."

"Thanks," Gage said, and when the guard
left, he looked back at Merry as he held up
the globe. "Thanks for your input."

"Sure, no problem," she barely got the
words out before he was on route to pay for
the globe before ducking out of the store with
the guard. Without a backward glance, he
crossed the walkway and veered away from
the charter service desk with the blonde still
behind it.

Merry could have kicked herself. Talk about
handling the situation all wrong! She should
have just walked up to him, introduced herself, and immediately asked for a ride on his
plane. "Should have, could have, would have,
but didn't," she muttered, angry with herself
as she quickly rushed after him.

Dragging her bag after her with one hand,
the duffel in the other, she frantically tried to
catch up to him as he cut diagonally across
the seating area. His long stride was eating up
the distance as he darted toward a side door
marked "Private," where another guard stood.

When he stopped to show identification to

the security guard, Merry called out, "Mr. Carson…Mr. Carson!"

He frowned as she sprinted toward him, stopping within a few feet of him. She let the duffel and suitcase drop by her feet. "I'm sorry," she gasped, breathless from the exertion. "I don't mean to bother you, I really don't," she said. "But I need to ask you something, and you got away too fast in the store."

He didn't bother hiding his impatience as he looked pointedly at his watch, then back to her. "What is it?"

Mary filled him in on her predicament. She spoke in a rush of words, trying to get everything in before he up and left. "I can't get out until tomorrow sometime, and that's not acceptable because I'm needed back in Wolf Lake now."

He hadn't moved while she spoke, and she barely paused to take a breath before going on. "Since you're on your way there, and you've got your own plane, I was wondering if I could hitch a ride with you back home?"

His intent gaze didn't change for a long moment; he shattered her hopes with a shake of his head. "No, I can't do that, and I'm in a hurry."

"Why not?" she asked before he could disappear through the door the guard had just pushed open for him.

"It's a company plane." He held up one hand, palm toward her when she started to protest. "The rules are, no one gets on board who isn't an employee or connected to the company in some manner. Sorry. Now I have to go."

Merry swallowed hard. She should have simply told him she was Merry Casey back in the day, that her dad had worked on his parents' ranch, fencing and running cattle. But she hadn't, and he'd made up his mind. But she refused to give up. "Mr. Carson," she began, but he cut her off again.

"No," he said as he slipped off his ball cap, smoothed back his thick dark hair with one hand then tugged it back on with a sharp jerk of the bill. The action served to shadow his eyes even more. "Rules are rules. Now, I really have to go."

Panic stricken, one last-ditch idea came to Merry—something that, if he agreed to it, wouldn't break any rules.

"Mr. Cason, please listen for one minute?"

"This is not open for discussion."

"I know, but I also know you're the head of your own company, so the plane is technically yours… And since you're the one who makes the rules, I think you could make an exception to break those rules just this one time for a neighbor."

He countered that with, "It's an insurance thing."

"You said you take clients up in your plane?"

"Of course I do, when it's called for," he admitted, "but—"

She cut him off by reaching in her pocket and pulling out her small wallet. She took all of the bills she had left from her trip, just over a hundred dollars, and held it out to him. "Please, I want you to do some work for me. I'm hiring you, right now, right here, so then I'll be your client."

"That's not going to happen," he said roughly.

"I want you to design and make a bulletin board for me with 'Kids Are Cool' at the top of the frame." She plowed on. "Four feet by four feet, a perfect square and painted in primary colors, nothing too cute or sweet. Just bright and beautiful."

His harsh expression eased a bit, and that seemed to soften the angular features of his tanned face. Even his eyes seemed a bit less intense. But he didn't take the money. "I don't do bulletin boards, only the buildings they hang in."

She stared at her hand, which was still thrusting the money toward him, and hated the unsteadiness that was starting to show. "It's a specialty job. I know you do them. A doctor at the hospital said you did one for him when the expansion was completed a few years ago. He brags about it, in fact—he said it was an add-on for the Radiology department."

"What doctor?"

"Dr. Moses Blackstar."

"He told you about me?"

She smiled at that. "Yes, he has. That work you did at the hospital is his favorite subject when it comes to you."

"So you're friends?"

"I'm on a government grant to The Family Center. I address the emotional and mental needs of challenged children, and he does the physical concerns. He's basically overseeing the grant, and that means the doctor and I work together a lot."

Gage cocked his head slightly to one side as if affording himself a better view of this crazy woman trying to hitch a ride with him.

"I won't even ask what's in Wolf Lake that can't wait a day, because I need to get in the air myself, and if you're a friend of Moses's, then I'll take that as a recommendation."

He took the money out of her hand, his heat brushing her skin for a second before he pushed the money in the pocket of his denim jacket. "Just let me know when you need the bulletin board by."

She drew back quickly, slightly light-headed with the massive relief she was experiencing at his sudden agreement. "Remember, all primary colors," she said a bit breathlessly as she pushed her now empty wallet back into her purse. When she looked up, he was already going through the open door and into the corridor.

"Come on. I can't waste any more time," he called back over his shoulder without looking, obviously certain she was following in his wake. And of course she was. She wasn't about to let him out of her sight now. She got her bags, and took off down the metal tunnel that echoed with each footstep she took.

At the bend, she turned, and almost rammed into Gage's back when he slowed to flat-hand a swinging door open to expose the cold gray day and a stretch of tarmac. As she stepped out, feeling the frigid air whip against her face, and gasping for breath, Gage stopped and swung back around. "Give me that," he said without preamble, and grabbed her suitcase, then turned and kept going. Merry was tall and her legs long enough to keep stride with most men, but Gage was not only long legged, he was a very fast walker.

She caught up to him again at the door to a flat roofed hangar set up against a ten-foot chain-link security fence. "There's a storm off to the east, and we need to be well out of its path before it gathers strength, but that'll only happen if we load up and get out of here quickly."

A storm? It did look like one might be coming, with the sun pretty much blocked from sight by a scattering of clouds. She nodded, yet not even thoughts of a distant storm could ruin her euphoria. She had never truly believed in miracles, but as she met Gage Carson's probing gaze, she actually felt she was in the middle of one right then.

In a few minutes, she'd be in the air and in less than two hours, she'd finally be home.

GAGE CARSON DIDN'T have a clue why he'd agreed to take this woman with him, except for her connection to Moses, and that arguing with her would have taken up precious time before he could get in the air. Moses and Gage had been childhood friends, spending boundless days on the Rez or on the Carson Ranch with Jack and Adam—Gage's brothers—and John Longbow, now the town sheriff. Gage would do anything for Moses, and since it had been clear that Merry Brenner wasn't going to give up easily, it had been most expedient to agree.

He crossed directly to his plane, a new aircraft with very few hours on it. It was a huge relief that the reason he had to put down in Pueblo, a slight hesitation at cruising speed, had been a simple fix.

He opened the door to the onboard storage area between the back passenger windows and the tail of the plane and tossed in the luggage. He turned to get Merry's other bag, expecting her to be behind him, but she was still over by the open double doors, staring nervously up at the plane. He crossed to take her other bag from her and said, "Let's get this show on the road."

It was then that she started babbling, just as she had when she'd been going on about needing the ride and Moses and custom jobs.

"I had no idea a corporate plane would be

so small," she'd started out with, and hurried onto, "It looks too little to fly, and only two really small engines, they don't look as if they could actually get any plane up in the air. I mean, the weight has to be a lot, even if it is so...so compact." At least she'd come up with a new word for small, he thought, and let her prattle on as he tossed her second bag in the compartment.

"If an engine goes out, can it keep going on the other one?"

"If it needs to," he said over his shoulder.

"But what if both go out?" she prodded. "Does it glide then?" She was slowly approaching the wing by him. "Well, can it?" she asked.

"Glide?" he queried as he closed the compartment hatch and secured it.

"Like one of those planes you make when you're a kid, all out of balsa wood and it floats in the air?"

"I never made one, but this plane can kind of glide for a short period, depending on the air speed, turbulence and other factors." He moved closer to her, and the minute he inhaled a floral fragrance that barely permeated the air around him, his first sight of her in the souvenir shop came back to him. The image of a tall and slender woman whom he could face and not have to bend down to make eye contact with, donned in skinny jeans, a suede jacket, chunky boots, and a dab of delicate perfume that had filled his senses.

He was studying her face now, her dark hair streaked with auburn, tugged back into a high ponytail, emphasizing a heart-shaped face dominated by striking green eyes. And there were freckles, dusting her clear skin over a flush to her cheeks that came either from the cold or from her being uneasy about flying. He didn't want a case of nerves on this flight, not with the weather starting to shift and change.

"You've never flown in a small plane before, have you?"

She blinked at him. "Of course I have. Actually, lots of times. Miles and miles and miles. How about you?"

"Obviously I've flown," he countered with his version of her answer to him. He saw her grimace. "I've been flying since I was twenty, and soloed before my twenty-first birthday," he added quickly. "Since then, it's one thrilling air ride for me after another."

"I bet," she muttered as she compulsively

twisted the strap of her purse around her fore-finger.

He didn't have the time to talk her into sit-ting back and relaxing so she could enjoy a "top of the world" flight that would be like no other in her life. The next couple of hours could be fun, but he didn't say any of that. He had a gut feeling that if he did, she'd start one of her bursts of nervous chatter.

So instead he stared right in those green eyes that had flares of gold at the pupils, and said as evenly as he could, "Let's get you home."

Her eyes widened slightly, and he had a mo-mentary fear that she was not only a babbler when she got scared or excited, but she was a crier. Thankfully that didn't happen. She managed a weak smile and said softly, "Yes, home," and went toward the side of the plane.

He came up behind her and cupped her elbow to help her up onto the wing. "Grab the door by the bottom, then ease back as you lift it." She did as he directed and the wing door went up. He was merely helping a client into the plane. No rules, even if they were his own rules, had been broken. He al-most laughed at that, remembering how she'd thought fast enough to con him into this flight with a bogus retainer.

He got onto the wing himself, let her get seated, and then warned. "Don't touch any controls. And be careful about the foot levers, just keep your feet off of them."

She nodded and shut the door. It only took him a minute to get behind the controls. He was aware of Merry buckling in as he contacted the tower, got his take off position and instructions for taxiing, then he started the plane. He motioned to the same set of controls in front of her. "If we have time, I'll give you a flying lesson," he offered to try and ease the tension.

She gasped at him with what sounded like horror, and he smiled. "Just kidding," he said.

Within minutes, they were on the runway, positioned for takeoff. Once they got clearance, it was flaps up and trim set for takeoff. He released the brakes and with the throttle fully open, the journey began. As the motor revved higher and higher, they gathered speed. At about sixty-five miles per hour, that moment came when the tires left the ground and there was nothing but air around the plane as the earth fell away.

He loved that transition—an addiction he

freely admitted to—he loved flying, having this plane at his beck and call. It was the best fringe benefit of his success. But one glance at his passenger and Gage knew she wasn't sharing any of his excitement at all.

She sat still, her hands gripping her knees, her eyes tightly shut, and he could see her taking deep breaths. Then her lips started to move silently. Praying? Oh, boy, he thought. "You okay?" he asked as they reached cruising altitude.

"Fine," she replied, barely breaking the rhythm of her breathing and quiet chanting. If she wasn't careful she was going to hyperventilate.

He eyed her. "I guess no one's pointed out to you during all those flights you had, that flying is safer than driving?"

She kept her eyes closed. "Sure, that's what they say, but no one adds that if you're in a car and there's a problem, you can pull to the side of the road, even if your motor explodes, but in a plane—" Her words cut off and she started that deep breathing and lip movement again.

Some kind of Zen thing, he thought, but said, "Never mind. Forget I mentioned that.

The engines are not going to explode, and I know what I'm doing. It's all good."

"Fine," she muttered, but went right back to her "exercises."

"So, you're going to Wolf Lake?"

She exhaled on a sigh and he couldn't tell if it was from him annoying her with questions, or that special breathing she'd been doing. "Yes."

He'd thought he could distract her, but now he wasn't sure that was possible. "And you know Moses."

"I told you that already, and I can't talk, I have to count," she said, her arms wrapping around herself so tightly her knuckles whitened.

"Count?"

"Please, yes, let me count." He did as she asked while he checked the GPS, banked southwest into the flight plan, then set auto pilot and sat back in the seat. Looking over at Merry again, he took in the whole picture and came to the conclusion that she was not the type of woman who would blow your socks off at first, but the kind that probably grew on you as you discovered more about her. He noticed the straightness of her nose, and the sweep of her jaw, a delicate angle. And those freckles. He'd never thought about it before, but the freckles in some way made her seem vulnerable.

He couldn't recall ever seeing her in Wolf Lake before, although he hadn't been back to town in a long time. Now, his older brother, Jackson, was dealing with the loss of his wife and not doing well. His other brother, Adam, had taken off for Chicago with a woman who had visited Wolf Lake around Christmas, and now he was helping the woman and father in a legal battle. He didn't understand much of what Adam was doing, but he knew it was so important to Adam that he left his job as a detective in Dallas, Texas, to go to Chicago with this lady called Faith.

Now Gage was on his way back, but not exactly for a visit. He looked at Merry, watching her lips moving again, and realized at one time he knew everyone in town, at least by sight, but now he figured there might be a lot of people who were total strangers to him. Just like Merry Brenner. The idea she was a friend of Moses's, well, he really did want to learn more about Merry and her association with the good doctor.

"You okay?" he dared to asked again.

"Fine," she breathed softly.

"Counting?"

"Yes."

"You know, I once heard that an interviewer's worst fear was a guest who gave one word answers. I think I finally understand what was meant by that."

He thought she might smile at that, or at least stop counting whatever she was counting, but she didn't. The only positive change was her flexing her fingers as if to ease the tension there. But her eyes stayed shut and the counting went on.

He checked the instrument panel, and then looked back at Merry. "Is there any point in my asking what you're counting?"

When a long moment went by with no response, Gage was ready to give up, get through the trip in silence and wish her good luck once they landed. What she counted was her own business. Then she surprised him by saying, "Bubbles."

"What?"

She exhaled, slowly rested her hands on her thighs and leaned back in the seat. Her eyes fluttered open, but they stayed focused on what was ahead of them, a growing cloud bank and thin beams of sunlight feebly cutting through them. "You know, the kind you blew as a kid that you could make from dish soap or get in those little plastic bottles?"

"Sure, but—"

She kept talking as if he hadn't tried to say anything. "When I was little, I'd get away from wherever we were living at the time, find some grass and blow bubbles while I laid on my back. I'd watch them float up and up and up, until they either disappeared or burst." She stopped and he saw her bite her lip. He could tell she wished she hadn't said that. "Like most kids," she added quickly.

He liked the feeling of her sharing, even if it she seemed to think it had been a mistake on her part. "My method of getting away was to go up to the lake at night," he admitted, surprising himself that he'd said that out loud to her. It wasn't something that had been brought up in any conversation for years.

"What would a Carson have to get away from?" she asked, finally turning to him. "You know the lake?"

"I was born in Wolf Lake. Obviously, I know the lake. I didn't see it until I was maybe six years old, just before we left, but I'd heard about it all my life. The magic of how the full moon turns that whole area of wild grass into a rippling ocean moved by the breeze."

She was born there? He shifted in his seat. She wasn't familiar at all. He tried to think of families he'd known in the past, but nothing came to him. "You know, I don't remember a Brenner family."

"How about the Casey family?"

Casey? Yes, he remembered a family named Casey, and a child, but he couldn't recall if the child was a boy or a girl. But he clearly remembered the father, Jerry Casey, a good man who had worked on the roads, and on some of the ranches around the area. Jerry had died young, and he couldn't remember seeing the mother or the child after that.

"Jerry Casey?" he asked.

When she looked at him, her green eyes widened. "My dad."

"I think he worked for my dad off and on."

"Yes, he helped with fencing on your ranch, and he ran some of your cattle."

So, he wasn't helping out a stranger after all, and it was indeed a small world. "So you left and got married?"

"Oh, no. I mean, yes, we left—my mother, me and my stepfather, Mike Brenner. I got his last name because he was in the Air Force, and the benefits were better if we were actually family."

He glanced at the control panel, then back at Merry. She seemed a bit less tense now. "So, you left and came back?"

"I left because I had to, and I came back because I wanted to."

"Why did you want to?"

"We were constantly uprooted. The air force reassigned my stepfather to lots and lots of places in this country and Europe," she explained. "A year here, a year there, and no real home." She grimaced slightly. "I hated it. Some people would love to roam the world, but all I wanted was some place to call home."

His choice would have been the roaming, going where he wanted to, exactly as he did with his business. "So, you returned to Wolf Lake?"

"Yes. When I graduated with a degree in Child Psychology, I did some clinical work, and met a lady who had a clinic in Arizona for Native children. It fascinated me, really making a difference and not being in an office setting."

She hadn't glanced out the front window for a few minutes, and Gage saw that as a positive step in keeping her calm. Especially since the clouds were starting to show signs of high wind, and he could feel the tugging at the plane.

"I'm certified to work with developmentally delayed children, and put in for several grants. Fate stepped in and I got an offer from The Family Center to work with the Native children and anyone else local in Wolf Lake."

"So you took the grant offer?" Gage asked a bit distractedly as he felt another tug at the plane and he checked the control panel. The sky around them was steel gray and darkening while the wind was gaining speed and changing direction. He flipped off the autopilot and took control again just as snow began to show up in the wind that was driving at them.

"Yes, I did, and moved back to town about six months ago."

"I was there when they put in The Family Center," he murmured, keeping a close eye on the sky in front of them. He flipped on the radio, got an update through his earpiece, and felt a bit uneasy when he heard that the storm, predicted to curve to the east and go south, had changed course to the west, almost curling around to get ahead of them in their flight path.

"Moses told me that when I arrived, he supervises the grant, as I told you before. I'm there for two years to study the effects of certain therapies that are being developed. There are about ten kids right now in the program and..."

Gage adjusted their speed and banked slightly away from the wind. He didn't realize that Merry had stopped speaking and was staring at him until she touched his arm.

"What's wrong?" she asked tightly.

CHAPTER THREE

GAGE FELT THE pressure from her fingers through the denim of his jacket. "Nothing, it's just a shift in the wind."

"What does that mean?" she demanded.

He glanced at her fingers on his jacket sleeve, then over to her green eyes growing wide with concern. "The wind shifts in direction, and that's what's happened. I have to compensate for it."

"And?"

"I'm compensating for it," he repeated, feeling her touch disappear from his arm.

"Didn't they tell you this could happen at the airport?"

"I was more worried about my plane," he admitted and immediately regretted that statement.

"What was—or is—wrong with it?" she asked, her low voice belying her growing panic. She laced her fingers tightly in her lap, but never took her eyes off of him.

"I had to check a few things," he said evasively. He wasn't about to tell her about the minor electrical problem that had been corrected. He could only imagine what she'd do if she heard that right now.

"What things?"

The plane was flying smoothly now, more at ease with the wind, but the clouds were getting thicker toward the south, and the heavy darkness that warned about coming snow, was ominous. "It was an easy fix. I was only down for a few hours."

She didn't respond, just wrapped her arms around herself again and closed her eyes. The counting started again.

"You know, I've been meaning to ask you something…"

The counting stopped and then she opened her eyes and turned toward him. "What is it?"

"Well, I was wondering why you keep counting the bubbles when it doesn't seem to be working for you?"

"Because I never mastered yoga or meditation. A therapist I trained with used it in therapy, and suggested it to me. Plain old diversion." She was rocking a bit now. "Count something that is beautiful and gentle and calming to you, and match the counting to

your breathing, and…" She sighed. "It's supposed to work. It did work on the commercial
flight today, but…it did work, it can work, but
it's not working now."

"I'm sorry," he said, having no idea what
it would be like to be scared of something as
incredible as flying.

"Now, can I ask *you* a question?" she said
almost in a whisper.

"Go ahead."

"Why did you buy such a small plane when
you've obviously got money and could get one
of those big silver corporate jets?"

He wanted to laugh at her question, but he
bit it back, instinctively knowing that really
wouldn't go over well with her at that moment. "It's what I wanted," he said, not about
to start discussing runway length and the fact
that he liked it smaller so he could fly alone
as much as possible.

"Why?"

He stared at her. "It's green. My favorite
color," he said, referring to the panel again.
The storm was approaching faster than he'd
anticipated, but worse than that, he could feel
a catch in the rhythm of the plane. A blip of
some sort.

The plane shook against resistance then,

and she exhaled on a long sigh. "I feel a bit green myself," she muttered, eyes shut again, and he just bet those bubbles were being counted, too.

"Listen, I've flown this route many times with no trouble. I know it so well I could close my eyes and land us safely at the landing strip on the ranch. I've done it before."

"You what?"

"I'm kidding," he said quickly. "It's just a joke. I'm wide awake, always am when I'm flying, and we'll be in Wolf Lake before you know it." Platitudes, he admitted to himself, but he was at a loss to figure out anything he could say that would put her at ease. That didn't mean that he'd stop trying, however. "We have radar, a flight tracker, GPS." He tapped the screen in front of him. "Every gadget we need to get there is in this panel and on this plane, so don't worry. It's all good."

The wind buffeted the plane to one side and she gasped, "What about that?" She pointed an unsteady finger at the storm clearly gathering in the distance. "That looks horrible."

He scanned the screen and said in what he hoped was a reassuring voice, "It's not pretty, but it won't get to us before we get to where we want to be. If worse comes to worst, we'll fly around it and take a bit more time to get home, or if it gets sloppy and spreads out, we'll climb high enough to go over it."

She was trembling slightly, he noticed, and he was flooded with a foreign feeling of protectiveness. He didn't like that at all. He didn't want to be totally responsible for her safety. He went through a lot on his own, answering to no one but himself, but this would be different.

Everything he'd have to do from here on out would be done for both of them, not just him. The usual rush he got from danger, or uncertainty, was gone since it wasn't only his life at stake anymore. Not by a long shot. One glance at Merry and his stomach clenched. He turned away from the sight of her before he gave in to an overwhelming need to touch her and say, "We'll make it." He wasn't a good liar, and he couldn't say those words with any conviction right then.

So Gage did what he knew, and got on the radio, trying to make contact with the nearest tower to give them his coordinates. How he wished he'd never listened to Merry in the terminal and never said he'd bring her back home to Wolf Lake....

When he heard a report from the tower

through the static about the changing direction and speed of the winds, and the mess they were heading right into, he knew he had to think fast.

"What are we going to do?" Merry asked in an unsteady voice.

If she hadn't been with him, he would have made an immediate decision and never second guessed himself. Never. But with her, he was going back and forth, contemplating about going up or heading off to the side. He hated uncertainty, knowing that his slightest hesitation could mess things up for them. "We'll go up," he said with more conviction than he felt.

"Good," he thought he heard Merry say as he spoke into the radio, telling the nearest tower what he'd do and asking for wind speed and direction. As he listened, he readjusted the controls and the plane started to climb. With the tower voice in the background, he could feel the small aircraft respond perfectly, and that gave him a sense of relief. It was a great plane. Then he felt the beginning of a drag, a sense of lost direction, right when Merry spoke again.

"Why are we climbing so slowly?"

The radio contact was breaking up, and he ignored it to check the radar. *Because the wind is so strong, it's pushing us back and down,* he told himself, but instead said, "The weather."

He had to concentrate, but was finding it harder than it should have been with Merry so close. He never should have let her get on board. Never. He didn't need this. It was why he had no wish to be in any long term relationship because he didn't want the responsibility or pressure. His job and his family were his only responsibilities, and business had been the main focus of his life since he'd started the company.

It still would be if the calls hadn't come, one after the other over the past month. Calls about mundane things from friends and family in Wolf Lake. But beyond all the banter, he knew their real purpose. His older brother, Jack, needed him and he hadn't been around.

Initially, Gage had planned on flying back for a day or two closer to summer. Then the request for a full bid on an entertainment complex southeast of Wolf Lake near the Rez had come from the town council, so he had made arrangements to travel there sooner rather than later.

Penciling in a week's stay in Wolf Lake, he'd pacified his obligations business wise and his own conscience. However, he never thought he'd be in this plane, with a beautiful, confounding woman, flying straight into a storm. When the plane shuddered again, he tried to feather it into the wind to get clear and the action didn't get any response from Merry. No gasp, no sobs, no petrified screams, so he chanced a look at her.

She was bent forward, her face hidden in her hands, and her back rising and falling rapidly. She was going to hyperventilate if she didn't stop. He tried to push away that growing sense of protectiveness and that effort made his words sound short and abrupt. "Sit back and stop breathing so fast. You're going to pass out."

Her hands dropped just a bit and he could see her green eyes flash angrily at him. "Thanks," she muttered, but did sit back and drop her hands to her lap.

He dismissed any apology he'd thought he should make, satisfied that she'd stopped counting bubbles and looking so terrified. "Make sure your belts are fastened and tight."

"You, too," she said, fiddling with her restraints.

He ignored her curt tone, and went on. "We're going to have to fight to get to the west," he told her, focusing on the panel in front of him. "That means jerking and possible dropping, but none of that means that we're putting down. Do you understand that?"

He heard one word as he kept scanning the screens. "Yes." She didn't ask any questions.

"Ready?"

Another single word answer. "Yes."

He didn't have to look to know her eyes were shut. "Okay, here we go," he said and began a painfully slow descent to the west. At first he felt it was working, despite two drops in altitude, and a jerk that snapped his head back. "It's okay," he said as much for his own benefit as it was for Merry's.

"Good," she replied, but he knew he'd spoken too soon. Things weren't okay. They were losing altitude at about the same speed he was losing control of the plane. The angry winds knocked them, the snow finally growing into thin flakes that were more like needles being driven at them. Visibility was failing and the compass was nudging toward the south, not the west.

"No," he murmured, trying to get control. The direction they were heading in was bringing them toward the mountain range that he flew over to get to Wolf Lake.

Now they were twisting in the air, icing on the outside direction adjusters made his control next to nonexistent. He heard Merry saying something, but the static of the radio in his ear drowned it out. He hit the button and heard more static. He felt a rush that came when he got in a tight spot, and he adjusted channels again, trying to get some clear connection between them and the nearest tower.

He gave his call identification, thought he heard someone say, "Roger, where—?" Then abrupt static was all he detected, along with the sounds of the wind beating against the plane, the whine of the engines and his own heart rattling against his ribs. He darted a look at Merry and was surprised to see she wasn't doing her bubble counting. She was gripping the sides of the seat, but her eyes were on him, filled with what looked like disbelief.

"What?" he asked when she didn't speak.

With a shake of her head, she rasped, "You're crazy."

He didn't know where that came from. "You won't be the first to call me that, or the last."

"I bet," she managed before biting her lip hard when the plane shuddered from the wind.

"How did you come to that diagnosis, Dr. Brenner?"

"All I had to do was see that excitement in your eyes," she said. "You're actually enjoying this!"

He wouldn't deny that, at least for now, and he hit her with his own question as the plane seemed to settle a bit. "Why exactly are you here?"

Very slowly, they were gaining ground on a southerly direction. "You know why," she responded.

"No, I don't know." *Make her talk. Keep her occupied.* "You're terrified of flying, yet spent a hundred dollars to get on this 'small, fragile plane'—your words, not mine—just so you could get home a day earlier than if you waited for a commercial flight." He read and reread the altimeter. "Now, don't you think that unless there's some certifiably pressing reason behind all of this, you might be a bit crazy to inflict torture on yourself by flying with me?"

When she didn't answer, he chanced a glance away from the screens to her. She was staring straight ahead, her teeth busy worrying her full bottom lip. "I just want to get home."

He'd blown it. All that anger was gone, and she looked as if she was on the verge of tears. He could kick himself for whatever he'd said that did this to her. "Okay, you're just in a hurry."

She was still silent and Gage felt the plane slide slightly as the altitude decreased enough for him to feel it. He hoped Merry wouldn't feel it, too. Wrong again. "What was that?" she asked abruptly.

"Just an adjustment," he replied, then tried the radio again. While he sent out his ID, it was met by the incoming contact. He went through a check, felt positive, and told the tower that they had stabilized and were now heading west. After giving their coordinates once again, he said he'd contact them at a designated time for an update and signed off.

While he settled back, letting the plane do the work now that circumstances were more normal, he had a thought, but didn't know where it had come from. Merry was doing anything to get home and the logical reason was someone was waiting for her in Wolf Lake, someone she was willing to risk everything to get to.

He kept a check on the information, but wondered why the conclusion he'd drawn, almost annoyed him. After all, what did he care what her reasons for returning home were? He'd known her for an hour at the most, and she was a "client." That brought a slight smile at the ridiculous way she'd managed to become a client.

"I told you, you're enjoying this, aren't you?" she demanded. "You're almost smiling."

He wasn't about to tell her why he almost smiled, that was for sure. So he went for sarcasm that usually served him well. "Yeah, I just love being in the middle of a storm with ice on the wings and a compass that can't figure out which way we're going."

Wrong thing to say again. "We're lost?" she blurted, his smile long forgotten now.

"No," he reassured her. "We're doing just fine right now. We'll be out of this mess in a bit, and home in Wolf Lake soon after that."

"GREAT," MERRY SAID on a shuddering sigh, her relief a heady thing. That was why he was smiling. They were in the clear, despite the growing storm, and he had it all under control. She'd been wrong to say he was crazy, since she was crazier than him. She should have waited at the airport. "I'm sorry," she muttered to him, trying to block out the noise outside. "Obviously you're in control." She closed her eyes tightly to stop the sight of the ominous grayness that surrounded them.

"We had a problem," he said evenly. "But we got through it. So, just sit back and count your bubbles."

She opened her eyes to glance at him at the same time he turned to her. Her heart lurched when she was met by a smile that crinkled the corners of his dark eyes and exposed a single dimple to the right of his mouth. For that moment, she forgot all about the storm and the wind and the plane. It all came back when the plane bucked, the action so abrupt that she felt as if her heart was in her mouth.

Gage quickly got the plane under control. "Merely fine tuning," he said, as the plane evened out again.

"You…you're doing fine," she breathed, needing that encouragement as much as she thought he probably did.

"Thanks," he said, flashing another grin in her direction. "I like that assessment better than the crazy one."

She wasn't sure if there was sarcasm or not in his response. "I trust you, I really do." And she meant it.

That brought a look her way that was dead

sober, the dark eyes considering her before glancing away. There was no response from him, only a soft whistling of a tune she couldn't recognize. She reasoned if he could joke about their situation, then that meant things had to be okay.

She exhaled, speaking to herself as much as to him. "You know, I'm the crazy one. I'm going back when I should have been patient. I should have called and let—"

She bolted upright. She hadn't called Marsala back! Since she hadn't heard anything from her, the receptionist probably figured Merry was still in Pueblo waiting for the morning flight out. She tugged her cell phone out of her jacket pocket and hit the power button. Her heart sank when she saw the battery was low and that no signal was available.

"Oh, man," she whispered, shoving her cell back into the pocket of her jacket.

"What?" Gage asked.

"Phone's dead, totally dead and I don't suppose you can jump out in midair and get my duffel bag out of storage?"

He barked a short laugh at that. "No, I'm not jumping out, but as a matter of fact, I can get to the luggage area over the backseats. But no one is getting out of their restraints until we're totally in the clear from this storm." He touched the screen twice, then turned to her. "Why don't you tell me why you're agreeing that you're crazy, too?"

"We're both going back when we should have stayed at the airport. You knew there was a storm, but you thought you could outrun it, and I knew they'd get me on a plane at ten o'clock in the morning, and I chose to flag you down instead. We both wanted to get to Wolf Lake badly enough to risk all this."

"Whoa, no. I'm going now because I have business meetings and I didn't have time to cool my heels in Pueblo. I really thought, from what I was told, that the storm was far enough away and on course to sweep to the east, not southwest." He scrubbed a hand across his face. "If I'd known, I would have stayed put, cancelled this trip and rescheduled the meetings."

"You weren't going home for your family?"

"It's mostly business, but I do need to see my brother and my parents. I couldn't get away at Christmas, and things are changing on the old homestead, so I decided to combine a business trip with a visit to the family."

She'd heard about Adam Carson leaving with the woman he'd met at the inn in town.

Something about heading to Chicago and they still weren't back, so Adam obviously wasn't the brother he was going to visit. "Jackson?" she asked as she leaned her head against the chair's high backrest and watched him closely.

"Yes, Jack."

When Gage didn't say any more, she thought again of the mention of business in his explanation. He was going back for business? She hadn't heard about any major construction going on, except for something about a hotel or something.

"You have business there?" she asked, thankful that the ride was fairly smooth at the moment.

He exhaled. "Yeah."

That was that; he didn't elaborate at all. "I would guess that since you didn't know about your bulletin board assignment until the last minute, that your business has to be on a grander scale than something in primary colors."

He chuckled again, a comfortable sound, despite the constant roar of the wind. "Every client is as important as any other."

"That's your motto?" she asked as he turned

to her, smiling, that single dimple showing up again.

"Maybe it should be," he said before he averted his gaze to look at the screens again. "So, what's waiting for you when you get back to Wolf Lake?"

Her stomach knotted. "My kids," she said simply.

"Your kids?"

"Yes, and I promised I'd be back tonight, before they went home."

He looked confused. "I thought you said you weren't married."

"I'm not. They're the kids at The Family Center. I told them that I would be back today. I made a calendar and put it up. Today is circled and they're watching for me. "I can't let them down. They've had too much disappointment in their lives already."

"So that's what's so urgent that you had to hitchhike to get back on time?"

She almost said an automatic, "Yes, that's why," but something else hit her out of the blue. Something she realized she'd known all along, but hadn't acknowledged. She simply wanted to get home as soon as possible. She needed to get back where she felt she belonged. "Partly," she conceded, but didn't elaborate.

"I suspect they'd be just fine if you hadn't found a way to get back," he said, but his tone had become almost distracted. "Kids are adaptable."

The tension in her grew even more. "Maybe. If they hadn't been thrown into lives that they either don't fully understand or can't cope with, maybe things would be different."

"Maybe they need to learn to cope," he said, tapping the screen right in front of him. She'd thought he was talking to keep her distracted, to make sure she didn't freak out, but his almost absentminded comment bothered her.

"Tell them that they need to suck it up and get over it?"

The edge in her voice finally caught his attention. "No, that's not what I'm saying," he countered. "I just meant—"

"Your reason for going to Wolf Lake is valid, and mine isn't?"

He held up a palm toward her. "Okay, okay, this has gotten off track. Let's get back to what I meant, not what you heard."

That made her snort. "Oh, a case of 'what are you going to believe, me or your lying ears?' Is that it?"

He stared at her, and then burst out laughing. She watched him, finally finding the humor in what she'd said, but she didn't laugh. The best she could do was offer an apology. "Peace?"

"Yes," he said, and she felt the plane turn slightly to her left, dipping into the snow streaked grayness around them.

"What are you doing? I thought we were managing to get toward the edges of this storm?"

"We are," he said, but without a lot of conviction in his voice.

"Then why are you looking concerned?" she prodded as the plane dipped even more. "Come on, you can tell me. I won't get upset, just tell me the plain, honest truth."

He hesitated, which didn't bode well for what he was going to say if he did what she asked. She braced herself and the howling wind was almost drowning out the sound of the motors. "Okay, we should be breaking out of this, at least, we should have broken out of it by now, but we haven't, and the mountains are there, far too close. So, I have to maneuver a bit, and it might make the plane roll."

"Roll?" She envisioned going head over

heels in the plane as it did a giant loop in the sky.

"Shouldn't have said that. I mean I'm going to have to angle more than normal, and you might feel a shifting of center. But I have to do it."

"Okay, okay, I can understand that," she said quickly. "Sure, that makes sense. Go ahead and do it."

Gage cast her a glance and said, "Thank you, I will." Then he focused his full attention on the controls.

Things seemed to be just what he said, that dipping, then leveling, then dipping again, mostly on his side, then she heard a muttered oath under his breath. He pressed something on his earpiece.

"What's happening?" she asked, but he wasn't talking to her.

He was back on the radio, speaking rapidly, but this time she could tell he was trying to make a connection. He said his call letters over and over again, waited, then tapped the screen several times before he started to talk again. A mishmash of unintelligible words to her. He must have made contact, but as far as she could tell, none of what he was saying was good.

When she thought he was finished trying the radio, she asked, "How bad is it?"

He shook his head as if to silence her, then he was speaking into the radio again. "Roger, roger!" He had made contact, listened, then shook his head. "Negative on that." He listened as he fought to keep the plane level again. "The edge?" he asked. "Temps dropped, too low."

Merry turned from him, wishing he was smiling now and enjoying this, despite how much that had annoyed her earlier. He was grim, intent on the words coming into his ears from the headset and the readings on the panel.

CHAPTER FOUR

Gage felt resistance in the controls that had little to do with the fierce wind and the snow sticking to the windows. He could see the temperature outside had dropped twenty degrees in less than a minute, and he knew what was happening. He switched radio channels to one he hoped to never see on any gages in a plane he was flying, 121.5 MHz—the international aeronautical emergency frequency.

"Mayday, mayday, mayday!" he repeated, followed by his call sign and his coordinates. "Extreme temperatures, engine involvement."

A voice from a tower two hundred miles north of their location spoke in his ear. "Roger that," the voice said, stating what he'd just told the person. "Got you. Can you maintain altitude?"

"Negative," Gage sent back. "Going down." He heard Merry gasp, but he couldn't even look at her right then as the voice said, "I read you five by five."

"Starting now," he said into the radio and eased back on the rudder, cutting his speed so the nose slipped lower. "Now!"

"Roger that. Assistance is on the way."

MERRY HUGGED HERSELF AGAIN, but she couldn't make herself close her eyes and imagine the meadow and the bubbles. She stared at the icy snow hitting the window, and the way the light was all but gone. Mountains? Had he said mountains? And they're going down? An image of a huge peak coming at them shook her, the visibility cut so drastically that she wasn't sure they'd see anything before they got to it.

She said a quick, silent prayer for both of them, and for the children. She looked at Gage. "Are we going to crash?"

"Not if I can help it."

"But you said —"

"I know what I said. I have to cover all eventualities."

She remembered something her father had mentioned years ago. "A couple of those Carson boys are big risk takers, going to be hard to control when they get older." He'd explained that there was no other reason why Gage and Adam ended up at the lake one night, hanging from an outcropping like two puppets, just because they'd wanted to climb the face of the cliff right after a rainstorm.

At the time, she hadn't given her dad's remark much thought, and couldn't recall anything other than he had been called out for the rescue party by the boys' grandfather, old Jackson Wolf. "You climbed the cliff at the lake and dangled there with your brother Adam until your grandfather found you, didn't you?"

He cast her a sharp glance. "What made you think of that? Adam and I missed the route we planned on the climb and got stranded. My grandpa found us. He said he had a vision or a hunch, but he came and got us down."

"I bet you enjoyed it until you realized how far you'd gone, didn't you?"

His expression got quizzical. "When you're a kid, you think you're immortal, and nothing can—" His words were cut off when the plane lurched violently, making her heart drop just as suddenly.

He was on the radio again, giving new coordinates, over and over again, and something else that she couldn't make out. She just knew that they were well and truly going down, not up. The plane shuddered ferociously, dropping more quickly than she knew it should. "Go back," she yelled. "Just turn around and go back!"

He ignored her hysteria, speaking into the radio again, giving what she thought were co-ordinates.

The plane dropped again, jarring everything in Merry, and she wanted to shake Gage and force him to turn around. But before she could do anything, he was speaking to her, not into the radio. "We can't," he said. "We're past that point."

"Are we going to die?"

He gave her one long look and said, "Listen to me. You are not going to die. I promise."

As strange as it seemed, she believed him. She really believed him. "Okay," she found herself saying. "Okay."

He reached over and covered her hand that was holding on to the seat for dear life. "Now check your belts, then hold on. If I tell you to get down, put your head on your knees and clasp your hands behind your neck."

"We really are going down now, aren't we?"

"Yes." Their eyes met for a moment, neither said a word, yet they seemed to be communicating just the same.

There was another sharp drop of altitude,

deeper into the driving snow that blinded them to everything. Gage barked out, "Look for any level place, anywhere that's flat!"

Before she could do more than blink, Gage was speaking into the radio again, "Mayday! Mayday!" he said urgently, followed by coordinates, over and over again

She scanned as much of the area as she could make out in the storm. Gage continued to shout into the radio, over the piercing roar of the laboring engine. "Merry! Find us a spot!"

She tried to speak, but her voice was lost to her. The engines faltered, then shut off. Only the rushing wind could be heard. "Glide, glide!" she screamed.

"Exactly," he said as the plane glided lower and lower. He hit some switches and reported, "Fuel, shut."

Merry stared out the window, her worst nightmare a reality. In this plane, with this man. This was all that was left of her life.

There was snow and more snow, backed by darkness. Merry strained to find anything of the ground below them, but just when she was ready to tell Gage there was nothing visible, he yelled, "Get down, head on knees, hands clasped behind your neck."

She did so without argument, bending at her waist to press her forehead to her legs. Her last glimpse out the window was of blurred shapes through the snow, a towering one directly ahead, as if rising up to meet them.

"Stay down no matter what happens," Gage ordered.

She heard Gage clicking something, as a numbing fear gripped her. She didn't want to die with this man, someone she barely knew, and the children...she couldn't even say goodbye to them or her mother and her stepfather. An aching part of her wished she had someone, truly that one person she'd always thought would come along sooner or later, a man who loved her, really loved her.

She heard the howl of the storm, felt the shuddering, a jerk, a violent upheaval and the plane dropping. With her eyes closed tight, she shuddered, whispering for her and Gage to be all right.

Her world condensed in one explosive moment when the plane hit something, and there was a cracking, ripping of metal, then the belly scraping violently against the ground before it sat upward, then crashed down again. It jarred every bone in her body. The impact willed her to go in the wrong direction, but the restraints wouldn't let her go, digging into her, stopping her. The pain was intense.

She couldn't scream, no words were there as the plane twisted to her left, spinning, snapping her head so violently that she felt a cracking blow by her ear. Then another snap produced more pain and disorientation. Before she could even try to assuage how she really felt, there was a gut wrenching jerk.

Then nothing.

No movement. No sound apart from the raging wind outside. Was this death? No, as pain seemed to be enveloping Merry, in her head and her ribs and arms. She tried to figure it out, the true agony came from the unbearable tightness of the restraints. No, she wasn't dead. She was hurting. "Thank you," she breathed, her words so simple but she meant them so profoundly.

She was grateful to be alive, pain and all, grateful for her mother and stepfather, the kids, and for Gage, who had done everything in his power to protect her. She stayed very still, almost afraid to move, wondering where they had landed.

She had to brace herself before she opened her eyes, a slit at first, then she blinked at what seemed like shadows, until she realized that the only lights were the security ones in the junction where the floor met the walls. The control panel was blank; there were no red lights, nothing was flashing.

She slowly, carefully, flexed her neck and shoulders, moved back into the seat and sank into the leather upholstery with a sigh. The pressure from the belts had eased, and she could breathe without too much difficulty.

"Oh, gosh," she whispered, trying to absorb the lingering discomfort in her arms and head. Alive. She was alive. They were alive! They'd made it. "Gage, we—"

She startled as she turned to him. He was twisted away from her, huddled against the window, his hat gone and his headpiece askew.

"Gage, Gage?" she said, her fingers fumbling with the buckles of her restraints, her voice sounding almost like a sob. "Please, Gage, look at me. We did it. You did it. We got down safe!"

He didn't move and the panic that she had fought to keep at bay during the last minutes of horror, welled up in her. "Gage…Gage." She pleaded for him to respond and reached for his arm. "Please."

Her fingers closed over the rough jacket sleeve, and she pushed closer, ignoring the way the partial console bit into her thigh. "Wake up, wake up," she begged. The horror she felt was almost suffocating her, horror that he was wounded or even worse. She couldn't even fathom the possibility that he was gone.

"You can't die," she wept. "Please, don't leave me." She tugged his dangling headset off and tossed it onto the backseat "Please, don't leave me!" It was then that she received her second miracle in one day.

A groan, barely audible over the sounds of the storm, caught her attention, then his right arm twitched. Relief was heady, and grew when she saw his hand move, awkwardly lifting up as if he was going to touch his face, then it fell heavily back on his thigh.

"Oh, Gage, thank you, thank you, thank you," she breathed.

Then he shifted, slowly moving away from the window and toward her, and relief surged through her again. But as he turned his head in her direction, the air almost drove out of her chest. There was blood, so much blood, all over the left side of his face. Blood matted his hair. Blood on the window. Blood dripping on his jaw, soaking his jacket collar, staining the whiteness of his shirt underneath.

FOR ONE INSANE MOMENT, Gage was twelve years old again, sneaking up to the "lake" in the middle of the night, climbing straight up the rocky face still damp from the earlier rain. Without warning, the world fell out under him. His hands were gripping the shale outcropping, and Adam was right with him, both of them screaming into the night.

Then everything he was thinking was gone and all he could feel was the pain. And the pain was real, very real, and someone was calling out to him, over and over again. He tried to move, to get his eyes to open, but all he could do was let out a low groan. That voice, calling to him, trying to reach through the misery in his head, but his hand wouldn't cooperate, not any more than his eyes would. His hand fell, and the voice got louder. He tried to think beyond the pain, and then it came to him—the crash, the gut wrenching pain, and Merry. She was talking to him, urging him to wake up, and he wanted to see the world, and to see Merry.

A touch on his chin and yes, Merry was speaking very close to him. "Just open your eyes, please, just open your eyes."

Gage fought to obey her. After several failed attempts, he finally managed to pry his eyes open. All he could see were shadows at first and then…

Merry.

"Yes," she said on a choked sob, "Thank you, thank you."

"What for?" he actually managed to get past his lips.

The dim light outlined her sweet face. But he didn't miss the tears that were trickling down her cheek. She touched him, her hand connecting with his jawline. "For…" She swallowed hard. "For getting us down," she said, then added quickly, "and for not dying. Thank you."

He got his hand to cover hers, feeling her shake, but she didn't move from the contact. "I hadn't planned on dying," he rasped.

With his free hand he felt along the side of his face, there was dampness there, but not from Merry's tears. One touch and he knew before he even saw his fingers stained with red, that he was bleeding. He groaned and gingerly felt his cheek again.

"No, don't," she said quickly. "It's…you're cut just under your hairline, and it's bleeding so much."

He drew back, exhaled and grabbed the edge of his seat to get into a better position.

A cut…not important. But what was important was him checking the plane, to make sure there were no fuel leaks, although he couldn't find any chemical odor as he tested the air in the cabin. But he had to be sure, and he had to find out how badly the aircraft was damaged.

But just the simple exertion of sitting up a bit, stopped him dead. His chest raged with pain, and he closed his eyes for a moment. He caught his breath and opened his eyes to Merry. "Sorry, a bit light-headed," he fudged.

"How can I help?"

"First aid. Backseat, underneath," he said thickly.

He watched her move back, shifting to one side, getting over the console, then she was gone. "Got it," she finally said. She reappeared up front with a large white tin with a red cross on its lid.

She looked at him again, barely suppressing a flinch, but he saw the expression on her face. "It's just a cut," he said softly.

That brought on a rush of nervous chatter from her as she awkwardly perched herself half on the console and half on her seat. She kept her eyes down on the contents of the tin once she snapped the metal fasteners open. "Yep, it's first aid, all right, and I can do this," she went on. "I've patched up a lot of kids after they've done something silly, and they lived to tell about it, so this should be a breeze..."

His head throbbed, and her rapid speech was grating, but he understood that in some way, this rambling was a coping method for Merry. Without warning, she stopped, and the silence amidst the sound of wind and driven snow, was almost deafening. Slowly, she looked up from the tin, and even in the low light he could see more tears shining in her eyes. He grimaced at the thought of her despair and him having no way to help her.

"I...thought for a moment that you were... that you were hurt worse than a cut." She caught her bottom lip between her teeth. "You aren't, are you? You're okay, right? Just the cut? Not any broken bones or anything else?"

He knew his ribs weren't right, but he guessed that was from the restraints. And his head, well he'd been told often enough how hard headed he was, so he guessed it was a simple cut. "I'm okay," he told her.

The exhaled breath said it all. "Good, good," she murmured and looked back down into the tin.

"What about you?" he asked.

She hesitated, then shook her head. "No blood or lacerations, so I'm fine," she said. "Just grateful that you knew what to do to get us down."

"I made a mess of it," he said flatly. "But any landing you walk away from is a good landing."

The rapid-fire speech started up again as the wind moaned and drove snow against the plane. "Bandages, antibiotics, wipes, cotton pads, tape. bandages…four, no, five of them." She pushed aside the perfectly packed supplies. "They even have gum and energy bars, pain pills and lollipops, of all things."

"We're covered," he said, shifting in the seat and feeling a stab of pain on his left side.

She took some things out, laid the tin behind her on her seat, then turned to Gage. "We…we just need to stop the blood, and get a bandage on it." She reached toward him, the tips of her fingers brushing at his hair, and a frown spread across her face. "You might need stitches."

"Whoa, you don't do stitches, do you?"

She drew back. "No, but I think when we get to Wolf Lake you should see your doctor."

"Good suggestion, when we get there." He wasn't going to say anything about "if" they got there. Now wasn't the time to give her a rundown on what most likely was going to happen.

She tore open a package that held a cotton pad. "I'm going to have to put pressure on the wound, so it might hurt."

"Go for it," he said, feeling a trickle of blood on his cheek. "It sure can't hurt as much as the results of one of Adam's dares that went wrong."

She eased the cotton gently onto his wound, her free hand brushing at his hair to clear it from the mess. He winced before he could stop himself. Lots of exposed nerve endings, he thought as he closed his eyes and let her do what she had to do. When she sat back with a sigh, he opened his eyes again. The blood on her hands startled him. She reached for a wipe and started to make the deep red disappear.

"Thanks," he said gratefully.

"What did Adam dare you to do?" she asked as she finished cleaning her hands, ripped open another package and tore off short strips of adhesive tape.

As she put on the bandage, he told her about his wild, but fun childhood. "The midnight run to the lake, and the cliff we almost fell off of," he murmured as she wiped at his jaw and neck with a cool cleansing pad. "Adam dared me to do that."

"I can't believe you accepted those dares."

"Sure did. And lived to regret them," he confessed as she gently fastened the adhesive strips to the cotton pad and his skin.

She moved back a bit and studied him. "You need clean clothes." She waved vaguely at his jacket and shirt that he knew were ruined. "They're really…" She crinkled her perfectly straight nose. "Really messy."

"I wish I had a change of clothes, but…" He shrugged. "If wishes were horses, beggars would ride."

Unexpectedly, his offhanded quote brought the touch of a smile to her lips. "And I'd need to learn to ride if wishes were horses."

His own smile nudged at him, despite the pain that seemed to be clamping around his head. "I'd teach you," he murmured, intrigued by the softening in her face, and how she turned from him as he spoke.

She drew away, maneuvered back to her seat, miraculously getting the tin with the first-aid supplies back on the console before she dropped down in her seat with a whoosh. Finally, Merry glanced over at him. "Just tell me what happened to make us…land," she said, obviously avoiding the word *crash*. "And what has to be done to get this thing going again."

He blinked, hoping against hope she was joking. She wasn't, so he answered her first question. "My best guess is, besides the storm, there was a problem with the electric and the motor was stalling, they couldn't get in sync again." He didn't sugarcoat his next words. "And thankfully it doesn't smell like there's any break in the fuel lines, or it could have been a whole lot worse."

He was going to continue to answer her, but was stricken with a sharp jolt of pain. He stayed very still. He had no choice. His ribs had chosen right then to feel like a hot vise around his chest. He kept that to himself. A broken rib was manageable if there weren't any other symptoms that developed.

"I wonder how we look from outside," he said, hating the unsteadiness in his own voice.

He knew the wing on his side had either been ripped off, or had been shredded, and since something was keeping the plane fairly level, shredded was his guess. He'd felt the torque when they hit land before he'd blacked out and come to with Merry over him, talking.

He'd been taught to undo the doors before

impact in an emergency crash, and he'd totally forgotten. Now he was glad he had skipped that step. The windows and doors seemed to be intact, keeping out the wind and snow, but the coldness was starting to seep into the interior of the plane. He wasn't sure how much he could move, but he had things to do, and he needed to do them now.

"Merry?" Gage said slowly, watching her closely. "I need to check the plane."

"What?" Now her eyes were wide with disbelief.

"I need to see what condition it's in," he said as he reached for the door handle by his left side, but that was as far as he got. Merry had his right arm clutched in both of her hands, and was leaning into him. He barely kept from gasping because of the pain and had to will himself to turn very cautiously back to her.

"No," Merry was saying emphatically, "you can't. It's a blizzard out there. You can't go out." She was still holding him and he could feel the pressure of her fingers through his jacket sleeve. She looked terrified.

"Hey, it's okay," he told her, but didn't make any move to get free of her hold on him. "I'm just going to go around the plane and get back in."

"No," she said again. "You'll get out there and disappear. You'll get lost."

He'd thought she was fairly controlled, that she was dealing with this as well as he could expect her to. But he'd been wrong. That unexpected sense of protectiveness surged through him. "Okay, okay," he acquiesced, and he felt her fingers ease a bit, but they didn't let go. "I'll explain how I'll do it, and…" He paid the price in acute pain to use his free hand to cover hers resting on his sleeve. "We'll get through this," he said simply, never breaking eye contact with her.

He saw her swallow. "Promise?"

"Absolutely. We'll do it together." That statement stunned him. He never joined forces with anyone if he could avoid it, but he'd meant what he said. "We'll get out of here."

He thought he'd handled that well until Merry sat back and spoke, releasing her grip on his hand.

"Clearly, you know what you're doing, so sure, of course, you need to see what you have to do to fix the plane. And if you think you're well enough to do it right now, I'll help any way I can so we can get out of here sooner rather than later."

He didn't know how to word what he had to

tell her, but it had to be said, despite the fact that it would wipe away that hopeful look on her face. "It can't be fixed," he said as evenly as possible. As the statement hung between them, the hope not only disappeared, but it was replaced by fear. He plunged on quickly. "We're lucky that the plane seems intact, that there wasn't a fire, but I need to check it to make sure it's going to protect us until we can get out of here."

"How can you do that?"

He had to admit that if he stood up just then, he might fall right back down again. His head was killing him, and nausea was beginning to rise in his belly. "I need to get the straps off," he said, not answering her question.

The relief from surviving the crash was rapidly being sucked away by the thought of what he had to do and what he most likely couldn't do. But he had to try. "I have to get out, now," he said, trying to speak firmly. "Do you understand? I have to get out."

Her tongue touched her slightly parted lips, then she finally said, "Yes, I do."

CHAPTER FIVE

"Good," Gage said, surveying the cabin. "My hat?"

Merry glanced past him to snatch something off the floor by his feet. His baseball cap had survived unblemished. He took it, slipped it on, and when the band came against his wound, he gritted his teeth and pulled it down. "Can you reach over and get the door handle up for me?"

She didn't ask why she had to do it when he was so close to it. That saved him from telling her that he couldn't do it himself and save any chance of further pain. He knew pain, and he knew that after enough of it from his ribs and head, he'd be unable to move at all. So, he had to get this over with as quickly as possible.

She stretched past him, over the console, her jacket brushing across his partially averted face. She twisted the handle, jerked it up and down. With a sigh, she moved back to her seat. "It's stuck. The handle doesn't even move much."

Not opening the doors before impact might not have been so lucky after all. "How about your door?" he asked.

She twisted, grabbed her handle and thankfully it clicked, but just as quickly, it shut again. "The wind, it's too strong," she said, staring at him with a "what do we do now?" look.

He struggled to get to his feet, but he pushed beyond it, getting by the console as Merry scooted back in her seat and pulled her legs up to her chest to let him have room to get to the door.

"Okay, pull the handle again," he said. When he heard the lock disengage, he added, "Push!"

He felt it give, inch by agonizing inch, until it was snatched out of his hand and surged up with a horrendous sound of metal slapping metal. Wind and snow drove into the cabin, followed by air so cold it almost hurt to breathe. He didn't hesitate, but ducked into the storm and onto the wing. He reached it without letting the biting pain stop him, got to the door, then yelled at Merry. "Get back. It's going to slam, and slam hard." And it did as soon as he got it halfway down and let go of it. The force of the slam made the plane shudder.

MERRY FELT THE impact of the door closing, then Gage was gone as if he'd never been there. She waited, willing to hear a sound, anything she could identify as a man moving around, but all she heard was the storm and her own rapid breathing.

She shouldn't have let him go out there. What could he possibly see? She jumped when there was a metal on metal sound, and held her breath as she waited, but nothing else came. Visions of a piece of the plane hitting Gage bloomed in her mind and she forced herself to close her eyes and lay on the grass, counting bubbles.

She tried to think of something positive, but the only thoughts that came were of the kids and her miserable attempt to keep her promise. That promise was shattered, but she'd make it up to them, she'd do anything it took to make things right, as soon as she could. If she ever could…

It felt like an eternity before Merry heard a heavy thump near her door. Before she could figure it out, the door began to move slowly at first, then quickly. Gage ducked down to look inside. Snow clung to his cap and shoulders. He looked grim and pale, with one hand braced against the door frame. "Move," he said abruptly. "Get over in my seat."

She moved as quickly as she could, so thankful to have him back that she would have done cartwheels if he had asked. She dropped into his seat, and had barely turned when she felt the plane shift as Gage dove into the seat she'd just vacated. Less than a breath later, the door slammed with earth shattering force.

He twisted slowly in the seat, then collapsed back against the soft leather, his head on the support, his eyes closed. She started to ask him what he'd found, but stopped when she saw how his jaw clenched and his chest rose and fell rapidly. With an unsteady hand, he pulled off the cap and tossed it behind him. The bandage on his head was dark with blood, and she could see Gage shivering.

He exhaled heavily, and said, "I'm back."

She felt his jacket. It was sodden and icy. Her eyes flicked over his snow encrusted jeans and books. "You need to get out of those clothes."

He started to move, then seemed to collapse against the seat. "In a minute," he said hoarsely.

"What's wrong?" Immediately, she felt stupid for even asking that when so much was obviously awry.

"Nothing."

The answer was as bad as her question. "Don't lie to me," she said, meaning it. "What's going on out there?"

"A storm," he murmured, his eyes still closed.

"The plane, what did you find?" she asked impatiently.

He didn't answer right away and she couldn't see his face too clearly with the screens all black and the night sky. The floor lights seemed about as substantial as a flickering candle. "What did you find out there?" she repeated, her nerves getting rawer by the second.

He turned to her and even in the dimness, when his dark eyes met hers, she felt the power of a connection. However, the next words that came from his lips sent her heart plummeting.

"Do you want the good news, or the bad news first?"

W HEN M ERRY SAID SOFTLY , "Okay, the good," Gage hated what he had to tell her, but that didn't stop him. To work together to survive, she had to know everything.

"The good news is…there's no fire, no fuel leaks, we might be able to get some heat in here, and we ended six feet short of one of the biggest fir trees I've ever seen." He couldn't even describe to her what he'd felt when he'd discovered how close they'd come to colliding with the huge pine.

As she pressed back against the door behind her, she asked hesitantly, "The bad?"

He took a deep breath and regretted walking around the plane in the heavy snow. It had taken its toll on him. His ribs were tight and sore and every time he moved, he had pain. "The plane is inoperable, one wing is shredded mess, the belly is ripped up, and we're pretty much being buried by the snow."

He could see her processing the information. "Okay. So, for sure you can't fix it?"

"No, it's done for."

She was clasping and unclasping her hands. "What can we do? There has to be something we can do. That *you* can do. You know planes. This is your plane…you have to know it and what to do with it."

He let her go on while he found the seat adjustment lever. Holding his breath, he pulled on it to slowly lower the back of his seat into a reclining position. The pain was worse, and he had almost reached his maximum limit. There was some relief from changing the chair's angle, however, and he welcomed it. "We will figure this out," he murmured, closing his eyes again. "Meanwhile, you said there were pain pills in the kit. Could you hand me some, then maybe I can get us a little heat in here."

"A headache?" she asked.

"Partly," he hedged.

He heard her rummaging around in the first-aid kit. "It says the dosage is two pills."

"One." He didn't want to have his thinking compromised.

He saw a single white pill on her palm, quivering a bit. He slowly reached for the medication. "There's bottled water under the seat where the first-aid kit came from."

She moved quickly, and came back with a bottle of water. He tossed the pill into his mouth, and then washed it down. "Thanks," he murmured, settling back in the seat again. But as soon as he did, he started to shiver again.

"Heat, you said something about getting heat in here."

"Yes, I think we can do it, but all it means is we can take the edge off the cold. No raging heat."

"Whatever," she said. "Just do whatever you need to do. Or tell me what to do. The sooner you get out of those cold, wet clothes, the better you'll feel."

She was right. His clothes and boots were damp and heavy. The shivering wasn't going to stop until they were gone. "The heater. It's there." He motioned to a spot below the main control panel for it. "It might work. I undid the main electric, but I think I remember the sales man telling me it has an emergency setting that isn't dependent on the main circuitry."

"All right," she said. "Relax and let me figure this out."

He closed his eyes again as she moved around, then he could hear her clicking something. "I think I found it," she exclaimed.

"Good," he whispered, all energy draining out of him as the pain intensified. "It'll take a couple of minutes to either work or not work," he told her.

He heard a click right before Merry asked

hesitantly, "Can I ask you how long you think we'll be stranded here?"

Gage had no legitimate answer for her question, but told himself to pick a reasonable time span, tell it to her, then get onto the really important issue—survival. Before he could give her an arbitrary hour, long enough for the storm to let up, and time for the GPS signal to be triangulated and the crew to get here, his body was shaken by a violent shiver.

Merry was there, stroking his face, her voice soft, "Oh, Gage, you're so cold. The heat should be on any minute now."

He couldn't talk, not when his teeth were chattering and his body seemed to be trembling inside and out. And the pain seemed to be everywhere. He swallowed hard, feeling sweat trickling down his temple, burning on the wound at his hairline.

"It's okay. It's okay," Merry cooed over and over again, even while he shook uncontrollably. "I just need to get you warm. Warm. The heater." He heard each word, but her image was out of focus, then gone. "Yes!" The single word echoed in the cabin, and he felt warmth from her hand on his face. "I did it! The heater's on. It's on. Warm air is coming out the bottom vents."

"Good," he managed again, and meant it when he could feel the hint of heat filling the air. It only made him shiver more as the temperature shifted slowly from cold to almost bearable.

"I did it," she said as her hand caressed his cheek again.

"Th…th…thanks," he managed to get out.

Merry put a hand on his shoulder. "Now, take off your clothes."

He was shaking, but he almost laughed at what she'd said. Almost. Although, that didn't mean that the pain wracking his body could stop him from smiling. That didn't hurt. "You…know, it's b…b…been a while since a w…w…woman said anything like that t… to me."

Despite his inability to speak smoothly, he was glad to see a slight tilt of her lips "Really? From the reputation that precedes you and your brothers, I'd suspect that it's happened more than you're admitting to." He felt pressure on his arm through the soggy jacket. "Come on, you need to get this off."

He glanced back over the seat and frowned. He was too tall to move around much where he was, despite the seat being on the incline.

"I kn…knew I sh…sh…should have gone for the bigger model," he muttered.

Without saying anything, Merry shifted toward him, leaning over the console, and started to methodically undo the buttons on his heavy jacket. She was so close he thought he could see the hint of gold in her green eyes as she worked intently and got the jacket open. There was a bit more warmth in the cabin, but he wondered how much of it was her body heat and how much came from the heater that had to be held on low to conserve energy.

"Okay," she said on a rush of exhaled air. "This is a good start."

His shivering was letting up, and he could actually speak without too much stammering. "You are a f…f…forward woman, aren't you?"

She hesitated, and then said, "Get over yourself. It's just a wet coat…" She bit her bottom lip. "But, if you prefer to do it yourself—"

"No, sorry, I can't," he admitted through clenched teeth.

"Oh, no, it's your ribs, isn't it?"

He exhaled. "You got me."

"You should have told me right from the start," she said, and even in the dim light, he could tell she was annoyed. It didn't stop her from reaching for his jacket cuff and pulling at it so his arm straightened in her direction. She kept up the tension, allowing him to slowly work his arm free at his own pace.

He had to twist a bit to get out his other arm, but the pill must have begun kicking in. The pain seemed a bit muffled and he managed to get free of the sodden garment without too much more discomfort. Afterward, Merry reached behind him, tugged the garment off of the seat, and held it up in her hand. "Where should it go?"

He considered that as he relished the touch of light heat on his bare arms. His first reaction was to throw the jacket outside, but that wasn't a wise one. "Hang it on the back of your seat and it might have a chance of drying out."

Once that task was done, Merry sat back, looking at him in the dimness. She flicked her gaze over him, and he didn't miss her grimace when she saw his shirt was covered with blood around the collar. He'd carefully felt for the lever and very slowly raised it to a partial sitting position. At any other time, he wouldn't think twice about crossing his arms, grabbing the bottom hem of the shirt and pulling it up and over his head to get it off. But that move would be impossible with his ribs.

As if she'd read his mind, Merry went to the first-aid kit, rummaged through it, then turned to him with the world's smallest scissors in her hand. "You do have clothes back in storage, don't you?" When he nodded, she said, "Let's get that shirt off. It's ruined anyway."

"You sure do cut right to the chase," he said. "Pun intended."

Her expression softened, but no smile came. "Military training, do anything fast and right, without too much loss," she muttered as she reached for the hem of his shirt with the scissors.

"You were in the army?" he asked as she started to cut, the back of her hand holding the material away from his body, but in the process brushing along his abdomen.

"Not me. My stepdad. He's in the air force, over in Germany until May. Then they're going to be sent to Portugal for some mysterious reason." While she spoke, she neatly cut the shirt from the bottom to within inches of his throat. Pausing, she hooked one finger in the neck and pulled it back a safe distance before making the final cut. "Don't worry...

I'm good with scissors," she assured him as she sat back and let the split shirt fall open on his naked chest. "I hardly ever draw blood."

"Good to know," he quipped. "And I'm not worried."

"Sure, you're not," she said, and a smile started to emerge.

But before he could see the full expression, her face darkened with concern as she leaned toward him. Involuntarily, he gasped when she touched his bare skin at his shoulder. "Wow, you're going to have some wicked bruises," she mused as she slowly outlined something on the area with the tip of her finger. "No wonder your ribs hurt."

He wasn't breathing now, and didn't until she drew back. She met his gaze, before quickly looking away. He could only guess at what she'd seen in his face. "Just bruises," he reiterated.

She came closer to cut the sleeves up to the collar on both sides, and then easily tugged at the ruined shirt to free it from behind his back. Without asking, she dropped it on the floor between his feet. "Oh, shoot, I should have asked if we can get to the luggage before destroying your shirt."

"We can," he said. "At least, I think you

can." Then he went on to explain about the double backseat, how each side reclined and the luggage area could be partially accessed from there. "There's a duffel," he said. "Navy blue, with the company logo on it."

"Okay, no problem," she replied and didn't hesitate getting over the console into the back the way she had to get the first-aid kit. She finally figured out how to get the seat forward to expose the luggage area, and in less than a few minutes, she had his duffel on the other backseat. "What do you want out of this?" she asked from behind him.

"Jeans, a flannel shirt, socks and there's thermals in there, two sets. Get them both out."

She rummaged around, and then climbed into the front and onto the pilot's seat with the clothes in her hands. Laying them on the console on top of the first-aid box, she looked at him. "What's first?"

The shirt, so I'm not sitting here half naked with a woman with tiny scissors close by, he thought, half wondering if he had a bit of concussion or not. He obviously wasn't thinking clearly, and he didn't believe it was because of Merry being there. Not at all. A mild concussion made more sense. Out loud he simply said, "The thermal top, then the flannel."

She held the thermal out to him. "You can do this?"

"With a bit of help," he said, and she came closer, leaning over the console.

"Sit up just a bit," she instructed and when he lifted his head, she slipped the thermal over his head. "Any ideas how to do the rest without you passing out from pain?"

"Just do it," he said and as slowly and easily as he could, he pulled the shirt down, wiggled his hand to get to the armhole, then, gritting his teeth, pushed his hand into the sleeve. He repeated it for the other side, then Merry tugged it down over his chest.

Gage sank back, breathing a bit harder than he had been, but it had worked. The flannel was easier to put on. He sat forward and with Merry's assistance was able to get his arms in the holes without too much problem. As he settled back again, she reached over to button up the front of the shirt.

She exhaled softly and studied him. "It's your call on the rest."

He glanced down where she was flicking her gaze, at his soaked jeans and boots. He could feel his feet squishing in his socks, and the chill was achingly persistent. After trying to heel and toe himself out of one boot, he finally gave up. No way he could bend forward enough to do it, and there was no room to lift his foot to pull the boots off. "This shouldn't be this hard," he muttered as he sank back in his seat. Merry hadn't moved. "What's that old saying? 'Life's hard, then you—'"

"Not funny," she retorted.

"I was going to say, 'Life's hard, then you get smart,'" he improvised.

Her smile came a bit reluctantly, and he had a stunning thought—that despite everything that had happened and what they were going through, she looked almost happy. He couldn't figure that out. A joke was a joke, but being stranded like this, didn't even come close to funny, despite his silly attempts at humor.

"Sure you were," she said, shaking her head in wry disbelief.

He honestly wanted to laugh himself, and wished he could, but he could still grin. Then Gage looked at her and knew that no concussion could make him think what came next. She was beautiful. At the airport terminal, he'd thought she was attractive in a quiet sort of way, but right then, things shifted. Her dark auburn hair had escaped from the ponytail in wisps that framed her face and brushed against her neck. Her eyes seemed incredibly green, the lashes luxurious, and her skin was almost translucent.

He muttered, "Oh, boy," and closed his eyes for a moment. One thing he knew was that, pretty or not, he found himself very grateful that he had Merry Brenner right there with him.

MERRY WATCHED GAGE as his expression morphed from a smile into a contemplative frown that stole that single dimple away. She had no idea what brought about that change, but she didn't like it. It tightened her stomach and made the sounds of the unrelenting storm seem more overwhelming.

Gage motioned vaguely behind them. "I need to get back there," he said. "We both do."

"Why?"

"We're going to have to shut the heat off in a bit. We can't risk getting too low on power, and it will stay a bit warmer now. Hopefully, the doors aren't damaged and leaking air. We don't need that. And I admit..." He lifted one booted foot a bit off the floor. "These boots are soaked."

They did look distorted from all the moisture they'd absorbed. "How will you get the boots off? I mean, you're in pain and getting in back to do it will be a bit tricky."

He didn't say anything as he slowly lowered the back of his chair again, until it was almost horizontal to the floor. He twisted just enough to look at the seat he needed to get to, before his dark gaze met hers. "I think I can slip back there without too much trouble. I have to push as much as I can and figure out how to move onto the seat."

"Okay," she said, stretching to grab her bag she'd pulled out of storage along with his, realizing how much bigger it was than his duffel. She pulled it into her lap and he was clear to try to maneuver.

She watched Gage, desperate to help him but knowing there wasn't anything she could do. When he was half on the backseat, half on the front seat, she dumped her bag onto the floor on top of the bloodied shirt and said, "Stop."

He looked at her, and she knew he was in pain from the slightly hazy, narrowed eyes that didn't appear to be able to focus right then. "Why?" he said in a low, rough voice. "I've almost made it."

She shifted toward his feet and grabbed a

foot. "I can help you now, to get your boots off, so you can relax better when we get back there."

She heard him take a shuddering breath and exhale sharply. "Okay, just do it," he said.

She got a grip on the left boot and warned him she was going to pull. Even without looking at him, she knew it was painful for him. But the boot came off and the other soon followed. Quickly she stripped off the cold, wet cotton socks and threw them after the boots. She got his clean socks on him, and then glanced up at Gage. She forced herself not to react too much when she saw the fine sheen of sweat on his forehead. "I'm sorry if that was painful," she said softly. When he didn't move or open his eyes, she asked, "Are you okay?"

"Sure," he mumbled.

"You're lying again, aren't you?" She reached for the package of pain pills. "You can have more medication. I think you need the second pill."

He started to shake his head, but relented. "Okay."

She shook out the pill, handed it to him and before she could get him the last of the water in the bottle, he dry swallowed the medication. Keeping his eyes closed, he resumed

what he'd started. Inching slowly and carefully, he got onto the backseat faster than she'd
thought possible. With a shuddering sigh, he
moved gingerly into the area behind the pilot's seat, and settled himself on the leather.

Merry got onto the seat he'd just vacated,
and watched him. He didn't have bruised ribs.
They were most likely fractured or fully broken. Pain was in the fan of lines at his eyes,
and the brackets at the sides of his mouth. She
didn't miss how he clenched and unclenched
his jaw. She was getting scared.

CHAPTER SIX

MERRY SPOKE SOFTLY. "You would have been better if you'd stayed in this seat. It goes all the way down. Now you're in the middle of the seat with nowhere to rest your legs."

"Ah, not so," he murmured. "Lower the pilot seat as far as it can go."

"What about your jacket?" she asked.

He frowned. "Put it on the floor up there."

She did so and slid off the seat, bent over the pilot's chair and found the lever. She lowered the seat, the headrest met the seat in the back, and she saw where he was going with this. "There," she said. "Can you shift enough to get on it?"

"Watch and learn," Gage said, then slowly moved to his left until he could stretch his legs out on the back of the now prone front seat for support. He sank back, fumbled with the adjustment on his seat and lowered the back enough to make something akin to a large chaise lounge. "This works for me."

She settled on the front seat. "Very nice," she agreed.

Merry watched him close his eyes, not moving, except for his chest rising and falling with each breath he took. She waited, letting him set the pace for whatever they were going to do. She worked at not jumping every time the plane shook from the wind. She had so many questions, but she knew she had to wait until he was up to answering them. Better that he dealt with the pain right then, than for her to rush anything.

She averted her eyes from the bandage, unable to look at the blood that had soaked through it. She thought the bleeding had stopped, but she wasn't going to check right then. Maybe when the pain pills really kicked in, she'd try to change the dressing.

A cut and some cracked ribs. Not good, but much better than it could have been. Then a thought struck her that made her breath hitch in her chest. What if he had a concussion? What if it wasn't just a cut? She remembered something about not sleeping; keeping the patient awake for…she couldn't remember the time limit. If he had a brain injury, he had to stay awake.

She leaned toward him and spoke quietly,

"Gage?" When he didn't respond, she touched his knee and shook it gently. "Gage?"

His eyes fluttered, eventually his gaze held hers. He looked less tense, his eyes heavy. "Sorry. It's just…" He shifted to sit up a bit more, but stopped and sagged against the seat. "Sorry."

"I had a thought," she said. When he started to close his eyes again, she spoke quickly. "No, don't do that. You have to stay awake."

"Why?"

"Because of your head. I was just thinking, how do we know you don't have a concussion?"

He was quiet for several seconds. "How do we know I *do?*"

"That's my point. If you do, you can't sleep. If you don't, you need to sleep."

"Catch 22?"

"Yes, exactly. I remember that no sleeping rule applies to a concussion. I just don't remember if one of the symptoms is dilated pupils, or constricted pupils. Nausea, I know that, dizziness, I know that, pain, too."

"Check."

"What?"

He opened his eyes wider. "Check my eyes."

"Oh, sure," she said, and shifted closer to him. His eyes were so dark in the dim light that it was difficult to see the pupils. When she managed to see them, they were dilated, but then again, there was no brightness in the plane, either, so it seemed obvious that the dark brown was little more than a thin circling of the pupil. "Shoot," she whispered.

"Well, am I going to live?"

That wasn't any funnier than his, "Life's hard…" quip. "They're dilated…a lot."

"And that means?"

"I don't know. There's only a little light in here, so they'd be dilated anyway." She moved on. "How do you feel right now?"

He seemed to be really considering the question, then said, "Cold, tired and bruised."

"Are you nauseated or dizzy?"

"No, just hungry."

She frowned. "I sure wish I could talk to Dr. Blackstone, but…" That brought a thought and she felt a jolt of excitement in her chest. "Of course, Dr. Blackstone." Her cell phone was dead, but she'd seen Gage on his cell phone in the terminal. "You have a cell phone with you, don't you?"

"Yeah," he said, then all but crushed her

hopes. "If you're thinking of making a call to Moses, then forget it. No service at all."

"How do you know?"

He shifted and she noticed he didn't really wince at the movement. Progress? "My cell's in the side pocket, by my seat up there. Check it yourself."

She did just that, and then watched and waited as the screen loaded. The last icon on the screen was for the signal strength, and it had a red circle with a slash through it. As if that wasn't obvious enough, a message flashed just under it. "No signal."

Muttering under her breath, she put it back where she'd found it and huffed. "Nothing," she told him.

Gage didn't say, "I told you so," which Merry thought was gracious of him. Instead, he said, "I guess we need to talk about what we're going to do."

"Do we have any choice?" she asked. "Don't we just sit and wait until they find us?"

"Pretty much, but we need to stay protected and warm until reinforcements come."

"That's covered with the heater working."

"That's another thing we have to discuss," he said evenly. "Like I said, we can't keep it running constantly. There's a limited amount of power for it and it has to be enough to last us for a while. We have to be careful and not get greedy for the heat."

"We have to keep the lights on, don't we, I mean, so they can see us when they search for us." She could hear the panic in her voice and tried to hide her worry.

"No, these lights won't help them. These lights barely could be seen if someone was within five feet of the plane."

"Then how can they be looking…?" Her voice trailed off, her heart lurching as a logical truth hit her. "They aren't looking for us, are they?"

"They will be, but they have to wait until light, they'll be able to follow our signal better. No point in trying while it's dark out."

That was totally rational, but it didn't help her at all. "Even when it's light, what if we're buried by that time? You know, snow all over the plane. No one will see us."

"We have a good supply of flares, and we have some fuel to make a rescue fire. At dawn, we can make that all happen. The smoke can be seen easily, if the wind stops." He sat a bit straighter, and despite the touch of warmth in the cabin, he shivered again. "First things first, we should focus on getting through the night."

"What about the radio?"

"No, it's gone. But the rest of the system for retrieval is in place, and the signal is going out. That's what they'll be searching for, and when we know they're close, we'll we have the fire and flares ready to go."

She looked down at his long legs stretching out along the prone back of the pilot's seat. His jeans were discolored from the cuffs to his knees. Reaching out, she touched the denim again. "Your pants, you need to…" She bit her lip.

"Yeah, I was just thinking the same thing."

"Can you…get them off? What about your ribs?"

"I think I can handle it," he said.

"Okay, where do you want me to go?"

He glanced exaggeratedly around the cabin. "Oh, I don't know. How about the first class area?"

"What?"

He pointed forward. "Just scoot farther up, and I'll take your word for it that you won't peek. Just give me the thermal pants and the jeans."

She felt the heat rush to her face as a vivid

memory of his strong chest and flat stomach, which she'd glimpsed when she'd cut off his shirt, came to her. Shoving the thought aside, she quickly picked up his jeans.

"The bottom thermals, too," he said.

She passed him both things. "What about the second set of thermals?"

"They're yours, probably too big, but they'll help a lot," he said as he took his clothes.

She turned away from him, and faced forward. Thermals for her? That meant she had to put them on. Well, duh, she thought. Of course she had to put them on and she would.

"You can change in first class," Gage said as if he'd read her mind.

"Great," she muttered, but didn't turn back to him. She could hear him shifting, his breathing getting a bit strained, and she closed her eyes.

She could imagine what he was doing, stripping off the wet jeans, putting on the thermals, then the dry jeans. After what seemed forever, she heard him almost fall back against the seat. Then a long, loud exhale of air. "Done," he finally said. "Your turn."

She twisted to look back at him. "Oh, shoot," she said when she realized that Gage was just zipping up his jeans. Looking away, she apologized fast. "Sorry."

"You can peek now," he said with just a touch of humor in the words.

Slowly, she turned again, relieved that he was really finished this time. The pain lines in his face seemed to have eased considerably, despite the exertion of changing his clothes. His wet jeans were in a ball on·the floor by the seat back. She reached for them and added them to the pile on the floor—his jacket and the bloody, shredded shirt.

She adjusted the lever to lower the back on her seat and sat cross legged on the soft leather. She looked over at Gage. The bandage was horrible and she leaned to her right and made a grab for the first-aid kit where she'd left it. "You need to change the bandage. It's totally ruined."

He gingerly tested the soaked bandage. He flinched at the contact. "I can do it," he murmured.

"No, let me," she said, taking out some cotton swabs, antibiotic wipes and three butterfly bandages. If the blood had stopped, she could pull the wound together in hopes that the scar wouldn't be too ugly when it finally healed.

He didn't argue, and didn't even flinch

when she moved back on the lowered front seat. She gently tugged the tape off his skin and slowly got the saturated cotton pad free from the wound. Thankfully the blood flow didn't start again. Carefully she cleaned the wound, before putting the three bandages along the cut strategically to make sure the gash was closed.

"Were you a medical doctor before you went into psychiatry?" Gage murmured, his eyes still closed.

"Psychology, and no, just the basics I had to take, but I've—"

"I know, bandaged kids up before."

She would never admit that she hadn't bandaged a man's wounds before, let him think that she'd done this any number of times in the past; that it was nothing special. When in fact, it was kind of special. She shivered as he slowly opened his eyes and met her gaze. Not only had she never bandaged a man's wounds before, she'd never bandaged a man who could make her breath catch in her chest merely by looking at her.

GAGE MET MERRY'S green gaze, an intensity there for a fleeting moment, and then instantly it was gone. She really was lovely. And he wasn't confused, certainly not by the pain or the medication.

Though he regretted taking on the responsibility for Merry, and then failing so miserably, a part of him was just plain thankful that she was here with him. He recognized the selfishness in that thought, but that didn't alter the truth of it.

"Thanks," he said and meant it. "I feel a lot better."

Merry shrugged as she moved back on the lowered front seat, but she seemed very serious, and offered no answering smile. So he finally asked, "What is it? The cut? It's worse or something?"

"Oh, no, it looks okay, or at least as okay as it can." She bit her bottom lip. "I was just thinking, you mentioned about the heater. So, do we make a schedule or just use it when we need to or what?"

"Yes, we use it as little as possible to preserve the power. The lights should go on forever, they're very low voltage."

"No radio at all?"

"No." He wanted to move past that quickly. "The heater and the flares and fire are our main means of survival. To keep the cold from getting too intense."

Her fine eyebrows lifted. "Too intense?"

"We don't want frostbite or worse."

She looked as if she'd never even thought about that possibility. "Of course not," she murmured. "Can we leave it on a bit longer?"

"Sure, for a bit," he said, before segueing to a new subject. "You really recognized me at the airport?" That still surprised him.

"Well, not at first, but then I heard that man who found you asking if you were Gage Carson. That's when I really knew who you were."

"I thought I'd changed a lot since I was a kid." He'd been a skinny child with unruly dark hair, tanned to the color of coffee, and always sporting a bandage after some mishap with his brothers and friends. "A lot."

That teased a smile from her. "Oh, you've changed, a lot, but there's something so familiar." She shrugged, her smile fading just a bit. "You look like how I imagined you would look when you were grown." She gestured with her hands. "I'd heard that you were a huge success with your own construction company, and then there you were getting on your plane to head to Wolf Lake. It seemed to be a…" She hesitated on the word, then flushed slightly when she said, "A miracle."

Some miracle. He cringed a bit at her words, especially since they were stranded in a storm in a plane he'd crashed. He hadn't even been capable of taking off his own boots. "Logistics."

"Excuse me?" she asked.

He realized he'd switched subjects again, and that it had surprised her. "Logistics. I couldn't even get my boots off and it's only simple logistics." He made a noise that sounded suspiciously to him like a snort, but then he realized it was about the only way he could actually do anything close to laughing. "I run a huge construction and design business, and yet even with all my engineering skills you had to pull my boots off."

She chuckled at that and he liked the sound of it. "Ah, yes, thank goodness for all my higher education," she kidded.

"I didn't get that far. My education is from living my life, the good, the bad and the ugly." He watched her as his eyes began to feel heavy.

Sobering slowly from his words, she shrugged, but didn't speak. Those beautiful green eyes looked down at her hands pressed to her knees, and he knew what he'd said had bothered her, but he didn't know her well enough to understand why. He was with a woman who had been a relative stranger to him just hours ago, and now their fates were intertwined in a way that he'd never thought possible. "Life is a great teacher," he said, noticing how low and slightly slurred his words were.

"Yes, it is," she said, sitting a bit straighter. "And it's free. There's no student loans for living your life."

"Said like someone who has student loans?"

"Whew, yes, some," she admitted. "But I did receive a few very good scholarships to help out along the way."

"I take it you were good in school?"

"Good enough. How about you?"

He grimaced and felt the bandages on his wound tug at the skin around them. "I hated it. I graduated high school just because my mother wouldn't let me drop out."

"But you've got the company and from what I heard from Moses, you're incredibly gifted when it comes to construction and design."

He settled his head against the back of the seat and let his eyes close. "Moses is a talker. No, I don't have a gift, just a knack for picking things up and doing them." He sighed heavily. "You did it the right way by getting a degree."

"I'm actually thinking of going back to school to work on some sub specialties."

"For what?"

"Simply put, to get a broader base to work with the needs of emotionally challenged children."

He whistled, a low, soft sound in the cabin. "I'm impressed."

"I haven't done it yet. I'm still trying to recover from just getting my degree and being certified."

He liked her voice, and wanted her to keep talking while he settled more. "It was a lot of work?"

"Yes, but it was worth it."

"Financially?"

"I wish. No, the salary's okay, but the payoffs aren't money related."

"Such as?"

"I was able to come home to Wolf Lake, where I've wanted to be since forever, and I'm actually renting the house I always dreamed of living in when I was little. I'm going to try to buy it, if the owner, Willie G., ever decides to sell."

"Willie G.," he murmured, as an image of the old man with long gray hair and darkly weathered skin came to him. Willie had been a fixture in Wolf Lake for as long as Gage could remember, and long before that. "Willie G. doesn't sell anything. He's into keeping all he can for his people on the Rez."

"Oh," she said and in that single word he heard real disappointment.

"But you never know," he found himself adding. "He might get to like you, and want you to stick around and let you buy the place. By the way, which piece of land is it? He's bought up a lot of Wolf Lake."

"An old Victorian two story. It's blue, just like it was when I was a kid."

"The one on the side street near the inn that Mallory Sanchez owns and runs?"

"Yes, that's it."

"I heard he bought it years ago off Momma Dot, a teacher who used to work at the Rez school."

"Good to know," she said. "I used to pass it as a kid and make up all sorts of scenarios about it, like who lived there and me buying it and…" Her voice trailed off. "I guess we'll see what he'll do down the road sometime."

"Yes," he said, not adding that he hoped they both had another chance to meet up with Willie. "Where's my headpiece?" he asked, deftly changing the subject again.

"Here somewhere," she said, and he felt her moving, then the seat by him shifting. He opened his eyes, watching her intent on what she was doing. She turned back to him and held out the headpiece, but he waved it off. "You put it somewhere safe. It's no use to us now."

He watched her slip it in a side compartment by the backseat, and he asked as she moved back to the prone seat, "Why is Wolf Lake so special to you?"

She didn't speak for a bit, but finally said, "It's always been home to me, and with my stepfather being in the military, we never put down permanent roots anywhere after we left Wolf Lake. Just places we stayed for a few months, or if we got lucky, a year. But no home."

"That must have been difficult," he said softly.

"That's an understatement. I went to eleven schools before I graduated high school. The only time I stayed put was for college, and that was staying in a dorm room with three other students, taking as many credits as I could every semester and working to get extra money.

"When I was done, I simply didn't want

to move again, not until the offer from Wolf Lake came in. Then, I got to go back home, and I'm being paid for it, at least for two years."

"Then what?" He really wanted to know what path she had planned.

"I don't know," she confessed. "I've never come up with an answer for that even for myself. But I really hope I can stay with the center in some capacity." She sighed. "And maybe buy Willie G.'s house."

The wind and snow shook the plane violently, and he realized how effective the pills were. Any pain from the sharp jerks was lost in a mellow haze. But Merry gasped, and gripped the sides of the prone seat.

"Tell me we aren't near any chasms or cliffs," she demanded with a panic-stricken look on her face.

"Just trees, lots of trees, especially that big one." He didn't know what was beyond the trees and snow, but he didn't mention that.

"I know, and it's six feet away." She sat back again and said, "Six whole feet."

"A miss is as good as a mile," he said. "In any event, you need to get those thermals on, then we should get ready for the night." He watched her tense up again, and he was almost grateful that he suddenly felt incredibly tired. His eyes fought to close as he rested back against the seat. But he kept them open.

"The thermals," she repeated and moved to pull them into her lap.

"Use first class, and I'll close my eyes." He almost smiled as she hesitated. "I promise not to peek and I'm a man of my word. I keep my promises."

Her face fell, and she bit her lip hard. Wrong thing to say, he realized, when she murmured, "At least one of us does."

"Hey," he said brightly. "You meant that promise. You did everything you could to make it happen. No one can expect more from you than that, even kids."

She closed her eyes tightly for a moment, then opened them, looking at him now. "*I* expected more," she said on a whisper, then shifted to the front of the seat and levered the back to an upright position. Without saying anything else, she shrugged out of her suede jacket, then grabbed the hem of her top and started to tug it up without saying anything to him.

That's when he did keep his promise and

closed his eyes. He didn't open them again, until he heard her say, "All done."

When he looked at her, she appeared pretty much the same, except she'd either taken the tie off her ponytail, or her hair had come free in the process of changing clothes. Either way, her thick hair fell a few inches past her shoulders, and even in the dimness, he could catch the coppery streaks in it.

Her seat back went down again, and she scooted into a comfortable sitting position. She looked at him expectantly. The soft waves of her hair framed her face, and he didn't even try to rationalize why his only thought right then was that she was stunning. No fancy clothes or makeup, and she looked incredible there on the seat, watching him.

"Okay, let's get ready," he said, and as her expression seemed a bit strained, he was almost thankful for the heaviness in his eyes. He needed to sleep, despite her worries about a concussion. "There's a side panel back here. Open it and get out the blankets and a thermal wrap, then we'll turn the heater off for a while."

He pushed himself to keep an eye on her,

until she'd retrieved the items he'd asked for. "Got them," she said a few moments later.

"Good," he replied as she faced him with the supplies in her hands. Yes, she sure was beautiful.

CHAPTER SEVEN

WHEN MERRY HANDED him a blanket, she was so close to Gage that she could see the pulse beating in the hollow of his throat. She quickly looked away and accidentally dropped the blanket on his lap. His eyes were on her, measuring her in some way she didn't understand, but she could tell that the medication was having an effect. "Sorry," she said, reaching for the blanket.

His hand moved to hold it where it landed. "Let it be," he almost whispered. "Now, we need to figure out the food situation."

"There are energy bars and suckers in the first-aid kit," she offered.

"If you could shut down the heater first, and then grab some bars and a couple bottles of water, we'll move on to the blankets."

She moved carefully to the console and soon returned with the water and snacks. Putting the bottles of water in the cup holders, she found the seat lever, and tilted it as far as possible, making the seat not as flat as the front seats, but enough to make things much more comfortable for both of them.

She stretched out by Gage and could tell that any heat she felt had to be from his body. The air in the rest of the cabin was cooling off quickly.

He looked so much more peaceful now than he had before, and she felt a degree of relief, then he whispered something she didn't quite hear. She leaned closer to him, asked, "Pardon," and heard him say softly, "Listen." Frowning, she stared at him, his eyes closed.

"To what?" she asked, then knew.

Nothing. She couldn't hear the wind or the snow blowing against the plane anymore. To check she looked out the side window. "Oh, wow," she breathed. "Storm's over."

As she turned back to Gage, his eyes opened and his mouth curved into a slightly goofy smile that she suspected had a lot to do with the medication.

"Wonderful, isn't it?"

She wondered if he meant the current weather conditions or the pain pills. Either way, his smile was endearing, and if his ribs hadn't been broken, she knew that she would have hugged him then and there.

"Absolutely wonderful," she agreed and hugged herself. "Now we just wait," she said, feeling a tiny spark of renewed hope.

"And stay warm," he added softly.

"Yes, definitely, stay warm."

Gage pointed at the blankets and she grabbed them. She shook out the top blanket, surprised to find that it sounded like crinkling plastic but felt like thermal material, colored a deep orange. It barely weighed anything. The other one was what she'd call a "real" blanket, soft and heavy, in a pale blue color.

"You'd better take off your shoes, then settle back and put the orange blanket over the blue blanket."

Merry glanced at him, found his eyes still closed, and then followed his instructions. Her boots hit the floor first before she tackled the blankets. Once they were in place, she repositioned herself in the seat. "Now what?"

"Scoot closer this way, then tuck the blankets around your legs and feet, as far under your body as you can."

Closer? She didn't have to ask what he meant, but felt oddly reluctant to get too close. She slid a few inches in his direction and jumped when he said, "I won't bite. Promise."

He was looking very comfortable, with the

blankets up to his chin and his eyes closed. Without saying anything, she moved over until his side was against hers and she could feel his body heat. That was the idea, she knew, and accepted it. "Good," he murmured. "Much better."

Awkwardly, she tucked the blankets all the way around Gage's other side, then his feet, and then she finally started tucking herself in until she was laying back, feeling as if she was in a cocoon.

"Done," she announced. A few minutes passed before she asked the question that was the equivalent of the elephant in the room. "Gage, what happens if they never find us?"

"They'll find us."

"But what if—?"

"What if the sun doesn't come up? Nothing we could do about that, is there?" His voice was low and showed no sign of anger or impatience. "They'll find us. It's all up to them now. We got down in one piece," he finished, ignoring the elephant completely.

"Yes, yes we did," she said, feeling grateful. They were both alive and relatively unscathed.

He caught her off guard by saying, "Sort of like Gilligan's Island, isn't it? They started on a three hour tour and look what happened to them. All we had to get through was two hours."

But there's only two of us, she thought, but kept it to herself. Then again, he'd gotten them down, and he seemed to know what he was doing. "Old TV shows aside, what can we do if no one ever shows up?" She needed to say it and she needed to get an answer.

GAGE DESERVED HER prodding after he'd so glibly thrown out the idea before that flying was so much safer than driving. Now, they were living the exception that broke that rule. "Okay, worst case scenario, we're stuck here and we'll have to walk out. But we won't have to face that for a few days, if ever."

Gage turned his head to the side until he could see her. She was like reading an open book. She was processing what he'd said, and coming to the conclusion that it might not be all that hopeless. When she finally spoke, he knew he was partially right.

"So we wait, then find a path to get down the mountain." Before he could agree and hope she'd drop the subject, she hit him with, "If not, we end up here forever." He could see the unsteadiness in her chin and tears at the corners of her eyes.

"No," he said emphatically. "No!" That got her attention and her eyes widened slightly as she turned more toward him. "We are not here forever. You are going to get back to Wolf Lake to see your kids, and I'm going to get back there to do my job and see my family. It's that simple. They'll find us, and we'll go home."

Boy, whatever had hit her in those words hit her hard and she started to sob. With her hands covering her face, she cried like her heart was broken. He tried to shift more toward her, but found even the pills couldn't stop the pain in his left arm when he moved. Slowly, pacing himself, he got his arm over his body until he could rest his hand on her shoulder.

When he made contact, she moved, too, but not away from him, instead, closer to him. Her head was on his right shoulder, her face tucked into his flannel shirt, and her tears were soaking the soft material. She cried so hard she was shaking all over and all he could do was touch her head with his chin and slip his hand to her back. Helpless. He'd never felt so completely helpless in his life.

MERRY GAVE IN TO every bit of fear and misery that had been building in her since the plane had gone down. She cried so hard she could barely breathe, and hated herself for giving in to her despair. She pressed against Gage, taking comfort in his closeness, and wished she could wake up and find this was all a twisted dream. But it wasn't. This was her reality, and thank goodness she wasn't in this alone.

Gradually she wearied of the sobbing, and became aware of the heat and strength she was nestling up against, and the arm wrapped protectively around her, never faltering. And a voice so low it seemed made just for her ears.

"We'll be okay, we will. I promise."

She hiccoughed sharply, gulping back the tears, but she didn't move away. She let him hold her, and she closed her eyes tightly, letting his heat seep into her. In that fleeting moment, she felt safer than she'd felt in her whole life. It was crazy, laying with a stranger, a man who hadn't wanted her on his plane at all, yet a man who had ended up being her only hope of getting home.

She slowly moved back, easing into the cold leather, not able to look at Gage right then. "I'm so, so sorry," she said in a voice that she barely recognized.

"Nerves are nerves, even if you're a shrink."

She grimaced at his choice of words, and let her head rest against the back of the seat. "Yes, they are," she admitted.

Gage brought the blanket back up near their chins. They were side by side now, his arm gone from around her, but his heat was still there. And she needed it desperately. "We'll be okay," he repeated.

She breathed deeply several times, an attempt to calm herself and regain control of her emotions. No words would come, so she merely nodded. And as she lay there next to Gage, something he'd mentioned before came back to her. "You…you said you had a job in Wolf Lake?"

"Hmm?"

"A job, I thought you said you had a job to get to?"

"Oh, yeah, well…a possible job."

She'd thought he was passing through on his way to another job close to Wolf Lake, or something like that. "In Wolf Lake?"

"That's right."

"What kind of job?"

When she turned her head to see his reaction, their faces were just inches apart. His eyes were closed. "Land development," he answered.

"Where?" she asked, trying to keep her voice even.

"Land south of town—a huge chunk of the Drey spread. Max Drey passed a few years ago, and the family decided to sell. It's a pristine piece of land, and it's in the right location for what the powers-that-be in Wolf Lake and the Rez want to do." He paused. "They asked for a bid from our company to develop the area for an entertainment complex."

She knew the Drey land and it was beautiful, sprawling and open, the epitome of what she'd always remembered about Wolf Lake when she was a kid. She'd heard rumors about something being done with it, but everyone she'd talked to hadn't wanted the town invaded by noise and pollution for some project that might never get off ground. Now, a Carson was actually talking about bulldozing his home as if it was just another job.

Staying very still, she asked, "Are you talking about casinos?"

"Exactly."

"Gage, no!" She abruptly sat up, taking most of the blankets with her. "You can't."

He stayed where he was, but his eyes were open now. "What are you talking about?"

"A casino?" She took a deep breath to keep

her voice from rising. "No one will want that in town, and how can you in good conscience do that to Wolf Lake, your own hometown?"

She could see that he was confused by what she was saying. "Hold on," he said, shifting in his seat to look more directly at her. "I was asked to come, to give a bid, to show a design model. I didn't come here to beg for the work." His face tightened. "Besides, you haven't been here for years. What makes you so sure about what should or shouldn't be in Wolf Lake?"

He was right. She'd been gone for twenty years, but that didn't matter when it came to right and wrong.

In the past, when she'd heard rumors about a possible gambling center, some hotels and restaurants, and more bars, a segment of the town felt it was "progress," while the majority felt it would never happen. She believed that putting an "entertainment complex" in a place like Wolf Lake would be like poisoning their water wells, then getting the locals to pay to drink it.

"So, I haven't been there for a long time, but I was born there. And even I know that it's a bad idea. A really bad idea."

"Tell the gaming commission and town officials. They asked for it," he said, closing his eyes. He made a display of stretching his legs, then putting the blankets back in place around him, tucking himself in as best he could. Despite her anger at him, she helped by rearranging them over his legs and feet.

She spoke as she worked, not finished with this diatribe by a long shot. "There are already a lot of problems with gambling and substance abuse in the area, and what you're doing will only draw in outsiders in droves with only their self-interest at heart. It's an uphill fight to keep some kids in school, what do you think is going to happen when they start trying to strike it rich gambling or get anything they want right within reach?"

He hadn't moved while she talked, and she was almost afraid he was purposely ignoring her. But she couldn't resist finishing with, "You don't have any concept of how damaging something like this could be to everyone in Wolf Lake." With that, she laid back down and retucked the blankets around herself.

A few moments later, Gage finally spoke. "I don't have an opinion on any of that. I'm only here to find out whether or not it's a good, sound business decision for my firm."

Merry didn't buy that. "That is either greed or ignorance, not indifference."

When Gage spoke again, she didn't look at him. She stared at the ceiling, but could hear the anger tingeing his words. "I'm a 'fly by the seat of my pants' businessman, and this deal feels good to me. Its effects won't hurt a soul, not if decisions are made reasonably and caution is taken. And there is such a thing as personal responsibility."

Merry bit her lip and forced herself to keep staring at the shadows. She couldn't believe that Gage meant what he said. Wolf Lake was where he'd been born and grown up. He couldn't be that unfeeling about the chance of something bad happening to it.

The kids. She squeezed her eyes tight to keep any more tears from falling. The poor kids. She'd never made it back, and didn't know when, or if, she could get there. And now this, this catastrophe of a business proposition, shrouded in the idea that it was good for everyone.

Nothing had worked out how she'd expected it to. Sick with worry about the whole situation, about the kids at the center and, unsettlingly, about the man beside her, she tried to relax. This wasn't the time for arguments anyway. They needed to focus on getting to safety. Gage was her only hope of survival, she owed him so much, and all she could do was give him a hard time about his ethics? She took a deep breath, then glanced to her left and saw Gage. His eyes were open and clear. "You're doing okay?" she asked.

"Sure," he murmured and his hand touched hers, as if to reassure her.

"Did we ever figure out if you should even be trying to sleep?"

"No, but I don't think it matters." He shifted ever so slightly to angle his body more toward hers. "Just try to put everything out of your mind and get some sleep. Worry doesn't get you far."

"I need to learn to cope, or whatever it takes, is that what you're saying?"

As soon as the sarcastic words were out of her mouth, she regretted them. She hoped that he didn't remember saying those same words about her kids when she'd told him about their inability to deal with disappointments in life. But all that hope was for nothing. "This isn't the same as kids being let down," he pointed out.

"No, it's not," she whispered in agreement. "Not at all." He would never truly understand what she'd told him about her kids, just as she couldn't understand why he was so blasé about a potentially harmful casino showing up in the middle of Wolf Lake.

"Are you warm enough?" he asked as she watched his eyes slowly close.

"Yes, but I'd love a roaring fireplace right about now."

He chuckled softly, whatever anger he'd felt moments ago, apparently gone. "At my parents' place, they have a fireplace in the main great room that's open in every direction. When we were kids, we'd all sit around it, and make Smores. I hated the taste, the sticky marshmallows and chocolate and broken Graham crackers, but it was fun setting the marshmallows on fire and watching them explode."

She studied him as he laid peacefully tangled in the blankets with her, and thought she could almost see the little boy who liked to burn marshmallows just to blow them up. "So, you never ate them?"

"No, never. But it fascinated me to take all the burned ones that didn't blow up, and stack them into towers. They really stuck together and I could get quite a few on the stack before it just looped over and fell."

"You were a builder even then," she said softly.

"I guess so."

"Can I ask you something?"

"Sure."

"Are you really okay with putting the gambling center in the town? Doesn't it bother you on some level, what it may negatively do to your friends and the community?"

His eyes opened as she spoke, and he waited until she grew silent before saying tightly, "No."

"Really? Not at all?"

He sighed with exasperation. "No, it's a job that the people there are asking me to consider. It's that simple." He took a rough breath. "And, to be honest, if I don't get the gig, someone else will. It's happening one way or another, regardless of who wins the bid."

"So that makes it okay?"

His anger was coming back. "Listen, can we agree to disagree on this at least until we get out of here?"

Chicken, she thought, but kept that to herself. "Okay." Now she had to figure out how to survive with the man beside her, who didn't seem to care at all about what happened to the only place she'd ever called home.

"Now get some rest," he said.

Sleep. She'd forgotten. "You can't sleep," she said.

He responded by saying groggily, "I have to. But I'll take full responsibility for whatever happens."

"Sure," she said to herself. "Another bad idea of yours." Still, she knew better than to belabor the point. He'd do what he wanted to do, and the fight had suddenly drained out of her.

MERRY SLEPT FITFULLY, waking in the near dark, hearing Gage's deep, even breaths so close to her. She started counting his breaths, waiting for a change, not even sure what that change would be. But she counted, and sometime toward dawn, she fell asleep. The next thing she knew, she felt something weird, as if someone had wrapped her up like a present, trapping her arms and legs.

She opened her eyes to bleak light and windows blurred by ice sheeting them on the outside. The world beyond was distorted in smears of grays and whites with shadows here and there. She jerked up, startled by movement over her. It was Gage, he was reaching for something beyond her.

"What are you doing?" she gasped, peering up into his face above her.

"Just making sure you were as warm as possible," he said and she realized he was kneeling on the bottom of her seat, his legs against hers, stretching over her. "After all, you did it for me last night even when you were furious with me." He actually smiled down at her, exposing his dimple.

She looked away. "Thanks, but I'm getting up," she said, and he moved back as she tried to sit up. "What are you doing up, anyway, and what about your ribs and head?"

"I'm fine," he said, but he moved stiffly as he drew back and sat leaning against the screen. "And it's morning."

That single word propelled her to sit up farther. "It's time, isn't it?"

"Yes," Gage said.

"Fires, smoke, whatever it takes to get noticed out there by the rescue team," she said, pushing at the blankets to get free of them. Everything else was of no importance, not even the conversation about the casino development, the worry and dread for her kids and for them. Today was their chance to get out of here, and she was ready.

"Let's get going, then," he said.

"What do we need to do?" It seemed she was always asking him that question in one context or another, but this time it seemed gravely important.

"Bundle up, and then make our way to safety," he said, turning away from her to reach down in front of the seat.

She barely bit back a gasp when she saw him double over in pain, but he didn't dwell on it. Instead, he pulled up his duffel bag, tossed it on the pilot's seat and rummaged through it.

"Did you take more medication?" she asked.

He nodded without looking at her.

She tugged on her suede jacket and gloves, then tied the scarf at her neck, leaving it loose enough to pull up over her face if she needed to do that once she was outside.

Gage looked at her. "Okay?" he asked.

"How about you?"

"Freezing to death," he muttered, as he tried to right himself by the door. Then he added something that made her almost smile. "I should have gotten a bigger plane while I had the chance."

"Can we turn on the heater soon?" Her face was already getting uncomfortable with the frigid air in the cabin.

He adjusted the control for the emergency

heat, and then told her, "It's on. We'll need it when we get back in here."

"How long can we leave it going?"

"We'll figure that out as we go along," Gage said and lifted his leg to get closer to the door.

A glimpse of his boot showed it still darkened and misshapen from the snow from the night before, and she had no doubt they were still damp and cold. "Don't you have another pair of boots?" she asked.

"Yes, I do, but didn't want to crawl all over you while you were sleeping to get to them," he replied. "Do you have a more colorful jacket with you?"

"No, I only brought the one."

He flicked his eyes over her medium brown jacket and white gloves, hat and scarf that all blended with her jacket.

She understood. "How about you? Anything that will make a color splash against the snow?"

"Yeah, I do. There's a surveying jacket that's really bright orange." He snapped his fingers. "And I think there's some watch caps, too, in ugly dayglow yellow."

She turned and moved the seats to gain access to the back storage area, the way she'd done the night before. "Where are they?" she asked.

"Near the back. Get the jacket, the boots and the hats should be with them. Also a pair of work gloves, leather, paint spattered."

She began to feel around, got the jacket and passed it onto him. Then she found the hats, two of them, the ugly dayglow yellow Gage had said they were. She saw Gage grab the jacket before she turned back to the storage area. When she offered the dry boots, with heavy lug soles, he had the jacket on, its brilliant orange almost painful to the eyes.

"Great," he said, taking the boots from her. "See if you can find a shovel. There's one with a collapsible handle in there somewhere."

She had a harder time finding the shovel, but finally located it, and a hammer and what looked like a tire iron of all things. She showed them to Gage, who was just finishing putting on his last boot. "I'll need the shovel and hammer, but put back the crow bar."

She pushed the seat back in place, and then turned to Gage. He had on the yellow cap now, and it almost covered the wound on his forehead. Despite the garish attire, his looks still made her pause. He tossed her a second hat, and she took off her light covering to replace it with the yellow wool cap. "These can't be missed by anyone looking for us," she quipped.

"Exactly," Gage said, in his bright orange and yellow ensemble. He moved around to grip the door handle. "Stay back when I open this. If there's snow against it, we're going to get some tumbling into the cabin. Bring the shovel with you."

She got the shovel before scooting along the reclining seat, and stopping right behind Gage. She waited as the lock clicked and the door began to swing up. She felt the frigid air, so cold it immediately made her face ache, invade the cabin. She tugged the scarf up over her mouth and nose and watched Gage move with painfully slow movements as he eased the door up, inch by inch.

It seemed like forever before the door was completely open to the world outside, but luckily only a minimal amount of snow came inside the cabin. Gage ducked out onto the wing and Merry was right behind him. Even so, she could feel the ice on the metal of the wing, and she grabbed the door frame to hold her footing.

The cold air hit her even harder, its temperature surely near the zero mark. The light all around was a dull gray, clouds heavy and low in the sky. Very little of the area was flat. Trees soared all around them, their snow burdened branches oddly loaded on one side, but merely icy on the other. Then she looked down and realized the snow on the ground was probably all of a foot deep, but the drifts against the plane had climbed to cover the bright green middle stripe.

One look at the trees in the path of their landing, and she was stunned at how impossible it seemed that they had cut through them, without the plane being destroyed. Then a glance toward the front and she knew that there was one more miracle to add to her list. The pine tree was massive, its top lost in the low clouds. And they were exactly as Gage had said, six feet from where they would have impacted with the plane. A life devoid of miracles until she'd been stranded in the airport terminal in Pueblo, had sudden become touched by so many.

CHAPTER EIGHT

"Merry?"

Gage's voice jarred her out of her thoughts, and she turned to him. As if he'd read her mind, yet again, he touched her shoulders with both hands and said, "Just remember, it's not what could have happened, but what didn't happen."

He was so close she felt his breath brush her cold skin as he spoke. "Yes, you're right," she said, fighting the urge to let herself just fall against him for support.

She turned as he let her go and inched toward the side of the wing. The snow wasn't very deep there, but the distance to the ground from the wing was still about three or four feet. "How do we get down from here?" she asked.

"I can manage it." Gage moved around her, going closer to the tip end of the wing. "We'll get the flares and fire material out of the safety storage, then get back inside."

Merry rubbed her arms briskly in an attempt to warm herself. "Okay, you're the boss," she said.

"I thought this was more of a partnership?" he retorted as he kicked at the snow on the wing. Then, in one continuous motion, he crouched, turned and lowered himself to the ground. The snow was thin in that spot and barely came halfway up his boots. He looked back up at her, and even though he didn't show any reaction to pain, she could tell that had taken a toll on him.

"Pass me the shovel, then come on down," he said, holding out a hand to her.

She lowered the shovel to him, but when he put his hand back up to help her down, Merry ignored the offer, not about to burden him with her weight when he was injured. Instead, she lowered herself to sit on the wing's edge and regretted it immediately when the cold snow and metal jarred her through her jeans. Faster than she intended to, she slid off the wing, hitting the ground with both feet. She felt snow go up her pant legs, but she was down and standing on her own.

"You should stay here and I'll shovel the snow away from the storage area." He looked around, frowning. "There has to be some level spot that's not too small," he muttered, more to himself than for her benefit, before he slowly walked around the side of the plane. He stopped about two feet from his goal and turned to her. "This won't take a minute," he said. And with those words he was shoveling, throwing snow behind him and away from the panel.

A small door appeared in the plane's side, then Gage froze. "Oh…keys for the storage section are in the plane somewhere."

"I'll go and get them," she offered, but he stopped her. "Never mind. This thing is ruined now, so—" He got the shovel up and pushed the tip of it into the crack that showed around the door. He pushed, burying the shovel tip a bit deeper in a growing gap, then left the shovel wedged there, lifted his booted foot and kicked at the shovel handle. There was a cracking sound when the handle broke, but at the same time, the door flew open.

"Who needs higher education?" he joked as he moved to the door, pulled it fully back and reached into the small opening. He brought out a red box, laid it at his feet, then a second box that was larger and a brilliant orange. It almost matched the jacket Gage was wearing. He left the door ajar, bent to get the smaller box and went to where Merry was. He left the box by her. "The flares," he said before he walked back for the larger box. When he brought it to Merry, he explained, "Fire goodies."

"Is that a technical term for what's in there?" she said, her spirits buoyed just by being out there doing something.

"You said you didn't want that technical jargon, so I thought I'd make this easy for you." The grin came, the dimple along with it, and Merry felt even better, despite the freezing air.

"Thank you, boss," she said.

"What's that all about?" he asked her.

"Well, you are in charge, aren't you?" She smiled back at him.

"Boss...yeah, I haven't thought much about that. I wish I could talk to my right-hand man," he said, wistfully. "So, all we need is a few hundred feet of visibility." He looked up into the heavily clouded sky. "And no more snow."

Merry swallowed hard, part of her wanting to just talk and not think about anything, but the other part pushing at her, telling her to take action and do something to facilitate a rescue. "What now?"

He crouched down and broke the seals on

the red box. "First the flares, then I need to see what's beyond those trees."

"Why?"

"In case we need to know later. I'd rather know now."

"That sounds vaguely like double talk, but I'll let it pass."

"Thank you," he said and handed her two of the long red flares. "Put them in your pockets, just in case we hear anything while we're out."

"What about making the fire?"

He glanced back and forth. "We can clear a spot around here, and keep an eye on it from the plane. We'll leave the rest of this here while we look around. Or you can go back inside and stay warm."

"No. I'm coming."

"All right," he said and shoved two flares in his own jacket pockets.

"If we hear anything, don't we need matches for the flares?"

"No. I'll show you how to do that with the cap in a bit."

She felt the weight of the flares in her pocket as Gage pointed toward the trees to the west. Drifts went halfway up the tree trunks, but the rest on the ground looked to be as thin as the snow by the plane.

"That way." He started off with Merry following in his tracks, literally, and into the trees.

The snow was even more sparse over there, but the branches looked weighted down on the edges. A short time later, they broke out of the trees and onto a long, narrow clearing.

Rimmed on three sides with massive trees, the clearing seemed to go off into nothingness on the last side facing west. With the clouds so low and the light so gray, she couldn't see very far, but she guessed if she could have, she would have been looking across a deep void to more mountains, more trees and snow.

"This could work for the rescue," he announced and crossed to the drop off. "There's enough clearance for a helicopter." He stared straight up into the clouds. "It could work." Then he started stomping around the clearing, making a large circle with the trampled snow. "What are you doing?" Merry called to him.

"Clearing this a bit, so we can make some sort of SOS on the ground. Rocks, branches, anything. An arrow's a good sign. Even just the arrow head could do it, pointed back in our direction."

"How could they see anything like that?" she asked.

"Helicopters get low, and anything could help." Merry hurried over and started stomping herself. While she beat down the snow, Gage added, "I'll look for anything we can use," and then he walked out of the circle and toward the trees again.

When he disappeared into the trees, Merry began to panic from the intense isolation. Without a second thought, she called out, "I'll help!" and plunged into the trees after him.

He turned as she hustled toward him, ducking the low branches. When she got to him, her first thought was the darn yellow hat actually looked good on the man. Dark eyes, dark hair. She thought he'd tell her to go back and finish what she was doing, but he just held out his hand to her and said, "Come on. Let's look around."

She put her hand in his, felt his fingers curl around hers through her wool gloves. Side by side they slowly scanned the area. After only a few minutes, Merry could feel Gage was slowing down and he was fighting pain again. She stopped and as he let go of her hand. "You know, we don't need to do this now. We should just go back and take care of the most important things—the flares and the fire—then do a search for rocks or whatever later."

He looked at her, and she knew that he knew that she knew about his condition. She almost laughed at that reasoning, but she was right. She knew it. He hesitated, then with a bare nod, he turned and started back the way they'd come.

She followed, with no hand offered to her this time. Keeping her eyes on his back under the brilliant orange material of his jacket, she watched in case he faltered, but he didn't. Then they were back at the plane, their boxes left where they'd been set. Gage crossed to them, started to bend, but stopped himself.

He pointed to the large box. "I should have thought of this before. Look in there. It should have fuel and things we can use."

Merry went around Gage and squatted by the box. She snapped the bail ties up and opened the lid. She saw an odd arrangement inside. Pieces of wood, maybe six inches long, bundled together on one side, white boxes about the size of what could hold a baseball divided the box in half, stacked three deep. A serrated knife, about the size of a butcher's knife, was sheathed in a plastic holder.

Two lighters, fuel for them and a plastic bag of what looked like black rocks, rounded out the inventory.

"What do I do first?" she asked, and didn't miss the way he was leaning back against the wing for support.

"Clear a space about eight feet across." He looked to the south and pointed to an area where the trees were thin and there was enough space for the clearing. "Stomp it down to level the area."

She walked in a circle, then began stamping the snow down. Glancing over at Gage, she saw him pick up the saw, take off the plastic and head for the trees. "Where are you going?" she yelled.

"Be right back," he said, ducking into the press of branches. "I want to try this." He held up the saw as he disappeared into the forest.

She tried to tamp down her rising panic by listening to the sounds of his movement just beyond her sight. When the snow was pressed flat to the ground, she stopped and heard a cracking sound, then the whoosh of something falling. "Gage!"

She took off at a dead run, hoping nothing bad had happened to him.

When she found him, he was standing by

a large pine and an iced branch was laying at his feet. He turned when he heard her, a questioning look in his eyes. "Did you hear a plane or someone?" he asked, crossing over to her immediately.

"Yes, uh, no, just thought something fell and I was…worried." She bit her lip to stop anymore babbling.

"Oh. The noise was just a branch I had to get some cuttings, we'll need to use them for the fire. The greener the better for smoke."

"Right. Sure, of course…green branches, smoke makers," she mumbled and grabbed the branch before he could bend to get it, then dragged it back to where she'd made the circle He caught up to her as she dropped the branch by the crushed snow and said, "I'll cut it up."

She noted how pale he looked. She didn't bother trying to finesse anything. "No, you won't. You're in pain again."

"Moving around will help loosen my sore muscles," he countered.

"No, it'll hurt you."

He touched her chin with the tip of his gloved finger. "Okay, sawing wood is out, but I can lay a fire." With that he went back to the big box, took out several pieces and came back to the circle. "Open the kindling and give it to me one at a time."

She hesitated, then a narrowed, "Don't mess with me," look from his dark eyes got her moving. She unwrapped a pack of kindling and handed him one stick after the other, while he made a pattern on the ground. The saw he'd used was on the ground by the large branch and he motioned to them. "Can you cut off a few of the smaller branches for me?"

"It's all ice," she pointed out. "It would smoke, if it could even catch fire."

She saw the frown distort his handsome features, then said, "It's the pills. I can't think straight. Of course that's not going to burn." He straightened very slowly, his shoulders slumped.

"Rest a minute," she said. "I'll be back soon."

As Merry headed into the wilderness, she heard him ask what she was doing. "Going on a scavenger hunt!" she tossed over her shoulder.

She ventured deep into the brush, veering away from the tracks that they'd left going and coming from the clearing at the drop off. Looking carefully, she found a spot where branches had broken off the tree and piled near its base. Snow and ice were thin on the top branches. Quickly, she pulled the upper branches off and found what she wanted. Branches that were barely touched by the dampness of ice and snow.

Five minutes later, she was back at the plane with her arms heavily laden by her find. Gage was leaning on the wing, his face tense until he spotted her, then he immediately brightened. "Did you take a survival course?" he asked as he met her halfway between the plane and the trees.

"I wish." She looked toward their spot for their signal fire. Gage had everything put in order, at least she thought it was in order. Walking toward the spot, she could see the kindling in a terribly small looking mound. As she dropped the wood, she asked, "Is that enough to get a fire going? And this wood is still a bit damp."

Gage was there, stepping past her, and nodded confidently. "The kindling does it all," he said. "It's treated, and it will make anything burn."

And he proved it as they both cracked off the smaller branches from the larger ones, and he laid them over the kindling. When he touched a wooden match to several spots, the kindling almost whooshed, then the branches began to light, one after the other, hissing and popping, but burning nonetheless. It was a fire, but not much of one, and it didn't look as if it would do any good. Then Gage took one of the boxes out and opened it, pouring some of whatever was inside into his hand and tossing it onto the growing flames.

Suddenly smoke was drifting into the dull sky, an oddly billowing cloud that rose up into the clouds. The smell wasn't unpleasant, almost a fire smoke smell with something tinged with pine in it.

"We'll need more wood," Merry said and started back toward the trees.

Gage followed, but stayed silent as Merry forged around a clump of tightly growing trees with what turned out to be a nice amount of protected branches they could use. He didn't make some macho attempt to carry anything, just silently watched her then fell into step beside her as they headed back.

"I'll cut more later." Merry moved toward the fire that was sending a steady stream of dark smoke up toward the clouds. She stopped, frowned, then turned to Gage right behind her. "Where can we put these?" she asked, nodding with her head toward the branches she was carrying.

He glanced around, then crossed to the plane and to the door he'd broken to get the flares and fire makings. "In here," he said, and when she got to him, he took the branches, shoving them inside the now empty space and forcing the door closed.

He faced her and Merry could see he was grim. "The snow won't get to it there," he said as he leaned back against the compartment's door.

She frowned at him. "More snow? There's another storm coming?"

"Let's hope not," he said, moving toward the end of the wing. "Every two hours of light, we have to renew the fire."

"Okay," she said.

"And if it gets windy, we have to put the fire out. It's too dangerous, even with all this snow around."

She nodded.

He took a deep breath and released it. His gaze held hers for a long moment. "Let's get inside and warm up a bit?"

"What about the flares?"

He pulled one from his pocket, and stared at it as if trying to figure out what to do. "This medicine..." He shook his head as his words trailed off and he headed about five feet away from the end of the wing.

A plain wooden stick the same length as the flare had been taped to its side. He pulled it off, pushed it in the bottom of the flare, then looked back toward her. "We'll put out four of them, push them in the snow as far as we can, space them about three or four feet apart, then if there's any sign of a search party, we've got the fire and can light the flares in seconds."

She yanked the flares out of her pocket, attached the sticks at the bottoms, then bent to push one into the snow near her feet. It went about four inches, then hit something as hard as a rock. "That's as far as it goes," she said, putting her head back to look up at Gage. "Is that far enough?"

"It'll have to be," he said and she repeated her action about three feet from the first. Gage went three feet farther, held out his flare to her, and she put it in place another three feet closer to the trees. "I hope they'll be able to see them," she said as she took the second flare from Gage, who had inserted the stake in the end.

"They will, believe me, these things are bright and high for about thirty seconds. Only light two at a time and wait for them to fizzle before lighting two more. We need to keep some with us at all times."

Merry took out four more flares from the box, closed it and returned to Gage to give him two. "Your stock," she said, then put hers in her jacket pockets. "And my stock." She hesitated. "Won't they get wet from the snow, and not light?"

"No, they'll light. They're made for bad weather and their ignition time is almost instantaneous. No extended burning."

"Good to know," she said, then asked, "Now how do I light the thing without a match?"

Gage explained it to her using one of his flares. He glanced over at the smoke from the small fire. "That will be useless if it snows again."

Merry felt some of the fear she'd been trying to suppress rise again. As if he sensed the damage his words had done to her spirits, he said more positively, "If anyone's close by and it's burning, they'll see it." He slowly started back to the wing.

She fell in step next to him, and without warning, he put his arm around her, pulling her to his side. At first she thought he'd been about to fall, but instead he just held her against him. "You did a good job…and we're going to be okay." His hold on her tightened for a second or so, then he let her go and they kept walking toward the plane.

She didn't know why he'd hugged her like that, but she knew it had been perfect timing. She had needed it badly, some affirmation that they were doing the right thing and that there was hope this would end well. Whatever had prompted the tender embrace, she was grateful for it.

Gage turned to her. "Come on," he said, holding out his hand. "Let's get out of this cold."

She couldn't take his hand, not when he was in such pain, but she wished she could. And she wished she could hold on to it until they were safely back home. Instead, she scrambled up onto the wing, felt his hand at the small of her back pushing to help her. Pivoting, she crouched and would have held out a hand to him, but he moved quickly, got himself up on the wing and made for the door.

But not before she got a glimpse of beads of sweat on his forehead, despite the fact the temperature had dropped even lower since they'd first come out.

She moved too quickly, almost losing her

footing on the icy snow, but she managed to get a grip on the hatch handle before Gage could bend to do it himself. She hauled up the door, and moved back to let him go in first, hoping he'd go right to the back where he could lay down.

But he stayed where he was. "Get in," he said through clenched teeth.

Arguing would just make things worse so Merry ducked into the cabin. He was right behind her and immediately secured the door. He struggled to sit down. Without looking at her, he murmured, "I can't think straight."

That's when she knew how badly he'd been hurt. Not just bruises, but yes, even a possible broken rib or two. "Try to get into the back so you can rest," she said.

He stared at his feet. "My boots."

He didn't have to say anything more. She toe and heeled out of her own boots, then leaned over and undid his, loosened the laces as much as she could before slipping them off of his feet.

He exhaled and said, "Okay, here goes." On his hands and knees he half crawled to the back, then shifted very slowly over to where he'd slept before. Merry had to make herself not reach out to help him get to where he wanted to be, and fortunately he made it without any problem.

Gage looked over at her, then positioned his stocking feet up on the lowered seat back in front of him. "Leave the boots ready to put on quickly," he said. "Just in case we hear something."

Merry agreed and settled into her seat. She kept reminding herself to stay calm. He needed her.

Gage checked his watch. "An hour and a half for the fire, then I'll tend to it."

She stared across the front seats to the windshield and could see the wavering motion of the smoke from the fire. It was still going. "We can see from here," she pointed out. "No reason to go out in that cold before we have to."

"You're right," he said and she could hear a heaviness in his tone.

"Do you want more pills?" she asked.

He closed his eyes for several minutes, long enough that Merry thought he hadn't heard her or was choosing to ignore her. His jaw was clenched, then she heard a hiss before he spoke. "No, I don't *want* any more pills, but I do need something to ease the pain…".

She heard the tremendous reluctance in his

voice and knew what it cost him to admit that to her. Quickly, she got the pills, and a bottle of water. He took the medication and then settled back again. "I hate not being able to think clearly."

She knew that anything she said to that would come across as patronizing, so she kept quiet. She shifted so she could watch Gage and could gradually see his breathing ease and the stress on his face lessen. From out of the blue, a smile suddenly tugged at his lips.

"What's so amusing?" she asked.

He shrugged, his eyes narrowed on her. "I was thinking about my assistant, Tark."

"And that's funny, how?" she asked. "Although Tark is an unusual name."

"His full name is Tarkington Davis, but that's another story. However, his nickname is Boom-Boom."

"He fell a lot or likes big guns?" she asked, totally at sea about what he was amused by.

"Neither. It's Boom-Boom because he likes the demolition part of this business."

"Okay, I get the Boom-Boom part. But I don't get why that's funny at this point in time?"

"What's funny is seeing you wearing his hat."

She yanked off the hat that she'd all but forgotten about wearing and looked down at it in her hand. *BOOM-BOOM* was sewn on the front of the hat.

"It could have been worse, I guess," she conceded. "I mean, what if his nickname had been Doofus or something like that?"

He chuckled and then caught himself immediately. "It only hurts when I laugh," he gasped, and despite what pain he felt, the smile still shadowed his lips. And she was enjoying that immensely.

She was about to tell Gage, but was shocked when he suddenly sat up, his gasp of pain a raw sound in the confines of the cabin. For a second she thought he was having a seizure, then he was actually pushing past her, on his knees, getting to the front seat and the door. "They're here!" he said as he pushed the door up and out, then stepped out onto the wing.

Merry fumbled getting upright, going after him as quickly as she could. She looked out the door, saw Gage at the wing's end, in his stocking feet and his hands fumbled in the pockets of his orange jacket. Merry understood he hadn't gone mad, no, he'd heard what she heard right then, a pulsating whirl of a helicopter high above them beyond the clouds.

"The flares are on the ground," she hollered, realizing he was going to try to light the flare he'd had in his pocket. "The ground!" she repeated, ignoring the stunning cold through her own socks as she ran to him, grabbed his arm and managed to knock the flare out of his hand. Top over bottom, it tumbled down and off the wing into the snow below.

She didn't think, just acted, lowering herself down to the ground, then darted toward the flares stuck in the snow. She sank to her knees by the closest one, trying to remember what Gage had told her about the cap and friction. But he was there, right behind her, going to the next flare. He worked quickly, then stood and had her by the arm, dragging her back out of the line of fire.

The flare hissed, followed by sparks and a strange noise. A burst of flame shot into the air, tailed by more red glow, soaring into the clouds and disappearing from sight. "We're here, we're here!" Gage shouted up to the heavens.

Merry thought she saw a change in the color of the clouds from leaden gray to an eerie glow, but it was gone quickly, the silence only broken by a fading whistling sound and then a growing wind. No sounds of helicopters, no engine sounds, nothing at all now. "Did they see it?" she asked, getting to her feet. Ignoring the damp coldness at her knees, and the frigidness of her socks, she grabbed Gage's arm. "They had to see the flare, didn't they?"

There was only his heavy breathing. "I don't know," he said in a low voice.

She held tightly to him while her eyes stayed fixed on the clouds over them, willing the helicopter to come back. But it didn't. "They're gone." Her whole body seemed to feel the disappointment.

Gage was still, and Merry thought he was still listening, waiting, maybe knowing something she didn't know about this kind of rescue. But when she looked up at him, she recognized that he wasn't moving because he was in a world of pain. His actions had cost him dearly. The pain had to be terrible, but that wasn't why his face was twisted in a heavy frown. He was staring at the fire, or what had been the fire five minutes ago.

The flames had since gone out, half buried by a huge dump of snow that had to have fallen, or been blown by the wind, off of one of the nearby towering trees. A bare wisp of smoke off to one side, was all that showed it had ever been there. The flare, the fire, nothing had worked right, and she felt all her hope start to slip away.

CHAPTER NINE

GAGE STRAINED TO hear the pulsating rhythm of the helicopter coming back. But it didn't. No sound beyond more snow falling off nearby trees. Soon he was berating himself for not thinking about snow falling from the trees onto the fire, he made himself focus on Merry, who was clinging to his arm.

It was the hardest thing he'd ever had to do, he realized, to meet her eyes and see the despair there. The pain burning through him, was nothing compared to what he felt when he saw the expression on her face. "They... they didn't see us, did they?" she asked. "The fire, it didn't work."

"No, it didn't," he admitted, the fiery ache in his side, growing with each passing moment.

He never should have run like a crazy man. He should have remembered the flares they'd pushed into the snow beyond the wing... should have taken the time to put on his boots.

He should have gotten off the wing slowly, instead of almost jumping for it. He should have...

He pushed all of those notions away, knowing his big challenge right then was just getting back in the plane, where there was at least some heat.

"This is useless, have to get back inside," he said through clenched teeth.

She hesitated, her eyes flicking over his face.

The pain was frustrating him, and his inability to do anything when the helicopter had been so close, made him sick. "I'll start the fire again after we warm up and the pills start to work. Then we'll wait. They'll be back," he said, lifting his eyes to the clouds. "They hit an area in a grid pattern, and that means they go over each section at least three times."

He sucked freezing air through his teeth, being careful not to expand his ribs too much with the effort. "This was just the first pass. There's two more for us to get it right."

She reached up to brush at his forehead by the wound. "You're sweating," she said gently. "You must feel awful."

Not any worse than the monumental failure he already felt like. "Let's get inside," he rasped and let her lead the way.

She raised herself up and onto the wing tip. "How can you get back up here?" she asked. "I could get the fire box."

"Forget it," he said tightly, and blocked everything except his goal of getting on the wing. He did it with one try, got up by Merry, and knew he couldn't speak right then, so he simply made himself move around her and get to the still open door.

He nodded for Merry to hop inside, then followed her, but knew he couldn't pull the door shut. Merry knew it too, and waited for him to get to his knees and crawl along the prone seat nearest to him, and then make his way to the backseats.

The door shut with a thud, as Merry stayed up front. "I'll get some socks for us. And can we leave the heater on for a bit longer?" Although it probably wasn't even near fifty degrees in the cabin, it felt almost balmy to him.

He agreed and was foolish to attempt to pull off his socks. Wrong decision, he admitted, when halfway through the motion, the cabin started to spin, and nausea rose in his throat.

Merry was there, helping him remove his

socks and put on a fresh pair she'd gotten out of his duffel. "Your jacket?"

He hated the mere idea of getting it off, but he knew that in the end, it would be better for both of them to get rid of their outerwear and let the thermal blankets do their job. He shifted and let her ease him out of it.

"Just rest," she said as he sank back into the cold leather. "Please, rest."

The pain was almost unbearable now, and he prayed the pills would kick in, despite his incredibly insane actions earlier. He'd heard the noise, recognized it and had gone into some sort of frenzy. He wanted to blame the pain, or anything else except his own idiocy. But he knew the truth, and it had been due to his own stupidity that he felt like this now.

Merry arranged the blankets over him, moving higher, she managed to cover his shoulder, then her hand touched his cheek. "No fever, thank goodness," she whispered.

"I'll be fine…in a few minutes," he said as he looked up at her hovering over him. "Then I'll redo the fire. Clear the snow and…get it going."

"Listen, boss," she said, leaning down to get closer. "You stay put. That pain is nothing to mess with, especially if you have a broken rib. I can do the fire."

He closed his eyes, hating that concern so evident in her expression. "No, I'll just…rest for a bit, then I'll…" He felt so weak, but persisted. "I'll do it."

"Uh-huh, you do that." She tugged the blankets higher over him. "But for now, just rest, please."

"I will…for a…few minutes," he murmured, feeling the pain pills starting to act.

"A few minutes," he heard Merry whisper, then a brush of heat caressed his forehead, the feather touch of her fingers. It felt almost like a caress, but it was gone so fast he couldn't quite comprehend it. And didn't try. He needed to wait until the aching receded to an intensity that was manageable, then he'd do what he had to do.

MERRY WATCHED GAGE as he dozed, and waited patiently until she saw the deep stress lines stamped on his features begin to gradually soften. There was something wrong, the ribs for sure, maybe the concussion that he'd passed off, or something else. She felt afraid and useless, with nothing she could do except keep him still and as warm as possible.

On impulse, she bent over him and cautiously touched his forehead, feeling the dampness there, wishing she could kiss the wound and make it all better—the way she did with her kids when they were sick. His skin felt cool and damp. That was better than feeling hot skin from a fever. She moved and stayed on her knees, backing onto the front seat and to the edge, so she could sit and put her boots back on.

With one last look at Gage, who seemed to be sleeping now, she opened the door, got out and lowered it back into place. She turned, hugging her jacket around herself more tightly, and carefully walked on the icy surface, going to the end of the wing. She got down to the ground, and took a deep breath of frigid air. She could do this. She *had* to do this.

Trudging to the now dead fire, she stopped and looked up, craning her neck so she could survey the snow laden limbs of the massive pines. She saw only two likely spots where snow could fall and possibly douse the fire again. She'd take care of it. She reached for some nearby snow, made a snowball, then spotted one clump of icy snow clinging to a branch high above. She drew back, then threw the snowball with all her strength.

Amazingly, she hit the clump on the first try, and sent it spraying down, part of it hitting exactly where the fire would be set. Searching for the other clump she'd spotted, again, made another snowball, took aim and threw at the tree. It not only didn't hit the clump, it hit a branch above it and sprayed snow down on her. She shook her head, got another snowball made, then tried again. This time she hit her mark.

Ten minutes later, Merry was watching the kindling catch, flames flare, licking at the branches she'd retrieved from the cargo space and crisscrossed on top of them. Carefully, when the flames seemed to be going okay, she got a handful of the black grains out of one of the boxes, tossed them at the fire, and immediately, black smoke billowed up, spiraling toward the clouds.

Two more passes. That's what Gage had told her. That gave them two more chances to be seen. She waited near the fire, watching it, willing it to make it through the clouds to where it could be seen from above. She took the time to close up the fire box again, checked the flares near the wing, replace the used one, then scrambled back up onto the wing.

She headed for the door and pulled it up,

feeling the warmer air instantly. Gage still looked asleep, but she could tell he'd moved around. The blankets were untucked and had slipped to the middle of his chest. Both hands were on his stomach, fingers laced. Pulling the door down and shut, she took off her boots, grabbed a couple of energy bars from the first-aid tin and climbed into the back.

Putting the bars on the seat, she stripped off her jacket, tossing it near the bars, then leaned over Gage to tuck the blankets back in for him. As she pushed the edge under his shoulder, she was startled when he spoke. "Nice pitching."

She drew back, and found herself looking down into midnight dark eyes that were touched by humor. She could tell the pain was being held at bay by the clarity of his expression. "How did you see me throwing the snowballs?"

"Out the window."

"I thought you were asleep when I went out."

"I almost was, but when you snuck out, I was curious to see you try to do the fire," he said, a smile shadowing the corners of his mouth now. "Man, you did a good job."

"Thanks, boss," she murmured.

"Boss? I kind of like you calling me that," he said.

"Good, as long as you don't call me Boom-Boom," she countered.

"I'd never do that. I just realized Boom-Boom sounds too much like an exotic dancer."

She smiled at that. "I've had a lot of strange jobs, but not that."

"I didn't think so."

"You're feeling better?" she asked, fighting the urge to brush errant hair back from his forehead.

"I'm not feeling any pain," he said, that smile still there.

"Good," was all she said. "Good."

He closed his eyes, but went on speaking. "I'm sorry for going crazy. I can only plead stupidity or a reaction to the pain. I don't know, but if I'd been thinking straight, I would have spotted that snow could fall from the trees and I would have knocked the clumps down like you did before making the fire. I really messed things up royally."

"You can't take all the blame. I'm the one who knocked the flare out of your hand," she countered. "I'm sorry, too. Besides, you said they'll be back at least two more time."

"Yes, they will," he agreed. "Two more chances."

Merry suddenly felt hungry and reached to pick up the energy bars. She offered Gage one. "It's not steak, but it's looking pretty good right about now."

That brought back a touch of a smile to his face, and she liked that—a lot. Freeing his hands from the cocoon she'd bundled around him, he tore the wrapper on his bar while she opened hers. Merry took a bite, and thought it could have been more savory, but that didn't stop her from eating every bit of it. When she finished, Gage looked at her with a lifted eyebrow.

"Wow, you actually like that?" he asked. She laughed. "I was thinking it was close to being cardboard, but it's food, or at least, it's what passes for food around here."

"Yeah, chewy cardboard," he said before popping the last piece of his bar into his mouth."

"Water?" she asked.

"Please."

She pulled two bottles out of the box pushed under their seat and gave him his. After they had both uncapped their bottles and taken drinks, Merry sighed. "This waiting is horrible."

"No, turning off the heater is what is really horrible," he said.

"Oh, we have to, don't we?"

"Yes, we should have turned it off sooner than this."

"I'll do it," she offered and scrambled up to the front to shut it down. She looked back at Gage. "Anything else we need to do before I get under the blankets?"

"No," GAGE REPLIED. "Just wait and listen." Then Merry came back to him. He watched her arrange the blankets again, pressing against him without him having to coax her to do it. She settled down with a soft sigh.

She'd held up well, despite the crying jag last night. That had been expected. But in every other way, she'd been a rock, doctoring him, doing whatever she had to without hesitation. She'd rebuilt the fire for them. He'd been the one to blow it. "They won't miss us a second time." He turned a bit onto his good side to see her more easily. "I promise you that."

Merry nodded, pulled off her cap, tossed it to one side, and brushed her loose hair away from her face. "Yes, the second time," she whispered. "We'll be ready."

If he'd been in this mess by himself, he knew that he'd be methodically figuring out what to do and he'd do it, despite the pain. But with Merry in the mix, he had a real need to tread more carefully, so he wouldn't see that look of despair on her face again. "I'm actually glad you paid that hundred dollars for the bulletin board so you could get me to let you on the plane."

A beautiful smile lit her face, making his breathing hitch for a moment and it had nothing to do with pain. "I'm so glad you went for my convoluted reasoning. I was desperate. Now this. The whole thing is awful, but if I was doing this alone..." She stopped and actually chuckled softly. "Whoa, back up. I wouldn't be doing this alone, because I'd never fly by myself, but if this world had gone crazy and I did pilot my own plane, I'd be lost alone."

He enjoyed the way her green eyes could sparkle. Shifting carefully to get his arm up to rest his head on his right hand, he looked down at her. The urge to kiss her came from nowhere and startled him. Not an urge, no, a need, but he confined his response to a caress on her cheek. "I would fly alone. I do fly alone, as much as I can, but right now..." He exhaled. "The world gets crazy, doesn't it?"

"Yes," she said softly as he drew his hand back. "Yes."

Her tongue touched her full lips and whatever control he'd had, was gone. Without hesitation, he bent over her and kissed her. He expected softness and heat, which were there immediately. What he didn't expect was a shocking sense of connection that came with the embrace.

A sense of finding something that had been hidden from him all his life, but that really was crazy. As crazy as him kissing her and letting his mind race with possibilities. When the idea of needing anyone, period, materialized, he always found a grasp on sanity. Reluctantly, he made himself draw back.

Her face was flushed, her lips parted, and her breathing matched his rapid cadence. "Crazy," he said roughly, then moved back farther. "I'm sorry, that shouldn't have happened."

He wasn't sorry, but he knew he had to say that, as certainly as he knew he had to move away and lay down. He had to keep his eyes on the ceiling of the plane. And he had to not touch her again. "It's the situation, and the medication," he reminded them, desperate for anything to explain himself to her. Even if it was a lie.

"Sure," he thought he heard Merry echo, then she shifted, making a small space between them. It felt like a huge void to him.

MERRY FELL SILENT and watched the faint light on the wall, trying to force her mind to stop fixating on the kiss. Then Gage apologizing for it, and being sorry, pretty much saying it was because of his condition…*their* condition. That made sense, actually, that bonding between people in life and death situations that wouldn't mean a thing when the danger passed.

She shut her eyes, hating how the sounds of the helicopter invaded her thoughts—Gage so frantic, then in so much pain, laying by him, him touching her face. His lips on hers.

She opened her eyes immediately, trying to think of something, anything but the man beside her. And she couldn't afford to doze off. She couldn't afford to miss anything outside that might let them know the rescuers were coming back.

"Gage?" she finally said in a low voice.

"Yes?"

"What time is it?"

She felt him move, getting his hand free to look at his watch. "Four o'clock. Maybe another hour of daylight. I was just thinking we don't need to ignite the fire again. It won't be light long enough to do any good, and they won't be flying too near sunset."

"What about the signal in the clearing you talked about? I can cut more branches and make some sort of arrow or something."

"We both will in the morning," he said, his voice slightly hoarse.

"Do you need more pain pills?"

"No."

She regretted the awkwardness between them as silence took over the cabin. Neither she nor Gage moved or spoke again as the light began to fade outside and the only glow came from the security lights. As the temperature dropped, Merry chanced moving a bit closer to Gage and to his warmth.

"Everything okay?" he asked.

"Fine."

"Cold?"

"A bit."

She heard the rough exhale before Gage moved, then said, "Lift your head."

She turned to him for the first time in what seemed hours. "What?" The growing shadows cut darkness at his eyes and jaw. "Why?"

He repeated, "Just lift your head."

When she did, he moved his right arm up slowly, and around her shoulders. "Body heat, remember?"

She did, pulling the blankets back up to cover them both, She gently settled against his shoulder. "Thank you," she whispered, his heat a blessing as the temperature became colder and colder.

"As I said, body heat," he murmured.

Closing her eyes tightly, she wouldn't let herself analyze why she felt safe this way, or why it felt so natural to be curled up against him. She just absorbed the heat that his closeness brought. "It must be the altitude, but I'm exhausted," she said, barely stifling a yawn.

"Thin air does that." When he spoke, his voice rumbled against her cheek.

"I guess the kids will be spending a second day at the center without me there," she remarked, as much to herself as to Gage. "I really blew that."

"I think you're underestimating those kids. They are resilient."

"Usually," she said, though she could think

of a few exceptions. "I just hope Marsala managed to explain things to the kids so they know I didn't do this on purpose. And that Erin understands."

"Erin?"

"One of the children. She's alone. Her mother's dead, and her father's in prison serving a life sentence. She doesn't have anyone."

Just saying the words tore at her heart. Erin clung to people, needing a family of her own so badly.

"They have Moses to help and he'll be great. He'll do the best anyone can under the circumstances. And you're with me, so that should help with any explanation about your absence."

She frowned into his chest, the softness of his flannel shirt against her cheek. "Neither one of them would have any idea that I saw you at the airport, let alone took off in your plane with you. The last Marsala heard I was in Pueblo waiting for a flight out. She wasn't expecting me until this afternoon, but when I don't show up, I have no clue what she'll think."

"The good part of that is, they don't know the mess we're in."

She bit her lip. "What about your family? They must be worried that you didn't show up."

He dropped a bomb on her. "They aren't expecting me now."

"What?" she asked. "Don't tell me this is all a surprise visit, and that they have no idea that you're supposed to be flying in?"

"They know I'm coming, but not exactly when—could be this week or maybe next, so there's a two week window there."

"What about those big important meetings you talked about?"

"They aren't for four days. I wanted to give myself time to check out the land, to brainstorm the design before discussing the project. But, the tower knows where we were going, and they know we were having trouble. And we know they're looking for us. The helicopter made a pass."

Her heart fell with one single thought that came to her. "But what if it wasn't looking for us? What if it was just out flying around, looking for something else? Maybe skiers or hikers or someone." She was clutching the blankets near her chin in a death grip now. "They probably didn't even know about us being down here."

GAGE COULD HEAR the desperation in Merry's voice, and wanted to put a stop to it right away. "Of course they know we're here. The signals are going out. Listen, we're doing pretty good. We've got the body of the plane intact, heat if we need it, and some awesome snacks, if you like peanut butter and chocolate chips fashioned into cardboard."

He shifted, moving his arm from under her to get up on his elbow to look right at her. "Are you a gambler?" he asked.

"Are you kidding me? After everything I said about the casino idea."

"I know, but this is different."

She frowned. "I don't have the money to gamble."

"What if no money was involved? Would you make a bet?"

"I guess so."

"Then I'll bet you that we're back in Wolf Lake in time for a big steak dinner tomorrow night." He looked at his watch again. "Say, six o'clock, back in town, warm and safe and full of good food."

She studied him from underneath ridiculously lush, dark lashes. "You mentioned a bet?" she asked. "What are the stakes? Just remember that I don't do money."

"You name what's at stake."

"Hmm…" He could almost see the wheels turning. When he was getting curious, she finally said, "Okay, I know what the stakes will be." There was a gleam in her green eyes that could have been amusement or could have been mischief, but whatever it was, it was better than that look of hope being lost.

"What?"

When she started to talk, he knew he'd been wrong about the look in those eyes. It wasn't from amusement or mischief, it was from the feeling that she had him right where she wanted him. "The bet is, if we are not back in Wolf Lake for dinner tomorrow, you will agree to reconsider your take on the so called entertainment and casino complex near town."

"What?" he asked, and he didn't bother to hide his surprise. "That's ridiculous."

"No, it's not. All I'm asking is you think it over, weigh my concerns, and the concerns of others in town, I might add, then make your decision." She pursed her lips. "I'm not asking you to tank it—I'm just asking you to really consider it from all angles before you blithely go ahead with this potentially damaging project. Is that too big a bet for you?"

He sat up more, never taking his eyes off of her. "What will it cost you if you lose, if we're home by six tomorrow night? Will you give up all opposition to the proposed plans?"

"No way, I'll fight to the bitter end," she said without any hedging."

"Then how about if you lose you'll have your opinions about it, but you never tell another person how you feel?"

She hesitated, and seemed to be stalling for time. "Stupid," she muttered. "Surely you've noticed that I talk way too much."

He grinned. He had noticed that, but found he actually had grown to like it more than he cared to admit. "All right. New terms then, if you lose…" He paused purposely before continuing. "If you lose, you have to take one flying lesson."

Her eyes widened with what he thought was either horror or shock, or both, then he realized it was palpable fear. "I…I don't know," she stammered .

"Oh, afraid you'll lose?"

"Well, nothing's one hundred percent, is it?" she challenged.

"Never mind. If you don't want to take the bet," he said, but knew she wouldn't let it go.

"No, no. I mean, I accept," she told him, then she pushed aside the blankets to hold out a hand for him to shake. "Deal?"

HE TOOK HER hand in his, the slender fingers feeling delicate until Merry squeezed his hand hard. "Okay, okay," Gage said, getting her message. "Deal."

The grip eased and he found he was reluctant to let go of her hand. "Did you ever think of going into business as a negotiator?"

She couldn't stop the giggle that left her mouth. "No, I wouldn't be good at that. I could only argue for something that was very important to me, not do it for mere money or power."

He chuckled as her hand withdrew from his. "Just the passion, huh?"

"Yes. And I am passionate about this."

"I noticed," he said, settling back in the seat again, finding that personality trait more than interesting. "I hope you'll make good on your side of the bet when you lose. Because I sure am looking forward to my steak dinner and signing you up for that first flight lesson. "

"In your dreams," she retorted as she, too,

settled back in her seat, and he watched her carefully tug the blankets back up to just below a satisfied smile on her full lips.

CHAPTER TEN

GAGE CLEARED HIS throat and averted his eyes from her lips. "What about your family?" he asked. "Do they know where you went and when you'd be back?"

"Since my mother and stepfather are in Germany, I only call them once a month or so. I just called them last week." She shrugged, moving the blankets up and down slightly. "They don't ever have to know about this. No point to it."

"If I ever meet them, they won't hear it from me," Gage promised.

Merry was surprised when a beeping sounded, and Gage pulled his arm free of the blankets to look at the face of his watch. "Time to give the mayor a call." He pushed a button to turn off the alarm, then tucked his hand back under the blankets. "I think I'll cancel that phone call," he said with a crooked grin."

"Jasper Barnes?" Merry asked.

"Yes, Barney. I was going to call him to let him know I was in town and maybe see him first off to get a feeling for what people really want."

"I've told you that most people don't want that type of business brought into town."

"Sorry. Bad choice of words. I was talking about the design—the type of design they want for the buildings, not their opinion of the project." Before she could respond, he slowly sat up and looked out the window. "I think I need to find those branches to make the arrow, just so it's in place in the morning."

She touched his shoulder. "You said you'd do it then, in the morning."

"Why wait?" he asked as he glanced down at her. His hand gently covered hers as it rested on his shoulder. "I don't want to mess up again."

"Oh, Gage, you don't have to—"

"Yes, I do," he stated matter of factly. "And I need to do it while those pills are having an effect."

"Then I'm coming, too," she said and sat up. "Let me get out first, so you can move a bit more freely." She shoved out of her share of the blankets, then looked at him. "Just promise me that if the pain starts up again, you'll tell me and you'll come back inside."

He hesitated. "I'll tell you if it gets too bad."

"No, just tell me when it starts up again," she insisted.

"And if I don't promise you that, what are you going to do?"

"Pin you down and tie you up and make you stay inside," she said.

"In your dreams," he quipped, and couldn't stop a smile. "Besides, I'm stronger than you."

She shrugged. "It was worth a try." Then she scooted onto the front seat, put on her boots and jacket, scarf and gloves. She grabbed the brilliant Boom-Boom hat, opened the door and stood outside.

"I'll be right there," Gage said as she stepped farther into the frosty air. The light was fading, and she wondered if they'd have enough time to do anything.

She waited on the wing, and Gage came out, moving easier than he had the last time. "Did you take more medication?" she asked.

With a shake of his head, he moved past her and slipped down onto the ground. He didn't wait for her to follow before he went to the fire ring, where the coals still smoldered. "We should get more wood," he said as the two of them started for the clearing. When they arrived at it, the clouds seemed even lower in the sky, dusk was on the horizon. Merry shivered, and this time he didn't hesitate to put his arm around her and pull her to his side. "Let's find things to make a sign," he said, releasing her. "You go that way and I'll go in the opposite direction, then meet back here."

Within minutes, they each had an assortment of rocks and large bows that had fallen from the trees. In a very short time, the limbs were laid out in a sprawling V that pointed in the direction of the plane's location.

"Done," Gage said as the last bough fell into place, and Merry could hear the slight breathlessness in his voice. Without thinking about what she was doing, Merry reached for his hand and felt his gloved fingers close around hers. She told herself it was to make sure they didn't stumble or fall, but deep down, she knew that the connection she'd just made was partly protective and partly wanting to be close to him again.

Silently they walked back to the plane, where Gage let go of Merry and made it onto the wing. Merry followed and soon they were settled in the back again, side by side, the air frigid inside.

GAGE FELT MERRY shiver and he wished they could have the heater on. But for now, they needed to conserve. Despite his stupid bet, he didn't have a lot of hope that they'd be out of the mountains by tomorrow night. Eventually he'd have to do what he'd promised to do if he lost the bet—rethink the whole project. He could and he would, but he doubted it would make any real difference to the outcome.

"It feels colder than it did outside," Merry mumbled.

"Come here," he said, reaching for her to bring her up close to his side. He knew that body heat, at any other time, wouldn't have been his priority for holding her close to him. But right then, his priority was their survival.

Again she didn't hesitate to shift closer to him, letting him put his right arm around her. She rested her head on his shoulder, her shivers running through her, but gradually slowing. "These blankets are great," he said. "The orange one is made out of some special material that weighs next to nothing, but can hold almost all a person's body heat."

"This is crazy, isn't it?" she asked.

He rubbed her shoulder under the blanket. "Crazy," he agreed against her silky hair. Very crazy how things had happened. Crazy how she'd found him at the airport, how he'd let her tag along on the flight, how they became stranded together in the middle of the wilderness, and how he hated himself for putting her in danger.

He felt her take an unsteady breath, then she settled into him without shivering. "Are you okay?" he asked softly.

She gave his a weak smile. "Just great."

He shuffled the blankets up higher, then reclined again and resumed holding on to her. "Relax," he whispered, desperate to reassure her. He squeezed her shoulder and felt his heart clench when she said nothing in return. "Remember, tomorrow is another day," he added.

She rested her hand on his chest, and he thought she laughed softly. "You're a bottomless trove of old movies and TV shows, aren't you?"

He closed his eyes, smiling at her words. "Useless trivia from nights of not sleeping well and watching old movies and a station that carried all the classic TV programs."

"The kids love the old shows," she said a bit thickly. "Love, love them."

Her kids. And she wouldn't be there for them tonight, either. He fought an urge to brush at her hair where it tickled his chin. When they got out of this, when he got her home, he'd make sure the kids understood what happened. That's the least he could do after letting this happen to her.

He started to say something mundane about kids understanding, but was saved from facing her wrath rooted in the fact she thought he didn't understand her kids' needs at all, when he heard her snoring softly.

He rested his cheek against the top of her head, and envied her. He'd been truthful about not being able to sleep well. He couldn't remember the last time he actually slept for a full night, and last night he'd been restless. Now, he felt sore, exhausted, and light-headed, but sleep eluded him.

He shifted a bit lower, easing her with him. He'd never been a man who needed people around, didn't need a woman to fill his bed during the long nights if he didn't want it. He did better alone. Now, though, he recognized that he needed this near stranger, Merry Brenner, with him, her warmth and softness against him, and that kind smile that stole his breath away.

He yawned and the last thing he heard before sleep claimed him was Merry sighing against his chest.

It wasn't long before he was awoken for some reason he didn't understand. The cabin seemed darker than it had been and the air was so cold it made him shudder beneath the blankets. He brought the blankets to just below his eyes. In the process, he all but covered Merry's face. When he went to peel the blankets back a bit, he heard, "Don't even think about it."

He smiled to himself and left the blankets alone. "Morning."

She stirred against him, stretching. Her green gaze still had the remnants of sleep, and her hair was tousled around her lovely face.

"Unfortunately, it is," she said, her words muffled by the blankets. "I don't think we slept more than half an hour.

"You're right," he conceded and he saw his breath spiral into the air. "Cold, isn't it?"

"Can't we put on the heater, just for a little while?"

"I don't know."

"Please, just long enough to take the edge off, then we'll be under the blankets and stay put. The way it is now, we're freezing and trying to warm up, instead of starting at relative warmness and maintaining it with the blankets." There was a plaintive note to her voice. "That makes sense, doesn't it?"

He met those green eyes, was about to say it wasn't the smart thing to do. Instead he said, "Fine, fine, for a little while."

"Yes!" she said, throwing off the blankets in a rush to climb to the front and start the heater. Once it was going, she came back, tucked herself under the blankets and pulled them up to her chin. "We'll let it run until we can't see our breath when we talk, okay?"

"Sure," he said, knowing that it would be futile to debate it with this woman. When Merry set her mind to something, she was a force of nature, and he needed to hold off for the bigger battles ahead. She was watching him closely, with a slightly befuddled look on her face, then said, "Cat got your tongue? We have to actually talk to see our breath."

Right then a vibration touched his skin, rocking him, a throbbing in the air, and he didn't need Merry to scream, "They found us! They're here!" to know what was happening.

MERRY HAD HEARD it first. A helicopter was somewhere overhead. It wasn't Gage who sprang up and scrambled for the door, grab-

bing boots to put on, then the jacket. It was
her rushing to the door, getting it open and
breaking out onto the wing.

Awkwardly she dropped to the ground and
headed for the flares. Over and over again in
her mind, she told herself what to do with the
cap, how to get that flare to light up and soar
through the clouds.

Bending over the nearest flare, she did what
Gage had told her, and stood back. The clouds
still hung low, the light was almost gone, dusk
was all around them, then there was a hiss, a
flash, then a soaring streak of fiery light surg-
ing up and into the sky. She stared hard above
her, barely feeling the hand on her shoulder
as she watched and waited, listening for the
sound of the helicopter that had been fading
away. It had to come back. It had to have seen
the brilliance in the air.

Gage was there, moving around her to light
a second flare, sending it arcing into the sky.
Then he straightened, stood back and looked
up. He stared above them, the helicopter
throbbing vibration closer, then the sounds
changed right when Merry was certain that it
would break through the clouds directly over
them.

Before that could happen, the noise headed

off again, going toward the clearing. Hope all but choked her, hope that they saw the flares, that they saw the arrow in the clearing and that was where they were going to land. Merry ran full tilt for the trees, screaming at the engine sounds that were fading, "We're here, we're here!" But the sounds kept going and she kept running toward them.

Then Gage was screaming at her. "Stop! Merry, stop! Stop!"

Ignoring him, Merry continued running, her head up, her eyes on the heavy clouds, and listening intently as the last noises of the helicopter faded into nothingness. Without warning, Gage caught her by her shoulders and stopped her dead in her tracks.

"No," she gasped. "No!" She struggled to get free.

But he didn't let her go. "I thought you were about to—" Gage bit off his words as he slowly pulled her back against his strong body. His arms wrapped around her and his chin rested on her head. "Thank goodness you stopped," he said.

It was then she looked ahead and was stunned to see Gage had stopped her less than two feet from the edge of the precipice that fell away to nothing below.

She was thankful that she was leaning back against Gage because her legs almost gave way from the shock of what she'd almost done. "Oh." The one word was all she could get out as she turned away from the vastness to press into Gage's chest. "They left," she mumbled against the roughness of his orange jacket and hit him lightly with her curled up fist. "They left and that was number two."

He held on to her, one hand rubbing her back. "They had to leave, even if they saw the flares. The light's failing, and maybe they're getting short on fuel, but they had to see the flares. You got there so fast. They'll return when it gets light."

She drew away, her eyes damp, but no tears falling. Surprising herself, she actually gave him a half smile. "You have to be so sick of me and—" She studied him and then lifted a hand to touch his face. "Thanks," she whispered.

She could see something in his eyes as they narrowed, then his head lowered toward hers. The fact that he was about to kiss her didn't surprise her. What *did* surprise her was that she wanted it to happen so desperately. But his lips didn't touch hers. They brushed her forehead as he whispered back, "We'll make it."

She could feel his heart beating against her hands that were still on his chest, in fact, she was thankful she couldn't move. Because if she had been free to, she would have wound her arms around his neck and brought him down to kiss him and never stop. When she looked up into his eyes, for a split second she thought she saw a fire in the dark brown depths, a fire that echoed in her. Then it was gone.

"We...we need to get back," she said, her voice slightly husky as she felt his arms let her go.

But the connection wasn't entirely severed. He took her hand in his, and silently led her over to the plane.

She almost lost her footing between the plane and the clearing, not because of the icy snow underfoot, but because for a moment, she didn't think she could go into the plane with Gage. She didn't think she could sit by him, and lay by him in the confines of the small cabin. But as they neared the plane, he erased that problem.

He let go of her and said, "Go on in and warm up," before he moved farther away from her. "I need to check a few things with the plane."

She didn't argue, but scrambled to get up on the wing, then went to the door and pulled it open and up. When it closed behind her, she took a deep breath and felt the tension in her middle ease a bit. Merry dropped down on the end of the pilot's seat, kicked off her boots and just enjoyed the warmer air for a long moment until she heard Gage on the wing, getting close to the door. She watched him climb in, lower the door, then sink onto the seat opposite her. "Did you find anything?"

GAGE LOOKED AT MERRY, cursing the fact that his pathetic excuse to "check out the plane" hadn't worked. That instant he'd seen her plunging through the trees toward the edge of the drop off, had spun him around emotionally. He'd thought it odd that he'd felt so protective of her before, but just then, it had been life and death, and it had terrified him.

The feel of her in his arms when he grabbed her to save her had been nothing short of wonderful, then that urge to kiss, being short circuited into a peck on her forehead. He'd been off balance ever since and now she had her eyes on him expectantly. What could he tell her? The truth? Hardly. "No, I didn't find anything," he said honestly and sat back, managing to remove his boots before making his way to a rear seat.

"What were you looking for?" she asked. He closed his eyes when a headache came out of nowhere, making him wince with discomfort. "Nothing specific," he admitted.

"As long as you didn't find anything bad," she said quickly. "I'm fine with that."

"Me, too," he replied and shifted to stretch out, but his ribs flared at the same moment the headache grew stronger. "Whoa," he breathed, forgetting about everything in an attempt to regroup and figure out what was happening to him.

Merry was close by, climbing onto the seat next to him, looking at him with concern.. "What is it?"

He couldn't talk for a minute and in that small span of time, Merry reached out and covered his hand with hers. "Gage, please, what's happening?"

He swallowed hard, before managing to say, "Headache."

Her look of concern seemed worse. "Oh, I don't think you can have any more pills yet."

"No pills," he said. "No more pills."

He'd thought the pain had been lessening, but obviously the running, the bending and movement had taken their toll on his ribs. The headache... He lifted a hand to touch the gash on his forehead. It seemed to be centered right behind the bandages. "Sorry," he mumbled, easing back to rest his head on the seat and close his eyes.

Merry got up, and he felt the blankets being spread out and secured around him. "The heater's doing fine, and you should be warmer soon. That should help." Despite everything, he shivered sharply, pain inundating him around his ribs and in his head. He bit his lip hard. Merry touched his forehead, then seemed to jerk back. "You...you need to rest, to not go out again," she said, but something different was in her voice now, something beyond concern, edging toward fear.

"Did I grow a third eye or something?" he asked, his voice thick from the exhaustion.

She hesitated for so long that he finally opened his eyes enough to see her, so close he could feel her breath touch his skin. "You... you feel kind of hot. I need to check..." Her voice trailed off as she found the first-aid kit off by the front passenger seat.

"Oh, good," she said with a touch of relief and turned back to him with what he thought was a strip of paper until she reached to lay it on his forehead. "A thermometer," she explained and stared at it, hard, for a long moment, then picked it up. He didn't miss how her eyes widened before she looked at him again.

"What is it?" he asked.

"A small fever…" she answered as she tossed the used thermometer into the first-aid kit.

"What is the definition of 'small,' just so I know?"

She looked at him as she shook her head. "One hundred and three," she said, speaking with what he could tell was as much control as she could muster.

How could he have a fever when he was so cold? He was feeling shaky, his hands so unsteady under the blankets that he pressed them to his thighs to stop the trembling. When he tried to speak again, words came at the same time as another shiver coursed through him. "N…n…not super hot, but warm, huh?"

"Hot enough," she said softly. "It's weird in this cold to think of someone getting too hot."

He had to agree with that, but he didn't get a chance to say anything before he began to shiver uncontrollably. He tried to stop it, but even his teeth were chattering. He didn't feel hot. He felt as if he'd been plunged into a deep freeze.

He felt Merry climb under the blankets and get up close to him. He was grateful for the extra heat. She carefully placed her hand on his chest. "I wish I knew if ibuprofen is safe to take after the pain pills."

Gage wanted to tell her, "Just give me some and I'll take the chance," but he couldn't stop shaking long enough to form any coherent words.

Her hand brushed his cheek, then touched his forehead, the contact soothing, despite his discomfort. "I'm going to check the labels, or any booklet in the box. I'll be right back," she said.

It seemed forever before she was there again, sliding under the blankets, her hand gentle on his forehead again. "You can take these," she said and he felt the touch of something against his lips. "Three of them."

He managed to open his mouth, felt the pills fall inside, then a cold water bottle was pressed to his lips. He almost gagged getting the medicine down, but he finally managed to swallow. He lay back and Merry nestled against him. "They'll work soon, I promise they will, and you'll be fine. It's probably a cold starting or something from this miserable freezing weather."

She was talking, but not convincingly. He was learning that she wasn't much of a liar, even for a good cause. Her left hand found his clenched by his thigh. She caught it and held it in her own. "Just rest. Just relax."

They laid like that for forever or maybe an hour, Gage didn't know. He wouldn't judge. But when he opened his eyes later, he was shocked that everything was blurred and he saw double when he tried to focus. He didn't say a thing about it to Merry, figuring it was a reaction to the fever. Besides, there was enough to worry about without adding impaired vision to their ever lengthening list.

He closed his eyes again and gradually he began to feel as if he was floating while Merry spoke to him. What she said, he didn't know, but he went with it, letting her voice wash over him. The sound of her words relaxing him more and more. The aching didn't follow where he was going, and as he went deeper and deeper into her voice, her words, all he really understood was she was the reason the pain stayed at bay.

CHAPTER ELEVEN

MERRY HELD ON TO GAGE, willing him to stop shivering. "You know, when we get back to Wolf Lake," she began, nervously talking so the silence around them wouldn't suffocate her. It helped and she found herself telling him things she'd barely thought about herself until then.

"I really think I'm going to make Willie G. an offer on that house. I mean, it can't hurt to try. It's a great house, even though it needs some work, and it's within walking distance of the Family Center. Three bedrooms, all upstairs, and what I think is a library or something downstairs that could be turned into another bedroom if I need it to be. I'll just make an offer and see what happens…"

She mentioned a money amount, and carried on. "I know Willie G. probably wants someone from the Rez to get it. I mean, he was nice enough to rent it to me, but that's a short term thing. I'm going to tell him that

I'm a native of Wolf Lake, born and bred right there, and I want to get back to my roots.

"Do you think he'd let me get it? I mean, I can't offer him too much, but it would be a fair price. He owns a few houses around town, a couple of mobile homes, and he seems to be kind of a canny old guy." She paused just long enough to catch her breath. "So what do you think? Is it a good idea or will he laugh at my offer?" Sometime during her ramblings about the house, Gage's shivering had stopped and he'd begun to breathe evenly. When he didn't respond to her question, she shifted to look up at him. His eyes were closed and the lines in his face were being erased by sleep. She raised herself on one elbow, brushed gently at his hair near the bandages and almost cried from relief when she felt a decided cooling to his skin. If things had been different, she would have kissed him, but she didn't dare do that. That could unleash a whole can of worms for her, and that couldn't happen.

She drew back a bit, letting go of his hand, and just laid beside him. She'd try to stay awake during the night to check on Gage's temperature in case he needed more medication.

Be patient, she told herself, *they'll be back*

tomorrow and they'll help Gage. She killed the "what if they don't come back" thoughts as quickly as they came, and she focused on home as the night deepened.

Her plans of staying awake failed sometime after she turned off the heater, checked to find Gage still cool and sleeping. As bitter cold invaded the cabin, she went farther and farther down into the blankets, closer and closer to Gage, until she barely had her nose and mouth exposed for air. The warmth from Gage was so soothing, and with him sleeping so peacefully, she settled in herself. The last thing she remembered thinking before she fell into a deep slumber, with her hand resting over Gage's heart, was that her feelings for this man were the definition of crazy.

She knew things were out of line, that feelings got heightened where two people were thrown together in a dangerous situation. And that those feelings were seldom real. But hers felt so real. She felt Gage by her side, and something in her heart rejoiced. There was a connection there, at least for her, but the circumstances were throwing things off balance.

This was a temporary reality, a manufactured existence, formed by the crash and the close confinement. That she wanted to just hold on to him had to come from her fear of being alone, the same way her fear of something awful happening to him, all but terrified her. Askew, totally and absolutely askew.

She carefully raised herself on her elbow to look down at Gage, and then kiss his partially parted lips. She felt the heat of his breath, felt his heart under her palm, steady and slow, and then she drew back. With one last glance at the sleeping man, she admitted that if things had been different, if the world had been normal at all when they'd met, there could be more.

She stopped that foolishness in its tracks. No, not with him. There could never be more, no matter what she felt. When they got out of here, he'd leave Wolf Lake, and she'd stay. Simple. There'd be nothing more to their shared time in the wilderness. A memory. But for now, they were here, together, and she'd hold on to him until it was time for them to let go.

MERRY WAS ENVELOPED in a deep sleep until she became aware of voices off in the distance, a jumble of sounds that seemed to be coming closer and closer. She stirred when there was movement, a shaking feeling, and Merry knew she was waking up into something that she'd dreamed of. Maybe she was still dreaming as a voice called out from close by, "Gage? Gage?" over and over again. Closer, clearer it came and she knew it was no dream when she opened her eyes to the same grayness as yesterday at the same moment the door of the cabin was swung open.

A man ducked inside the cabin, saw Merry struggling to sit up and get free of her blankets.

"Who are you?" he demanded, but didn't wait for her to answer when he looked to her left. All of a sudden, his face broke into a huge smile, and Merry thought she saw tears well in his eyes. Then he turned to yell, "It's Gage! He's in here!"

Gage's brother Jack Carson barged inside, pulling the other man out of the way. She'd recognized Jack immediately—a man with the same skin tone, body type, dark eyes and hair of his brother, not to mention that single dimple near his mouth when he smiled. He was a Carson through and through.

Then he was scrambling to get in past the front seats to reach his brother. "He's got a fever and he was hurt during the landing.

His ribs. His head," Merry was saying as she moved back to let Jack get closer.

Then Dr. Blackstar was there, looking in, first over at Gage, then he glanced at Merry, his mouth dropping open with surprise. "Merry," he said and held out his hand, motioning for her to get out of the plane with him.

She fumbled for her boots and jacket and climbed over the seat to the door. Pushing her arms into the heavy jacket, she turned to leave and almost fell into the doctor before she could actually make contact with the wing.

The cold was bitter and a wind swirled all around, backed by that ever present pulsating roar that she knew now had to be a nearby helicopter. Moses helped her down off the wing, then stood to look at her closely. "How did you end up here with Gage?" he asked.

"I was stuck in Pueblo, and he was there with his plane. He gave me a ride, so we could both get back."

Moses nodded. "Okay, now how are you? Any injuries?"

She shook her head. "No, but Gage hit the door or something and the restraints really bruised him up. But he got us down in that storm." She had to stop and clear her throat, then hugged her arms tightly around herself while the doctor waited patiently for her to continue. "He was unconscious for a short time afterward, and he got a gash on his forehead. He's had headaches, and his ribs are really bothering him. He can't move very quickly unless he has the pain medication that was in the first-aid kit."

"Why isn't he up and awake like you are?" Moses asked with a deep frown. She could feel his need to get back in the plane to his friend.

"Last night, he spiked a sudden fever. He was really cold, then he was shivering, and he felt hot. I gave him some medicine, and he's been sleeping for hours."

He motioned past her to a man in a jumpsuit who was approaching them from the trees, carrying a heavy box in each hand. "Tell Lester to take care of Miss Brenner, get her warm and check out her vitals. I'm going to see about Gage."

"Yes, sir," the man said. After setting the cases down by Dr. Blackstar, he motioned with his head for Merry to follow him back the way he'd just come. She was reluctant, needing to be there to find out about Gage, but knew that this was the beginning of the end for them. Their time together was all but over, and any feelings that had begun to develop between them, wouldn't be going any further.

And as wonderful as it was to finally be going home to Wolf Lake, it was also tinged with a sense of bittersweet sadness. Swallowing hard, she silently followed the short, compact man who was wearing Search and Rescue badges on his clothes. "Name's Patrick," he called over his shoulder.

She just kept following him. At the clearing, the space had been transformed from an empty expanse with a crude arrow in the snow to a landing area for a huge helicopter. The air current from the sweeping blades blew snow off the trees close by and even the thinning clouds were being spun up and out by the pulsating swings of the rotors. She paused, hesitant about getting into a machine that looked so fierce, especially without Gage. If she could have, she would have waited right there for him and the others to come, but another man jumped out of the door of the copter and hurried to her.

"Come on. Let's make sure you're okay." The new man introduced himself as Lester and said quickly, "Let's get this nightmare over for you."

She felt something in her crumble. Nightmare? Yes, it may have started that way, but it had ended in something she couldn't define. Lester had his hand on her arm, urging her up and into the beast. Turning her back to what was behind her, she got on board.

GAGE COULDN'T FIGURE OUT what was going on at first. Merry had disappeared, replaced by Jack, of all people—two Jacks, actually, since his eyes still seemed to be blurred. What was his brother doing here, talking nonstop, asking questions he couldn't even try to reply to? Then Moses was taking Jack's place, playing doctor with his stethoscope and thermometer and more questions.

Gage was able to sit up, moisten his dry lips with offered water, then croaked out, "Where's Merry?"

Moses motioned behind them. "On the rescue helicopter. She's being checked out by the EMT. She told me what happened. Now, we're going to get you out of here, and you can fill in the blanks for me." Moses moved back to let another man into the plane. Lester Waylon. Gage had known him for years.

Instead of getting out of there on a stretcher, Gage was able to get out on his own two feet, all the way to the clearing with Moses supporting him on one side, and Jack on the other. Thankfully, he made it there in one piece, and with their help managed to navigate the step up into the helicopter.

The first thing he noticed was Merry, and relief flooded through him. Then he realized he wasn't seeing double anymore, and he marveled at how stunning she looked. She saw him right away and a smile spread across her face, making her green eyes glow. Actually, stunning didn't begin to describe her at that moment.

Then hands behind him eased him into the nearest chair. He almost fell into it, his legs finally giving out. Moses and Jack were right beside him now, his brother crossing to sit by Merry, and Moses taking a seat where he could be directly across from Gage. Lester climbed in, headed up to the front, then the doors were closed and the rotation of the overhead blades increased along with the volume of noise all around them.

Gage watched Merry gripping the arm rests on her seat, her eyes closed and her lips barely moving, but he knew what she was doing. She had to be terrified, a case of where the cure is worse than the sickness, but she withstood it. They lifted into the steel gray sky, dipped north at first, then did a half turn back to the southwest. They were on their way home, finally.

Moses dominated Gage's attention on the ride, asking him question after question about how he felt, what he thought happened, how they'd survived. But Gage never stopped being aware of Merry sitting one seat away from his. Jack spoke to her a few times, probably interrupting her bubble counting, but beyond that she was silently coping with the flying.

Jack stood abruptly, bent over to avoid striking his head on the roof of the copter, and went to speak to Lester. The next thing Gage knew, Merry was taking the seat beside him, settling in, then looking at him. It was all he could do not to stroke her hand where it rested on her thigh. "How many?" he asked.

She frowned, but that cleared as she understood. "Beyond what I can count," she confessed. Then a wide smile touched her face. "You're feeling better?"

"A lot. Now that we're on our way back, I'm just fine."

"Yeah, me too," she said. She seemed to be

hesitating for some reason. "You win," she stated.

It was his turn to be confused. "The bet?"

She nodded. "I suspect that you'll have your steak dinner and be warm tonight."

"*We'll* have it," he corrected her and didn't miss the slight shock in her expression before she shook her head.

"As hard as this is for me to say, I will keep my end of the bargain, since you won. I will take one flying lesson when I am able." She blew out a sharp breath. "One."

He should have told her he wouldn't make her do it, but instead, he said, "Good, because a bet's a bet."

"I will try to do it before you leave, or when you come the next time, maybe. "Just let me know when you'll be in town." There was no smile on her face now.

He didn't have any idea why those words hit him so hard, but he could barely catch his breath.

He'd leave.

Yes, he would. And he'd return once in a while, more often if his company won the bid for the development project. But Merry would be in Wolf Lake, forever, if she could. Now he wondered if he shouldn't find a reason to venture back to Wolf Lake even after his business was complete.

When Merry leaned closer and her hand covered his, the contact made him feel unsteady. More so when she whispered into his ear, "Thank you for everything. I mean that. Thank you so much." She tightened her grip on his hand for a moment, then drew back. But before she turned away from him, he could tell her green eyes were bright with unshed tears.

MERRY BIT HER lip hard and turned away from Gage as Moses gestured to get his attention. The two men bent forward toward each other and Merry stared at her hands tightly clasped in her lap while they spoke. She was going home. She'd be there soon. This was what she'd prayed for since the crash had happened, but now it was a reality and she felt slightly disoriented, less focused on what she wanted to do and more focused on what she'd done.

Merry wanted to talk, to put whatever was going on into words, but there was no one to talk to. Just the stranger in the seat next to her. A man who had, over a few days, touched her on some soul-deep level she hadn't even known existed before. At some point, she'd thought they might have died together. But they weren't going to die. They would live. They would both go home. Gage would do his work, and she'd do hers, and their lives would follow separate paths.

Jack startled her when he touched her arm, abruptly jerking her out of her thoughts. She turned to look at him.

He was smiling, showing that Carson dimple. "Are you doing okay?" he asked her.

"Oh, sure, just…" She didn't know how to put how she felt into words right then. *Sad, relieved, scared, worried, happy?* Nothing fit exactly. "I'm just glad Gage is doing better."

"We weren't sure what we'd find, but then those flares went off last night. The pilot was low on fuel, or we would have tried to make contact then." Running a hand roughly over his face, he shook his head. "After what you two went through, it's incredible that nothing too serious happened to either of you, beyond a demolished plane that's insured.

What an understatement that "nothing serious had happened," Merry thought. All she had to do was look at Gage and she knew that her life had shifted in some way she couldn't begin to understand. She didn't know if it was for the good or the bad, but it would never be the same again.

She sat back, hugging herself when the pilot called over the speakers, "We're almost there. Get ready."

Merry looked past Jack out the windows, seeing the whole sprawling desert floor sweep into sight. She could make out the ragged pattern of the Rez nestled into the mountainous high country, old and secure in its place with snow dusting the rough terrain around it. The town spanned the low country in the distance, a nucleolus of houses and buildings in the middle of the land, with ranches spreading out from there.

Home.

Jack touched her arm again and motioned to something the helicopter was sweeping toward. An ordered pattern of endless pastures and empty crop fields below were dotted by majestic buttes and mesas, draped with thin snow. "The ranch," he said. "Moses called ahead to have everything ready."

"Good," she said, thinking that Gage might need some extra care for his ribs. "I just want to get home."

"You'll have to talk to Moses about that," Jack said.

The doctor must have half heard their conversation, because he cut in then. "We'll see when we get there, after I check you completely." Moses smiled at her. "I know you're anxious to see the kids, but they can wait a bit longer."

"That's why Merry got on the plane with me to begin with. Her kids," Gage stated. "She was worried to death that they wouldn't understand she'd been delayed, especially the little girl, Erin."

Merry heard Gage's words, and she couldn't believe that after those first catastrophic hours in the plane, the kids had slipped farther and farther down her list of concerns. Her first reason for being with Gage had shifted to her world revolving around the man, not the waiting children.

"They have no idea about any of this, since we didn't even know Merry was with you, but they'll be thrilled when Merry's with them again," Moses said.

As they flew lower, approaching the back of a sprawling multi-storied adobe house, Merry looked over at Gage. By virtue of her nomadic upbringing, moving all over and saying goodbye to friends before they could almost become friends, she had left so many people behind. But she knew that walking away from Gage would be harder after these few days than it would have been after two years.

The helicopter started to hover, and Merry looked out and down, seeing Gage's mother and father, holding on to each other, their eyes riveted on the huge machine landing by a massive barn ringed with stalls and snow spotted pastures. She was surprised to see a tall woman behind the Camerons, then she recognized Mallory Sanchez, Willie G.'s niece and the owner of the old inn in town. She was waving wildly at them, her long dark hair swirling from the blowing air currents.

"We made it," Moses exclaimed as the helicopter landed easily on the packed earth. The motors were switched off and were gradually winding down. There was an almost strange silence for a second before Herbert Carson, a large, gray haired man in denims, was opening the door. He was up in the chopper before anyone inside had time to move. He rushed over to his son and hugged him with unabashed relief.

"Hey, Dad. Watch the ribs," Gage warned, but not with much conviction. His father drew back a bit, then said, "Welcome home, son," and turned to call out to his wife, "Your boy looks good, sweetheart!" His eyes fell on Merry with obvious shock as he turned back from the open door. "Miss Brenner? What —?"

Moses cut in. "We'll explain later," he said to the older man.

Merry stayed where she was as Gage eased up and out of his seat with Moses offering him support by taking him by the arm. Gage stopped and looked down at her, then held out a hand that she could see was slightly unsteady. "We're home," he told her, his ragged voice betraying his emotions.

She reached for him, holding his hand in both hers, then nodded. "Yes, home."

He hesitated before letting his brother and the doctor get him out of the helicopter. Merry watched his mother hug and kiss him. Then Mallory was there, hugging Gage, before stepping aside to embrace the doctor. She beamed up at Moses. The two men took either side of Gage, and Mallory fell in behind, following them to the house.

Merry stopped and closed her eyes, wanting to take in everything that was happening. They were home. Home.

A hand touched her shoulder, and she expected it to be one of the EMTs, Luther or

Patrick. But Lark Carson was less than a foot from her.

The woman had a timeless beauty, with tiny stature and midnight dark hair that was starting to streak with gray. Her jeans and shirt were denim, but both had significant applications, hand done, that displayed her Native heritage. "Miss Brenner?" she said. "We had no idea you were with our son, but I think we should be thankful that you were."

"I'm thankful he got us down in that storm," Merry responded.

"If he had been up there on the mountain alone… I don't know what would have happened."

Merry remembered that horrible moment when she'd seen the blood, and then Gage lying there unconscious. "Your son knew just what to do, and we made it."

Lark slipped an arm around Merry's waist and urged her to continue following the men. She and Lark fell in step, and the older woman never let go of Merry. "We have a guest room that is yours as long as you need it," she was saying.

Merry stopped at the edge of a huge stone terrace that fronted multiple glass doors set into the adobe on one side of the house. Gage and the others were already going through the open space, but Merry looked down at Lark hesitantly. "Oh, no, I'm not staying. I need to get back to my place."

Lark motioned to the house. "Let's get in where it's warm and we can talk about this."

There was nothing to talk about. When either Jack or the doctor headed back to town, she was going too. "I really appreciate the offer—" she began, but Lark cut her off.

"Good, you'll love the west guest room. With three boys, I never got to decorate any room in a feminine way, but this guest room became my pet project just a few months ago," she spoke, not giving Merry a chance to argue.

But when they passed through a great room with the fireplace Gage had spoken of in the middle and came to a wide staircase framed with an intricate iron rail, Lark finally paused for breath before asking, "Can you make it up the stairs?"

"Yes, of course, but I thought we would go right to the hospital."

"I'm sure if either one of you needed emergency care when you were found, Moses would have made sure you went directly there." She patted Merry's hand and offered a kind smile. "Thank goodness he feels it's safe for you and Gage to be here. Also, if you knew Gage, you'd realize he wouldn't go to a hospital unless there was no other choice. He's always been like that, all the boys are."

Lark peered up at Merry. "Now, I have a smaller room down here, but it's not nearly as nice and it doesn't have its own bathroom." When she smiled this time, Merry was taken aback to see a very small version of the "Carson dimple" appear by the older woman's lips. "I know you're looking forward to a hot shower or long bath or both."

Merry was desperate for either one of them at that moment. She heard voices from upstairs, male voices, and then a door was closed and the sound was cut off. "When will Dr. Blackstar be leaving?"

"Not for a while. Moses is going to check the both of you thoroughly, and then make a decision about further treatment. That's going to take him a few hours at least."

"I'd like a hot bath," she admitted, then realized she had nothing with her. Her luggage was still back at the wreck. "But I left my things on the plane."

"Your bags are here. They got them before you all took off. I'll have your luggage brought in, and taken up to your room."

Merry hesitated, wondering if she was just being weak and foolish, her better judgment to leave quickly, being distorted by the lure of a hot bath. "I really need to get back to town," she said. "I work with these kids and they—"

"Oh, yes, I know all about that. I've heard from people at the hospital and the center about your program there. They say you're making a difference with those young lives that are so challenged, and bless you for your work there."

"They need to see me, and I really want to see them and show them I'm okay."

"Oh, I don't believe that Moses would have told them about the airplane crash, because he didn't even know you were on the plane until they found both of you in the wreck." Lark patted her arm again. "They certainly need to see you, but they need to see a rested, healthy you. And they will, just as soon as possible. But right now, you need to freshen up and get some food in your stomach."

Merry couldn't deny that she just wanted to strip off the clothes she'd been wearing far too long and soak in warmth. And she was starving too. "Okay," Merry agreed, for now, and started up the stairs with Lark by her side.

At the top, they turned away from the source of the muffled voices, and to a room at the other end of a hallway that was lined with photos and paintings—a lot of them were portraits, some distinctively Natives, some not. She almost wished she had the time to look at each one, but she kept going. A moment later, she stepped into a spacious room, with a wall of windows that let plenty of light inside. A four poster bed was decidedly feminine with lavender linens and a bank of pastel pillows arranged against a white wooden headboard.

Merry could have fallen face first onto the bed and not moved for a week, but a bath was her priority. Lark took her into the adjoining bath with a vanity that looked like an antique chest, and a large, claw-footed bathtub. After setting out towels and toiletries on the vanity for Merry, Lark surprised her by reaching out to draw her into a hug. "We are grateful you are both back safely."

Merry had been taken off guard by the show of affection, but she found she actually liked it. Then Lark stood back, swiped at her eyes and said, "Get in the tub and I'll tell

Alma to bring up your things. Are you allergic to any foods?"

"Oh, you don't have to—"

"Of course I don't, but I will," Lark said firmly.

"Thank you. No, I don't have any allergies."

"Oh, one last thing. Your parents. They need to know you're okay." She pointed toward the nightstand. "The phone by the bed works, and call anywhere you need to, to let them know you're okay and where you are."

"Thanks, but my folks never even knew I was on the plane, either. I'll call them from my house when I get there."

Lark nodded. "I'm glad they didn't have to go through that worry," the woman said softly, before leaving.

Finally alone, Merry quickly stripped off her clothes, grimacing at the thermals and the still wet boots scattered on the floor. Minutes later, she was in the tub, with luxurious, warm water up to her chin. The tears came then. She wasn't sure why she cried, whether out of relief or just plain nervous tension seeping out of her, but she didn't fight them.

CHAPTER TWELVE

MERRY FELT RELAXED and safe and closed her eyes. A soft knock caught her attention and she yawned before calling out, "Yes?"

"Ma'am, your things are on the bed," a woman said through the bathroom door. "Can I get you anything else?"

"No, thank you," she responded and waited until she heard the soft click of the outer door closing before slipping lower into the water. Shutting her eyes again, she just soaked in the sweet scent of the water and exhaled deeply. She would have fallen asleep if she hadn't slipped a bit more and got bathwater in her mouth. Coughing, she got out of the tub and dried herself on a huge white towel that was obscenely soft. She towel dried her hair, then tossed the towel on the vanity and reached for a second towel to wrap around herself as she headed out into the bedroom.

Her purse and small suitcase were all resting on the bed that had been turned down to expose silky lavender sheets. The bank of decorative pillows had been neatly stacked on the floor to one side, leaving two thick sleeping pillows against the white headboard.

A covered tray sat on the nightstand, and Merry caught a hint of something savory. Her stomach growled with hunger as she crossed to lift the cover. There was a ceramic bowl of rich, creamy looking soup, accompanied by a carved turkey sandwich on a thick French roll. A cup of steaming coffee topped it all off.

After quickly dressing and pulling her hair back into a ponytail, she climbed into bed, reached for the tray and began to eat a meal that was as delicious as it smelled. Warm both outside and in, she laid the tray of empty dishes on the nightstand before sinking back against the pillows.

GAGE WASN'T IN BED. Despite Moses warning him about staying still, letting his bruises and ribs heal, Gage was on the phone with his head office. He downplayed the crash, said he'd be up and running in a day or so. Then, he added with emphasis, that he didn't want them talking to anyone about what had happened, no matter what news media outlet approached them. "No comment," was the phrase of the day. Period.

He hung up and turned to find Moses coming into the room. "Work?" the doctor asked.

"Always. How's Merry?"

"Taking a hot bath and eating something, I was told. I'm giving her time to settle before going in to check her out."

Gage went to the window and looked out onto the front of the house and to the winding driveway. The gates weren't visible from the house, but he knew what was there. The media had heard about the crash, specifically, his involvement, and that he'd had a mysterious woman passenger he'd picked up in Pueblo. "Are they still set up there?"

"Yes. After Mallory left and got a ways down the road, she called and said that there were three crews and that another was joining them. A couple of reporters stopped her as she was going out, and yelled questions at her. Asked her name and wanted to know if she was the last-minute passenger added to the flight." Gage winced. Part of his reason for not heading to the hospital had been the reporters camped out there. "They're like vultures," he groused, turning back to Moses.

"I'll give them what they want, and get rid

of them. There's no story beyond the survival angle. It's a human interest piece at most." He grimaced when he flexed his shoulders under the navy flannel shirt he was wearing with his fresh boots and jeans.

"You're not going to throw Merry to the sharks or vultures, are you?"

That stopped him dead.

"No, he's not," a female voice replied. His mother had just come into the room and she crossed to him, flicking a glance at Moses. "No one is being thrown to the sharks, least of all that girl in the guest room. Can you imagine if they found out you two were there together? They'd be insatiable." She came closer to Gage. "What do you think would happen then? Your lives would probably become nightmares with all that attention from the press."

None of that was going to happen on his watch, especially to Merry and her kids. The sooner he dealt with the reporters, the faster he could get on with his life, and Merry with hers, and the kids would be spared any disruption of their routines. The notion of those innocent children being harassed as part of this story turned his stomach.

Merry was so protective of the kids that

she had boarded a plane she was terrified of flying in, and spent days struggling to survive on a mountain in freezing weather. And all because she'd been desperate to get back to the center.

He looked at his friend. "You're on their radar, too, Moses. They're already at the hospital. They'll be rabidly following any connection to the crash, so you'd better keep your guard up, unless you want your fifteen minutes of fame?"

"I don't have the time," he muttered.

"I just told Merry that Moses hadn't told the kids about the crash, because he hadn't known Merry was on that plane. No one around here knew it or knows it, except the men on the helicopter."

It made sense to Gage. Whoever had tipped off the press about him having a female passenger wouldn't have known it was Merry and wouldn't have known her name, either. What was on record on the original flight plan was that he'd been on board alone. He hadn't the time to change it, although it might help them out now. If they played their cards right, Merry wouldn't have to be any more involved publicly for the moment.

"All we'll have to do is keep Merry's identity to ourselves, at least until this blows over," Moses chimed in.

"Exactly," Gage said, happy they were all on the same page.

Lark started for the door. "That's settled then. I'll go down and talk to your dad. He's out with Lester and Patrick. He can tell them about our plan." She looked back at Moses. "You talk to Mallory right away and let her know?"

Moses nodded and his mother walked out of the room. Gage saw the frown on Moses' face.

"Oh, shoot," Moses said. "I was supposed to call her anyway." He pulled out his cell and punched in numbers fast, then exhaled as he put the phone to his ear. "Hey, Mal, it's me. Where are you?"

He visibly relaxed as he told Gage, "Just getting to town now." Then he went back to Mallory, quickly explaining what they were doing. "Thanks, love, I—" He glanced at Gage, and Gage couldn't help stop chuckling. "Call me, and I'll come and get you for the Carsons' steak dinner." Moses hung up. "She's in complete agreement," he said.

"*Love?* Is that what I heard?" Gage repeated, unable to resist teasing his friend about how close he and Mallory had become.

Willie G.'s niece had been Moses' first love in high school, then Mallory had found Henry Sanchez, setting off a whirlwind courtship and eventual marriage. Moses had licked his wounds and gone on, never marrying, only dating occasionally, but two years ago, Henry had died suddenly. After another two years of allowing Mallory some space, Moses had decided that he wouldn't lose her again. It seemed his plan was working.

"So?" Moses countered.

"So, nothing. I just commented. I think you're very lucky to get a second chance," he said and meant it.

Moses' face turned somber. "I do too," he said, then asked, "Do you want me to tell Merry what's going on?"

Gage shook his head. "No, I'll do it. I owe her that much." He started for the door. "And I should do it before handling the reporters at the gates."

"Are you sure about doing that interview? You're up to it?"

"It'll be much better to give them what they want, and then they'll fold up their tents and slip off into the night. It'll be worse trying to wait them out."

Moses conceded, "It sounds like a plan,

I guess. *My* plan is to go into town, check on my patients and get back before you've eaten all those steaks." He studied Gage. "You know, on second thought, I could take Merry with me now and get it over with."

"And if they follow you? They already have to know you're my doctor. That's pretty much known anywhere in town."

"Well, it's your call, or, more accurately, Merry's."

Moses was right—he had no right to make decisions for her. But he wanted to be the one to speak to her about all this. They'd discuss the situation, he'd say what he needed to say and she could decide what she wanted to do. "I'll tell her what we think, and see how she wants to play it out."

"I'll be with your parents and Jack downstairs for fifteen minutes. Let me know by then if I'm going to have a passenger on the way back."

Gage nodded and Moses headed to the door to leave. When his hand touched the handle, Gage stopped him. "And Moses?" The man he'd been friends with since what seemed like forever, turned to him. "Thank you," Gage said simply.

Neither man had to define what that "thank

you" was for. Moses smiled and shrugged. "You'd do the same for me," he said, then left the room.

Gage raked his fingers through his still shower dampened hair as he headed from his bedroom to Merry's room. Outside her door, he listened for a minute, trying to hear movement, or maybe the sound of the shower still going. But it was silent. He rapped on the closed door with his knuckles and waited, but nothing happened. He knocked again. Nothing.

He started to leave when he heard a soft thud, then Merry called out, "Yes?"

"It's me, Gage."

There was the sound of movement, then soft footsteps coming to the door. The barrier swung back and Merry stood in front of him. His breath caught in his chest at the sight of her. Her hair was back in a ponytail, with tendrils already being freed to brush her forehead and cheeks. A simple chambray shirt and jeans, looked great on her. And the green eyes were sleep heavy, their long lashes shading any expression in them.

She yawned, covering her mouth with one hand. "I'm sorry. I sat down and just fell asleep. I didn't mean to."

He knew then that it might have been smarter to let Moses explain things to her. No, not just smart, but wise. But it was too late to back out now, since he was already standing at her door.

What was he doing? She survived an ordeal with him. They were friends. He hoped they always would be, and he'd see her again whenever he visited Wolf Lake. He'd want to see her, and who knew? Maybe, just maybe, they could be close. Why not?

"We need to talk," he said.

She moved back to let him in, then he watched her sit on the edge of the bed. She yawned again, her fingertips pressed to her parted lips as she looked up at him. "Please, sit down," she said, patting the spot next to her on the bed. "Tell me what you want."

He hesitated, thinking that what he wanted right then, could never be said between them, at least nothing as blunt as, "Don't leave." Slowly he sank down beside her, but kept some distance between them.

MERRY SAT BY GAGE, wondering why he looked so good to her in a navy flannel shirt, jeans and boots. Not the Western boots he'd ruined in the snow, but another pair with silver toe tips and some tooling on the side. She couldn't make it out, but she thought it might be the initials of his business. A new dressing on his wound was starkly white against his dark skin, and his hair was combed straight back, showing the strong angles of his handsome face.

Fine lines at the corners of his eyes gathered when he narrowed them to look at her. "So, how are you doing?" he finally asked.

"Fine. I'm just anxious to head back to my house."

He was silent for so long, she started to feel uneasy, but then he said, "I need to explain something. And get your decision, then let Moses know." He glanced at his wristwatch. We've got fifteen minutes to talk it over."

She was confused. "What is it?"

"There's a contingent from the press outside, waiting to find out what happened on the plane."

She'd never thought of that, but Gage was a highly successful businessman and the Carsons were well known in the state. "They want your story?"

He nodded, ran a hand over his face, flinching when he nudged at the bandage. "It seems that way." There was a pause that didn't feel right to her, then she understood. "Your story too, if they discover you were on that mountaintop with me."

Her jaw nearly hit the floor. "Me? Oh, no, no, just forget all about that," she replied in a hurry. "Besides, your mom said that no one knew I was there until we were found."

"That is true. No one else knows you were there except a handful of people we trust to keep quiet. But there's a chance reporters will stumble on something, and Moses and I both agree that you shouldn't be dragged into whatever problems that could cause." He was so serious, studying her with dark as night eyes. "I can deal with it, and Moses could if he had to. But what about you...and the kids?"

"I could take the heat, but I sure don't want to," she said. "I mean, that's the last thing I want. I want to get back to the kids."

"And what about those kids of yours?"

She felt her heart sink. The kids. She had one horrific moment when she thought of microphones pushed in their faces, questions shouted at them. She said they wouldn't understand her disappearing and not keeping her promise, but she knew that they also wouldn't understand adults going after them relentlessly to get their "angle" on some stupid story. "Oh, no," she breathed. "That can't happen. It can't."

She hadn't been aware that she was shaking, until she felt Gage put his hand on her shoulder. "Hey, they never have to be involved. We just have to get past it without anyone being the wiser. Then there's no reason for them to go anywhere near the center, or you." He cleared his throat. "The worse that's going to happen is Moses might get some of the fallout because of our friendship and him being my doctor. But he can handle it, and he won't let them get into the hospital, where they could cause any problems."

She knew that was true, but how would she get back to her kids? As if Gage had read her mind, he spoke up. "Moses says he can smuggle you out of here when he leaves."

She laughed at that, just a bit this side of hysteria. "All covert and top secret, huh?"

"If you want to do it, he's…"

A knock on the door stopped Gage and Merry turned to see the doctor stride into the room. "It's all off," he said. "At least until you talk to the hoards at the gate."

Gage stood. "What happened?"

"Just talked to Mallory again, who, by the

way, is pretty put out. Once she got to the inn, two reporters came barging in, wanting a story about her relationship to you, to the Carsons, and demanding to find out what happened on that plane. She told them to leave."

"Oh, man," Gage said. "That's pretty bad."

Merry looked anxiously from one man to the other. "They'll follow us, won't they?" she asked Moses.

"I'm pretty sure they'll try, and since I'm no stunt driver, the odds of me losing them between here and town, are slim to none." He frowned at her. "I'm coming back for the steak dinner, so perhaps when it's dark, we could try to get past them then."

"I'm going to give them everything I can apart from Merry's involvement and maybe that will get them off our backs," Gage said. "Or, at the very least, distract them so you can slip past without being the center of anyone's attention." His intense gaze shifted to her. "What do you want to do—try to make your escape now, or when Moses leaves later? Or do you have any other ideas of how to handle this?"

She wanted to shout, "I just want to go home!" but stopped and fought the urge to get in Moses' car and take her chances. The chances, she reminded herself, weren't just hers.

"I can't go. I can't risk possibly involving the kids in this," she said in a voice that, despite her attempts to steady it, broke more than once. "I think I should wait until after Gage speaks to the reporters."

Gage hunkered down in front of her, his hands on his knees. "Are you sure?"

She nodded slowly. "If or when they find out who I am, they'll know everything—what I do, where I do it, and about the children. It's what you said, they'll go after the kids." She narrowed her eyes. "Look at what they're doing to Mallory, for Pete's sake."

"She's right, Gage. They're going to follow Merry until they get something."

Gage turned to look up at the doctor, then stood. "That's why I need to get down there and give them a few details." Merry met his gaze again. "Once I speak with them, I'm sure things will calm down."

Merry hoped against hope he was right. Things had gone from bad to worse. "How did they even know about the crash so fast?"

"I'm not sure," Gage replied.

Flattening her lips, Merry felt her anger

building. "Those reporters at the inn, if they're still hanging around outside, bothering Mallory and her guests....that's got to be against the law," she said. "You can't just do that to people."

Gage snapped his fingers as he turned back to Moses. "That's it!"

"What is?" her friend asked. "Stalking. Merry's right—it's illegal, totally illegal. I think one of us needs to call John and let him know what's happened at Mallory's. He could do something, I'm sure, at least in town."

"John?" Merry asked, looking from one man to the other.

"John Longbow, the chief of police."

"Oh, right. Do you think he could stop all of this?"

"Not the reporters at the gates because they aren't on private property, or trying to break in. Freedom of the press in action and all that, but it can't hurt to get some help for Mallory."

Moses said quickly, "I'll go and call him." He addressed Merry. "If you're not going with me, I'm leaving, but I'll be back shortly and maybe then I can give you a checkup just to make sure things are okay."

She nodded, barely covering a deep yawn. She'd never felt so tired in her life. Gage came closer and bent down again in front of her. "You need to rest. I know I woke you, so why don't you go back to what you were doing, and I'll see what I can do to dull the Fifth Estate's need for a story."

"Thank you," she whispered, "and good luck."

He reached out and clasped her hands resting in her lap. "It'll be a breeze, trust me." He squeezed her hands tenderly before drawing back. "There's no big story here at all, and they'll figure it out and that will be the end of it. They'll be heading in droves for the last train out of Dodge."

"What?"

"A figure of speech. You know, like the old Westerns where the bad guy takes the last train out of Dodge when he knows he's beaten, and if he stays, he's not going to do well with the hero?"

"Old movies again," she murmured.

"I told you, I'm a person who can't sleep much, so old movies serve a purpose. They help me pass the time, and they give me things to say to others—trivia, interesting little tidbits of…" He shrugged. "Trivia." He smiled at her, flashing his dimple.

She found a smile easy to come by right

then. "You have a lot to offer, besides a bit of trivia," she teased.

He touched her chin with the tip of his finger. "You look so much better," he said almost on a whisper.

She felt some heat in her cheeks. "I feel better, but so darn tired."

"Do what I said, rest up." He stood, then motioned her back onto the pillows. "You'll be able to see your kids soon, I promise."

She did as he said, scooting back toward the pillows against the white wooden headboard. Sinking into them, she sighed, and covered yet another yawn. "When things settle down, Gage, I'll keep my side of the bet. I'll even get you a stamped receipt from the instructor to prove to you that I keep my word."

"Good, I'll look forward to you giving it to me," he said, reaching for a crocheted throw that lay across the foot of the bed. He spread it out over her. "But right now, all I want you to do is relax."

She closed her eyes, laced her fingers behind her head. "Yes, boss."

"Very funny," he said, then turned away. "I need to get down to the gates," he told her. "Then I want to call Moses to find out about John, if he can do anything for Mallory."

"Good luck," Merry said, but suddenly she thought of an idea and sat up straight in bed. Gage was ready to open the door as she exclaimed, "I've got it! Why didn't I think of this right away?"

She swung her legs over the side of the bed, sleep forgotten. "My kids! It's okay."

CHAPTER THIRTEEN

GAGE WAS STARTLED by her voice, then turned and she was scrambling off the bed. He had no idea what was happening, but he could see the huge smile on her face, the way her green eyes shone. She grabbed his arm with both hands. "The kids, the kids, I can phone them!" She waited, looking up at him as if she'd told him she could walk on the moon.

"Of course you can," he said, pointing out what he considered the truly obvious, but wondering why he hadn't suggested it to her after they'd arrived at the ranch.

"But I didn't phone them," she murmured, her smile starting to slip. "I didn't."

"Then do it and call them," he urged as he took her hands in his again. "Use the house phone."

She stared at him, then slowly shook her head and held tightly to him with a grasp that was starting to tremble. "I should have," she said, her face pulling into a pained frown.

He had an uneasy feeling and wished Moses was still there. Delayed shock? Total fatigue? He didn't know, but he sure could feel the pull on his arm as she began to slip toward the floor.

He caught her, managing to keep her on her feet by holding her against him. Wishing he could just lift her into his arms to get her to the bed, but he knew his ribs would never tolerate that. Awkwardly, he walked her backward to the bed.

"I'm horrible," she was muttering against his chest. "I forgot. I forgot. Those poor kids, I forgot them all." And with those last words she became a dead weight in his arms.

Thankfully they were at the bed and, favoring his ribs, he managed to get her up onto it and resting against the pillows. He stood back, watching her, making sure she'd just fainted and hadn't truly passed out. Her breathing was easy, her face free of the misery that had been there seconds ago. He pulled his cell out of his pocket and punched in Moses' number.

With it to his ear, his eyes never left Merry. After two rings, Moses answered with, "I just got here. They followed me, too, so I am not going to the hospital right now. I'm at Jack's office and Maureen is going to get me out of here, one way or the other."

That all came in a rush of words, and when it ended, Gage said without preamble, "Merry passed out."

Moses shifted gears without a blink. "What happened?"

Gage explained it to the doctor as he sat down on the side of the bed by Merry. Automatically, he brushed at loose tendrils of hair that rested on her forehead. She felt cool, and the trembling was gone. When he finished explaining what had gone on, Moses said, "Probably pure exhaustion, both physically and emotionally."

"She's out like a light," Gage said, gently stroking her cheek.

"Any fever?"

"No."

"Breathing?"

He watched her chest rise and fall, then with a sigh, Merry turned onto her side and resettled. "Yes."

"I mean, is it fast, slow, shallow?"

"No, yes, no. Even and steady." He took in her dark lashes fanning out against her skin. "Fine."

Gage heard a long sigh over the phone.

"She's okay. She probably used whatever she had in her game book to cope with the whole survival situation. Now she's paying for burying all that anxiety and fear."

"Bubbles," Gage said softly, struck by how very vulnerable the woman on the bed looked to him at that moment.

"What?" came the reply in his ear.

"Nothing. Just…is it okay? Is she okay?"

"I'm sure she will be. I'll do a full work up when I get there, if or when I get there."

"What about John? Can he help you out?"

"I don't think so. Mallory still has her 'stalkers' at the inn. John got the guys to move down the street a bit, but they're still out there, watching."

"Is Mallory there alone?"

"No, she said Willie G. came in for a bit, and he's there with her."

"Good. I'm finally going to go down to talk to whoever is left at the gates." Then he had a thought. "Hey, if Willie G. is at Mallory's, chances are he came in on that big bike of his."

"Yes, he would have."

"If he did, call the guy and ask him if he'll help. He could get to Jack's office in the back, and if you're ready, he'd have you on that bike so quickly no one would know what's going on."

"That's a good idea. He might like some excitement."

"You bet." Willie G. had come down from the Rez to the lowlands when the town was formed forty years ago. He had little if any patience for people who didn't respect others and the fine community the locals had created here.

"Moses, get him. Go and do what you need to do, then try to get back here as soon as you can to check Merry over. Just let me know what's going on in town, good or bad."

"Will do," Moses said before he broke the connection.

Gage slipped his phone in his pocket, then stood for a very long moment, just looking at Merry. With the power of a punch to the middle, he realized that if any woman he'd ever met could have changed the man he was, it might have been Merry. Sadly, he was sure that was as close as any woman would get, and a feeling of regret settled deep inside him.

Leaning over her, he inhaled her lovely, sweet scent, then touched his lips to her silky smooth cheek. "Rest well," he whispered, determined to get her to her kids as soon as he could, no matter what he had to do to make that happen.

Minutes later, Gage approached the heavy metal gates on foot, hit the security pad and input the code. The barriers started to slowly part. The sun was almost hidden behind heavy clouds, and the air had a real bite of cold in it. But he didn't notice too much more than the fact that the broadcast vans were clustered across the road in a dirt packed field, and about a dozen reporters were running toward the gates as they opened.

He stepped through as voices erupted with questions, and bright lights snapped on, all but blinding him. He ignored the yelling, standing just two paces from the open gates, and held up his hands. When the voices died down enough for him to be heard, he raised his own voice. "Hello, everyone, I am Gage Carson and this is my parents' home, so I expect that to be respected."

He barely got out the words before the reporters started up again. Coming closer, they thrust microphones into his face and threw a barrage of questions at him. Again, Gage waited, then when he got a chance to cut in, he said, "I will answer all your questions, on one condition."

That brought instant silence and all eyes on him. "I was the one that flew the plane, the one that made an emergency landing in it, and the one who was stranded on the mountain in it. I am the one who survived because the plane was one of the best in the world, and because another storm didn't come." He'd noticed the gathering clouds rolling down from the mountains even as he spoke. "I'm the one who was rescued and got back here."

The reporters looked expectantly, waiting for his punch line. "It's me. All me. My friends and family and people in the town, don't know anything I haven't told them or will tell them. If you want me to answer your questions, my condition for that is, you leave the rest of the people around here alone."

He stopped, waited, then a gray haired reporter spoke. "We just want the story," he pointed out.

"Do you want the real story, or a story about what people thought, or guessed, or felt?"

"Both," the man said without hesitation.

Gage pulled a huge bluff, and he turned to go back through the gates. "Drive safely," he tossed over his shoulder, with a dismissive wave behind him.

Before he could take more than two steps,

the voices were pummeling him again. He turned, hesitated, then went back.

"Listen, I understand your job, what you have to do, but you have limits, too. I'll be leaving here in a few days, and probably won't be back for months. I'm the one you want the story from, and I'm willing to give it to you all, but not if you involve everyone around here in your hunt for whatever truth you think you're going to find."

The gray haired man spoke again. "I, for one, find that agreeable. This isn't about corruption or anything criminal going on. It's a good story of survival. I'll abide by your conditions."

There was a murmur from the others, some back and forth, then they all agreed with Gage. His relief was immense, but he tried not to show it. Instead, he motioned around. "Go ahead, what do you all want to know…?"

It took over an hour before the questions and follow up inquiries were asked, then Gage held up his hand. "I think that's about it." A woman he hadn't really noticed came closer, She was slight and dark, in a jacket with the insignia of another local TV station on the lapel of a navy blazer.

"One last question?" she asked him.

He nodded.

"Did you ever think that you'd die up there, alone?"

Something in the question struck him, making his chest tighten. Then, unbidden, images of Merry flooded through him. Images of her lying next to him, talking through the darkness, holding his hand when he was miserable, responding so sweetly to his kiss.

"No," he said honestly. "Never had one thought like that," and he swallowed before finishing with, "I'm back. I'm fine, and I'm getting on with my life in a few days."

A shattering roar came up behind the group of reporters, who parted to reveal a huge motorcycle, emblazoned with Eagles and the American flag. It glided forward, the engine throbbing and cut right through them and up to Gage.

The rider flipped up the front of his bright red, white and blue helmet, and Gage suddenly came face to face with Willie G. The epitome of the Native, his long gray hair was flowing around his shoulders, his hawkish features frozen with disapproval. The shirt he was wearing, a splashy tie-dye in brilliant colors, hung on his wiry frame. At sixty-plus, the man was, and always had been, a force to be reckoned with.

As the throbbing engine died, Willie G. raised his voice. "Your project you came to see about, is it still a go?"

Gage was really confused now. "As far as I know they are still wanting bids on it and my company is still in the running."

"And you, brother, can live with that? Ruining your people's land, their peace and their heritage?" he demanded.

Gage flinched at the words. "Willie, I'm not here to—"

Still straddling his huge motorcycle, the old man stopped him with a raised hand. "I come to talk to you, boy," he said, loud enough for everyone to hear.

Gage didn't know what was going on, but he had a gut instinct to go with the flow. "Good, come on in and talk, then," he said and motioned up to the house.

A reporter shoved a microphone in front of Willie G. and got a snort for his effort. "Just your name, sir?" the reporter asked, drawing the microphone back to his chest.

"I am Willie G. and this is my town," he said, and gestured for Gage to get on the bike behind him.

Gage didn't hesitate. He climbed on the back, held to the seat, then Willie started up the machine. He went slowly through the gates, let Gage hit the "close" code, then with a twist of the accelerator, the engine roared.

The ride to the house took less than a minute, and Willie pulled up in front of the formal entry area. He put down the kickstand, took off his helmet and hung it on the handle before he climbed off. Gage was already standing, looking at the older man. "So tell me, what's up?"

Willie spoke as he pulled his long gray hair back and secured it with a leather tie. "Merely asked you some questions, boy." His dark eyes met Gage's. "Truth. Truth."

Gage patted Willie on the shoulder. "Let's go inside and get out of the cold."

The two men went through the entry and into the main room, centered around a massive stone fireplace. Lark Carson was there talking to Alma, the housekeeper, and both women looked up at Willie and Gage as they came toward them.

Lark beamed, holding out both hands to Willie. "Oh, Willie, so good to see you."

"It sure is," Moses said from the hallway that led to the east side of the house.

He stepped out into the large room, his hair ruffled, and he was wearing a heavy leather jacket. "This old man is crazy," he said, pointing a finger at Willie.

Gage looked from the doctor to Willie, then back to Moses. Things finally fit. "He brought you out here on that bike?"

Moses exhaled roughly. "Shoot, he sure did. Almost killed us both more than once driving like a maniac at over a hundred miles an hour."

The older man chuckled. "You boys are so soft. Talk about speed, when I was your age, I—"

"You could outrun a train and be at the next stop in time to serve the passengers high tea," Lark put in with a soft burst of laughter.

Willie gave her a mock bow. "You remember."

"I remember a young Willie riding his bicycle straight down the Pontu Pass road with brakes that didn't work."

Willie smiled warmly. "Good memory, Lark."

"One remembers abject fear when one was on the back of that bike," Lark said with a grin.

"You didn't really go down Pontu Pass like

that, did you?" Gage asked before she turned to leave with Alma in tow.

She showed a coy smile. "In another life, son, in another life." She glanced at Willie. "And you're staying for dinner, right?"

"Oh, yes, lady, I am." He crossed to her and the housekeeper. "And I am going to do the cooking of the steaks."

Lark didn't fight that offer. "Then come on," she said.

The three left the main room and Gage turned to Moses. "Still can't believe you rode with that lunatic, but I sure am glad you made it back in one piece. Merry really needs you to look in on her."

"I already did that," Moses said, taking a seat on the sofa. "Went right up as soon as I got here."

"And?"

"She's okay, just exhausted, both physically and emotionally. Everything else checked out, and she rolled over and went back to sleep."

Gage felt some relief. "That's good. She wants to call the kids, can't believe we hadn't thought of that one sooner."

"How'd it go with the press?"

"I thought it went well until Willie roared

up and confronted me about the bid I'm here to make."

"What?"

"Yeah, scared the heck out of me when he talked about my company basically desecrating the land." He shook his head. "Is he for real on that?"

"I'd guess he might be, but he was trying to draw attention down there and away from me. He told me so, when he dropped me off by the stable." Moses chuckled. "If he wasn't Mallory's uncle, I'd say he's a bit, uh…reckless?"

"He always has been if he took my mother on the back of his bike down—" He stopped, unable to say the words out loud. "Unbelievable," he said instead, then started for the stairs. "I'm going to check on Merry."

Moses waved at him to leave. "I'm going to sit here and forget about the ride I just took."

MERRY FELT WONDERFUL. Warm and protected and so comfortable. Then she woke with a start, not understanding where she was or what was going on. Shadows were everywhere, but she could hear movement near the foot of the bed. Then a light clicked on.

Gage. And she understood everything—the bedroom, the warmth, and the ease that she had felt for that single moment before she remembered…*everything*.

"Oh, hey," she said a bit thickly, still sleepy. Yawning, she pushed up on her elbows.

Gage came closer, into the halo of light that fought the shadows all around. He was still in the same clothes, but he looked tired, his hair spiked a bit as if he'd been running his fingers through it.

"How are you?" he asked.

"I…I fainted?"

"I didn't know at first," he said as he sat on the bed, studying her. "Scared me, actually."

She closed her eyes. "I'm sorry."

"No, no," he said, his hand finding hers by her side and closing over it. "Don't be sorry. You went through a terrible ordeal. There had to be a time when it all took a toll on you, and you've had it. It's over."

She sighed heavily, giving in to a need to hold on to him by turning her hand over in his and lacing their fingers together. She remembered the phone, her not thinking about calling her kids, because she'd been worried more about Gage and his medical ailments. The kids had been pushed aside and she felt suffocating guilt from it. As if he read her mind, he murmured, "It was pretty normal to worry about what was right in front of us, and not fret so much about things at a distance, things we couldn't change." His grip on her hand tightened for a moment, then moved out of her hold and found its way to her cheek. He stroked her with the back of his fingers, an achingly gentle touch. "You did remarkably well, believe me."

She opened her eyes, finding him less than a few feet from her, and her breath caught in her throat. For a moment she felt as if she was floating in the air, her only anchor being Gage. Then his touch left her, and she felt her breath release in a rush.

"Are you up to coming down for the steak dinner?" he asked.

"Oh, I don't know. I'm so tired still," she said honestly.

He hesitated, then cupped her chin in the warmth of his fingers. "You aren't hungry?"

She was, but not starved. "Maybe I can get something later," she said. "I'd only put a damper on the party by falling asleep at the table if I go down now."

He chuckled softly. "Okay, just take it easy. When you're hungry, Alma can bring something up for you."

"Thank you," she said, then remembered. "The press conference? Did you do it yet?"

He nodded. "It's done. Hopefully it worked."

He didn't sound convinced, but she didn't have the energy to question him any further. "Good. At least Moses got back safely."

For some reason that brought a full smile from Gage. "Oh, he survived all right." Then he added, "He rode back on Willie G.'s motorcycle, at, according to Moses, a hundred miles an hour."

"Oh, wow," she said, imagining the doctor on the back of the huge motorcycle that Willie G. rode around town. "He never mentioned it to me when he came up here earlier."

"I think he was still in shock," Gage said, still grinning. Then he looked at his watch, "Well, I guess I better get down there and grab some steak before it's all gone."

"Good idea," she said softly.

Before he went out, he looked back at Merry for a long moment. "Rest," was all he said before going out and closing the door.

Merry laid there feeling alone. Pressing her hand to a low growl in her stomach, she almost wished she'd gone down with Gage for the celebration dinner. Instead, she was there by herself. Alone. She glanced to her side at the house phone, but didn't pick it up. She'd have to search to find the numbers she needed.

She closed her eyes, feeling tension in her neck and shoulders starting to flare. She thought about laying on the grass, blowing bubbles into the sky, counting each one as it rose into the clear blue above the meadow. Then from nowhere, she was in a tiny plane with a handsome, dark-haired man, laying by her side, holding his hand, feeling each breath he took.

She sat up quickly, buried her face in her hands and muttered about how stupid she was being. The professional side of her knew that it really wasn't stupid to be feeling things she knew she shouldn't about Gage. It was an impossible situation; not just opposites attracting, but total incompatibles attracting. There was no middle ground for them to meet on. But that didn't stop her from hoping there could be.

She knew about strange alliances being formed under duress of survival. That's what it was, she thought, but that didn't make it any less real for her. She already missed him, even before she left this house. Even before he left Wolf Lake again. She missed him.

The door opened without any warning, and Gage came in, carrying a large tray in his hands. "I got to thinking…the whole dinner from the bet, it was for both of us. Me to gloat at winning and you to be duly chastised for being so wrong."

He got to the bed and put the tray on the nightstand. "So, I brought the dinner up here for you, so I can sit and gloat and you can watch me gloat."

Turning from her, he crossed to the armoire near the bathroom and opened the upper doors. "Mom said she left a lap tray up here, and…aha!" There was a rustling noise, then Gage was back with the tray. He pulled the legs down and put it on Merry's lap where she sat amid the pillows. "Willie G. cooked the steaks, and I have to say, he's a genius when it comes to good, plain cooking. He's also a talker, a big talker."

She'd knew Willie G. was a storyteller, mostly about the past, the history of the town and the reservation near it. "He sure is entertaining."

"And opinionated," he added as he removed the cover off the tray. "Very opinionated."

His tone told her that there was more to his Willie G. encounter downstairs than just storytelling. "Sounds as if he irritated you just a bit," she murmured as she watched him transfer a plate of food to her lap tray.

He cast her a sideways glance before reaching for cutlery and a napkin for her. As he laid down the fork and steak knife by her plate, he murmured, "Smart lady." He picked up the other plate he'd brought with him, and made room for it on the nightstand. He crossed, grabbed a chair sitting by the armoire and brought it back to the side of the bed. He finally sat and said, "There. That's better."

"What did he say?" Merry asked, watching him cut a chunk of steak and then spear it with his fork.

He was quiet as he chewed, then took a sip from a small glass of water that had a lemon wedge in it. Swallowing, he shrugged. "Let me put it this way, he's a man whose mind is made up about many things."

She'd heard about Willie's dissatisfaction about controversial changes around town, including the project Gage had come to bid on. "Oh, he hates the idea of the development, doesn't he?"

"He makes you look like a wimp."

"A wimp?"

"Yes, a wimp." He ate more steak and motioned her to eat up.

"I've never been called that before," she conceded with a smile, ignoring the food that he was obviously enjoying.

He stopped for a moment, meeting her gaze. "I can say you are definitely not a wimp, not after what you survived."

"But I don't want to go up against Willie G., huh?"

"No. He's one of those guys who would have chained himself to a tree to save it from being cut down."

She chuckled at that. "No wonder you brought the food up for me. A tactical retreat."

"Partly," he said and motioned to her food again. "Eat while it's hot."

She did as he requested, and soon realized that the potato casserole was every bit as good as the succulent meat. But her appetite failed her after just a few bites. Gage was watching her as she laid down her fork. His food was more than half gone.

"You don't like it?" Gage asked. "That kind of takes the punch out of my victory if you don't enjoy the meal."

"It's great food and I like it very much, but I realized I'm not really hungry," she murmured, sinking back into the pillows. Then a question came to her. "You said you left to get away from Willie G....partly. What was the rest of your reason for leaving and bringing up my dinner?"

She saw him hesitate, then he laid his knife and fork across the top of his plate, and sat forward in his chair. His dark eyes were level with hers. "I know I said I came up to gloat about my win, but it's not true." She heard him take a breath before he dropped a bombshell on her. "I came up because I missed you."

CHAPTER FOURTEEN

GAGE HEARD HIS own words and recognized the pure truth in them. He had felt like a fish out of water eating downstairs while she'd been up here alone. Hearing Willie G. make his case, reminded Gage about Merry's passion about the same subject. She'd been gone twenty years at least, but she loved Wolf Lake and the residents, especially her kids.

He didn't begin to understand that bond with her and the children, but maybe it happened between the caregiver and the ones in need. He didn't know, but he knew that she loved those kids, and the town. He watched her, the widening of her eyes as he made his statement, then the way she dropped her gaze to her barely touched meal.

"There was no one to make a bet with down there?" she asked in a low voice.

"No, Willie's always up for a bet or two, and Jack's been known to do a bit on that front."

He decided to make a joke of his words, to take the depth, he knew had been in the confession, out of them.

She didn't respond to him until he reached to get the tray and lift it off her lap.

"It's odd, isn't it?" she said so softly he almost didn't hear her.

"What's that?" he asked as he put the tray down on the floor by the nightstand.

"You and me, meeting like that, then crashing and surviving. I wouldn't have believed it if someone had told me that would all happen within a matter of hours."

He sat back down, touching the edge of the comforter with his fingertips. He knew the feeling. Out of nowhere, his life had been altered. "Yeah, me too."

"But miracles happen," she said. "You know, I don't remember too many miracles in my life…and then in one day, there was the first, then another, then another." She spread her hands on her thighs, and stared down at them.

He hadn't thought about miracles much in his own life, but now that he stopped to consider it, the landing could qualify for a miracle of sorts, he guessed. The trees could have torn the plane to pieces, but hadn't. They could have frozen to death. They didn't. And the second storm that he knew was going to come at any time, would have buried them. But it had stalled, and they'd been rescued. He'd concede a miracle or two in that mix.

"I'm not going to fly again," she said out of the blue. "I figure, you get a reprieve one time, but it's pushing it to do the same again and expect the same result." She hesitated, color touching her cheeks. "I mean, after I make good on the bet, then never ever again."

"Where is this all coming from?"

She rubbed the flats of her hands up and down on the denim covering her thighs. "I don't know. Just thinking, and then you said—" She cut her words off with a fluttery shrug of her slender shoulders. Green eyes turned to him, shadowed by lush dark lashes. "How long are you going to be here?"

"At this house?"

"Wolf Lake."

"I'd guess a week at the most—that should provide sufficient time for meetings and going over the proposed site to get ideas for a bid."

She closed her eyes for a moment, then pushed toward him as if to get up off the bed. "I need to get changed for bed," she said, as she dangled her legs over the side.

He quickly shoved his chair back and stood. Then he held out a hand to her. "Come on."

She took his offered support, gently eased her up to her feet, then on impulse, he kept pulling her until she was in his arms. "You're right about miracles," he whispered. "They don't happen very often." He rested his chin on her hair and closed his eyes. He savored the feeling of her face pressed into his shoulder, and the way her body molded to his, before reluctantly letting her go. "Tomorrow you can talk to the kids, or if things work out, we'll get you back to town."

"Thank you," she whispered, then ducked past him and went to the bathroom door.

"Sweet dreams," he called after her, watching her pause before entering the small room. But she didn't look back, instead she stepped into the bathroom and closed the door after her.

Gage stood there for a long time just staring at the door, then he heard water start to run and he turned, picked up the tray with the leftovers, and headed out of the bedroom. Closing the door behind him, he turned to head downstairs, walking away from his foolish notions as he went.

Before he got to the head of the stairs, his mother was coming toward him.

"Here, let me take that," she said, lifting the tray from his hands.

"Is Willie still down there?"

"Oh, yes, he's been talking your dad's ear off." She frowned up at him. "He didn't upset you, did he?"

More like ticked him off, he thought wryly. "No, he didn't. I'm just too tired to go over the same ground again and again with him." He bent to kiss his mother on the cheek. "Thanks for the great meal. Now, I'm going to bed."

"Good night," she said as he headed down the hallway to his room.

He'd showered and climbed into bed just before Moses came in with a summary knock that he didn't bother to wait to have answered. "You ran like a chicken," he said, grinning as he came near the bed.

Gage sat up. "Call me a chicken, but I couldn't take that anymore."

"Willie sure came down on you, didn't he?"

"I sort of expected him to be on the 'don't do it,' side of the debate, but figured with him spending most of his time at his restaurant, he wouldn't be around here or the Rez enough to really get into it."

Moses almost snorted a laugh. "He's involved up to his neck with everything around here."

Gage studied his friend. "How about you? Do you have an issue with what is going to be done?"

Moses shrugged. "I don't necessarily like it, but it's business, and to be honest, Wolf Lake needs some funds for infrastructure stability. It could be a positive thing."

"You really believe that?" he asked. "Your whole life has been in this town."

"Yours, too," he countered. "And if you're good with it, and other good folks around here are, too, I think it's worth giving it the benefit of the doubt. At least until there's something concrete to vote on."

"And when they solidify a deal, with whoever wins the bid, you're going to back it?"

"I will until I see something that lets me know that it will be harmful."

Gage wished Merry could be so sensible about the whole deal. "Merry just hates it," he confided.

"I gathered that out the first time she spoke to me about it." Moses smiled. "She's a smart lady, and passionate about whatever she gets involved with."

"I couldn't agree more," he murmured.

"You should see her around the kids at the center. They're the center of her world, no pun intended."

"Well, I sure hope to see her in action there soon," he said, and meant every word.

"Well, better wish me luck. I'm about to take my life in my hands and head back with Willie. I just wanted to touch base with you and see how you're feeling."

"Tired," he said honestly, "but I'll be fine by tomorrow. I've got to get ready for the meetings with the council elders and the mayor, et al."

Moses hesitated, then turned and went to the door. He swung back around before opening it. "Pain, do you need anything for pain? Or how about the wound…do I need to look at it again, check for any infection? I can go down and get my bag and—"

"No thanks…I'm fine," Gage said with a grin. "Now, quit making excuses not to jump on that bike and roar out of here. You're such a chicken."

"That's why we're such good friends," Moses said. He gave a brief wave and then left, closing the door behind him.

"Smart and passionate," Gage echoed

Moses' words about Merry. That was a nice combination, all rolled up in one beautiful lady. "Very nice indeed," he thought, still smiling at the idea when he finally fell asleep.

MERRY WOKE TO wind and the noise of something hitting the windows. She blinked, pushed herself up and was shocked to see grayness outside, along with snow hitting the window panes. Pushing her tangled hair back from her face, she glanced at the clock by the bed. Ten-fifteen! She must have slept for twelve hours at least.

Scrambling out of bed, she padded barefoot to the bathroom and fifteen minutes later, she was dressed in a red cowl necked sweater and her last pair of clean jeans. Stepping out into the hallway, she stopped, heard voices in the distance from the lower floor, a door closing, then quiet. She headed for the staircase and went down.

Following soft sounds of something being brushed, she found herself in an expansive kitchen, lined with beautifully crafted cabinets, stone countertops and what looked like restaurant sized appliances. Lark Carson was sweeping the tiled floor, but stopped to look up when Merry came into the room.

She smiled broadly. "Oh, my dear, you look wonderful this morning!" Gage's mom put the broom aside and came over to Merry, making a show of studying her. "And how are you feeling?"

"Like a whole new person. It's amazing what a good night's rest can do."

"Oh yes, this *is* a good day!" she exclaimed. "You have a bounce in your step, and everyone is safe and sound. I am very thankful." Then, unexpectedly, she got on her tiptoes to kiss Merry's cheek. "Very thankful."

"Yes," Merry agreed as she looked around at the almost empty space. "Where is Gage?"

"Gone," Lark said. "What do you want for breakfast? Eggs and bacon, cereal, some fruit?"

"Thanks, but nothing right now." She glanced at the windows that showed the heavily falling snow. "I was hoping I could get a ride into town by now. I never expected another storm."

"Of course you can, as soon as someone comes back. Herbert left to see a friend, and Jack went back to town last night." She frowned slightly. "He took this whole thing very hard," she confided, then looked at Merry with a smile. "Moses and Willie G.

left last night, and Gage was gone at sunrise, before the snow started." She frowned again. "I don't know what's going on with this snow. It's February, for heaven's sake, and it's snowing and cold."

"I don't remember a lot of snow when I lived here," Merry said. "But one year, there was quite a bit and we actually got snowed in for a whole day. I was maybe four or so."

"I remember that huge blizzard like it was yesterday. Threw the whole town into a tizzy!" She brushed a hand over her dark hair twisted into a low knot at her neck. "If you don't want breakfast, how about some coffee or tea?"

"Tea sounds good," Merry said.

Lark got busy putting a kettle on the eight burner stove, then sat with Merry at a huge glass table in a breakfast room to one side of the kitchen. Multiple windows overlooked the back of the ranch and everything was gradually turning white under an angry sky.

"I heard this storm was stalled in Colorado before it got here."

Merry took that in. "Well, it's here now."

"In full force," Lark said, then looked past Merry as the door across the room from the breakfast area opened. A gust of cold, damp air flooded in and Merry saw Gage taking off his baseball cap to slap it against his thigh to get the clinging snow off of it. He stomped his boots on the floor, then looked up and spotted the two women.

Lark was up right when the kettle started to whistle shrilly. "Get in here," she said to her son as she headed toward the stove. "Sit. I'll get you something hot to drink."

Gage walked in stocking feet into the kitchen, slipped off his snow blotched leather jacket and dropped it over the back of the nearest wooden chair. He kept going to the breakfast area and made a beeline for Merry. "So, you're awake?" he said as he pulled out a chair across from her and sat down. "Last time I looked, you were snoring peacefully."

"Me?" she questioned. "Wrong person. I don't snore."

"That's what they all say," he murmured with a smile that exposed his dimple. The man only had to do that for her to forget how to think straight. "Where did you get to, and why are you running around with your ribs hurt?"

"I'm fine. The ribs barely hurt now, and I had business in town."

That sobered her. "Oh," was all she said as

Lark returned with two steaming cups of tea on a tray with cream and sugar.

"Thanks," Merry said, then realized there was no cup for the older woman. "You aren't going to join us?"

"No, I need to figure out where my husband got to. He left earlier this morning to see some friends, but he's not there yet." She glanced at a huge clock on a wall by the windows. "He's probably just talking to folks, maybe stopped to get coffee or something." She was talking almost to herself, mulling over ideas of why he wasn't where he should have been. "Just running late."

Gage wrapped his hands around his mug, but didn't lift it to drink. "Dad's never been good with schedules, not since he retired."

"You're right, but with this weather..." Lark looked concerned. "His cell phone is going straight to voice mail, and that hardly ever happens. The last time that happened was...." She looked stricken.

Gage held up his hand. "No, Mom, don't go there. Please, I'll call John and see if he knows anything."

He got out his cell phone, connected with the chief of police, and explained what he needed. Then, listening intently for several moments, he thanked him and ended the call. "The chief just got back from a massive pileup west of town, and, you won't believe this, but he saw Dad stuck in the backup from it."

Lark pressed both hands to her heart. She crossed over, and kissed Gage on the cheek. "I'm sorry to overreact," she said, glancing at Merry. "But he had a heart attack a few months ago, and…"

"I know, I heard about it, but he's okay, and maybe he doesn't even know his phone is dead or not turned on," Merry suggested.

"Exactly," Lark said.

"I'll go to the office to call a few people. You two enjoy your tea." Her eyes moved to Gage. "Let me know when you're ready to leave with Merry, okay?" She left them, heading farther into the house.

"Your parents have been together a long time, haven't they?" Merry asked.

"Yes, and she's had a lot to worry about with Dad in the past," he said. "Hopefully that's all over."

Merry didn't ask for any clarification. She knew a family matter when she heard about it. After Gage finally took a sip of his tea, she asked, "What's happening at the gate and in town?"

He gave her an easy smile. "This storm, that at any other time could have been bad for us, has turned out to be a blessing. There's no one at the gate, not with snow coming down like it is, and in town, it's full of skiers making their way to the slopes." He took a breath. "I heard that the inn is fully booked and most other places to wait out the storm. I haven't spotted any broadcast vans in a while." He drank more tea and the smile came back. "I think my fifteen minutes are over and you're free to leave."

Words she'd wanted to hear so much, any yet.... *Free to leave.* "That...that's terrific," she said, and was surprised to realize she was forcing a smile and enthusiasm for how the situation had been altered by the snowfall. "Did you know about this storm?"

He looked blank for a minute. "That it was coming, you mean?"

"I mean, when we were in the plane, did you know anything about it?"

He looked away from her as he fingered the handle on his heavy mug. "No, but I worried about another one hitting us up there. Who wouldn't have been?" Then he looked up at her, his dark eyes narrowed, and he changed the subject. "I went by the center earlier."

He said that so casually, but it really took her aback. "Why?"

"To see those kids you've been talking about so much." With an exhale of air, he added, "You have your hands full with them, don't you?"

She chuckled. "Oh, yes, but believe me, they're worth it…and they've improved so much in the past six months."

"Wow, I don't want to think about what those six months entailed." Gage rested his elbows on the table, the mug cupped between his palms. "I spoke to a lady there by the name of Merlot. I think that was her name."

She smiled with amusement. "You probably talked to Marsala."

He laughed. "I knew it was a type of wine. Yes, Marsala."

"And what did she have to say?"

"A lot. But I did get to tell the kids that you're just fine, that you got delayed because of the weather, and that you'd either call them or be back sometime today. Hedging my bets there."

She never dreamed he'd do that for her. "They're not all upset?"

"Didn't seem to be, although I think I met

Erin, the little girl you spoke about. Bright red curly hair?"

"That's Erin," she said fondly. "She's okay?"

"I don't know. She just stared at me and stayed right beside a kid named Joseph, who really did seem upset that he—"

Merry filled in the rest of the sentence. "Didn't have a huge red van to go driving around in to look for me, right?"

"How did you know?"

"Search and Rescue has always been his dream, and the focal point of everything he does. He's truly into rescuing anything he comes upon. I've never figured out the origin of that obsession in his life, but it's very real to him."

"He's pretty adamant about it—getting a red van, I mean?"

"Yes, he is," she conceded. "He's one of the kids that really needs so much, but has so little."

Gage drank more tea, and she followed suit. Then he set his mug down on the table with a soft thud. "Sometimes I forget about the poverty in Wolf Lake. It's something no one really talks about, or that they really see, unless they're doing work like you're doing."

"That's par for the course," she said, holding her cup just inches from her lips and watching Gage over the rim. "Out of sight, out of mind, and…" She glanced around the spacious kitchen. "You haven't had to deal with any of that."

He exhaled. "No, I guess not."

"And you aren't around here much anymore, so it would be easy to never see any of it."

He narrowed his eyes on her again, almost as if he didn't like what he saw at that moment. "Maybe I'm just blind," he muttered.

"I didn't say that."

"No, you didn't," he said and stood. "So, do you want to get out of here now?"

She realized there had been a bond of closeness between them while they talked, and now it was gone, as if it had never even existed. "Yes, I'd like to," she said. "Give me five minutes and I'll collect my things."

He didn't move as she left the room, and she hurried upstairs to get her jacket and luggage, and put on her boots. When she came back down, arriving at the bottom of the staircase, she met Gage and his mother coming out of a side room. They both looked up at her, then she hurried quickly over to them. "I'm ready."

Gage took her bags from her. "Me, too," he murmured and headed toward the back of the house.

Lark stopped Merry from following by laying a hand on her arm. "Take care of yourself, and come back and see us soon?"

"Thank you," Merry said, knowing she probably wouldn't, but it was nice to be asked. "For everything."

"I think I owe you a thank-you for Gage's present to me when he got back—the snow globe?"

She'd totally forgotten about that.

"He told me you said you thought it was just what I wanted."

Merry reddened a bit. "I thought you'd like it."

"I love it," Lark said, gave her a hug, then stepped back. "I was thinking about those kids of yours… I know young'uns around here love horses, but most can't afford to keep them anymore. Do they like to ride?"

"Absolutely. Despite some of their limitations, they ride when they can."

"Well, we have some very nice horses that would be good for children to ride, and they need exercise. I was thinking, when the snow lets up and it clears a bit, bring them on out for a day to ride, or hike, or just play."

"That's so nice of you. They'd love it."

"Good," Lark said, patting Merry's shoulder. "Call me as soon as you think you can arrange it."

"I will," she said and hurried off in the direction Gage had gone.

GAGE WAS AT the back door when Merry came around the corner into the kitchen. "Over here," he called to her, and she went to where he stood. "Got everything?"

"I think so," she said.

He didn't move. There was something he wanted to say, but wasn't sure what would happen if he did. He blurted, "Just because I'm not here a lot, that doesn't mean that I'm cavalier about what happens in Wolf Lake."

She seemed taken aback. "I'm sorry, I never meant to—"

He turned away and stepped aside as he got the door open, then let her step out before he did.

She started to go past him, then hesitated, and whirled around to face him. "Listen to me," she said in a tight voice. "I never meant that, at least not the way you think. Surely it's the case that since you're not around, Wolf Lake has to be lower on your list of priorities."

He had to admit she had a valid point, but that didn't stop him from feeling off balance. "Well, I guess that's irrelevant because I won't be here much, and you'll be busy with your kids."

He wasn't sure what he'd expected, but it wasn't to see the tears suddenly welling up in her eyes. Before he could say he was sorry, she ducked her head and rushed away from him. "Merry?" he said, trying to catch up to her in the falling snow. "Hey, just a minute."

"The truck? We're taking that?" she asked, pointing to the black pickup they used at the ranch.

"Yes, but—"

She pulled the door open and got in, slamming it behind her. Rushing around to his side, he opened the back door, tossed in her things, then climbed in behind the wheel. "Hey, I thought we were friends," he said, starting the truck to get the heater going.

She gazed out the window, ignoring his words, or not hearing them. He didn't miss the way she clasped her hands firmly in her lap.

"Did you hear me?"

That's when she turned, her eyes clear now. "I heard you."

He drove slowly toward the gates. "Can't we be friends after everything we went through together?"

"Sure," she said without any conviction in her voice. "Why not?"

"Forget it," he muttered, and pressed the release for the gates as they got close to them.

As the barrier opened for them to pass through, Gage stole another glance at Merry. She was sitting upright, staring straight ahead. He wasn't sure what had just happened, but he knew that right then he was looking at a stranger.

CHAPTER FIFTEEN

THEY DROVE TO town through the steady snow-fall in total silence, neither one breaking the tension between them. When they hit the main street, Gage finally chanced a glance at Merry. She hadn't moved, but her teeth were nibbling on her bottom lip. He didn't want this at all, not certain exactly what he did want, but he knew he didn't want her to ever look at him with that coldness again.

"So, straight to the center?" he asked mildly.

"No, home, my home," she said in a voice barely above a whisper.

"The house on Rock Line?" he clarified, remembering her telling him about renting Willie G.'s place.

"Yes, please."

He drove past Wolf Lake Inn. It was one of the oldest adobe structures in the area. The original part of the building had housed the first hotel in town. Now, Mallory kept up its history as much as she could.

"So, you really want to try and buy the house you're renting?"

"Yes," she replied.

"I wish you good luck in getting Willie to let go of anything he owns in this town."

"You think I don't belong here, so he won't sell to me, is that it?"

Where had that come from? "I never said that."

She kept staring ahead.

He knew where her house was, on the street with the elementary school, and veered off the main road onto the side street. That's when he realized that the main street must have been cleared earlier, because the side street was deeper in snow. His truck took the challenge, but he knew any car wouldn't, unless it had four wheel drive. He saw the old Victorian ahead and on the right, snow drifting up to the wraparound porch. The driveway that led to the garage was a slight indentation amongst all the powdery whiteness.

"Your car's in the garage?" he asked.

"Oh, shoot," she said, slumping back in the seat.

"What's wrong?"

"It's parked in the long term lot at the Santa Fe airport. I don't know why I didn't think about that at all."

He came to a stop, and let the truck idle as he turned to her. "You had way too much going on."

She put her head back against the headrest on the seat and closed her eyes. The action exposed the sweep of her throat, and he knew that his stupid idea of being friends wasn't what he wanted at all. He wanted more, and most importantly, he didn't want to lose contact with her. "Go on inside and change, do what you need to, and then I'll run you over to the center when you're ready."

She sat up and turned to him. "Oh, no, I can't ask you to do that. I'll call and see if someone over there can come and get me."

"No. I'm here, and I don't mind waiting, I don't have anywhere to be just yet."

She stared at the house and then at him. "All right. Thanks," she said and grabbed the handle to open the door.

She got out quickly and trudged up her front steps that were thick with snow. After fumbling in her jacket pocket for the keys, she finally unlocked the door, and then, without a look back at the idling truck, disappeared into the old Victorian.

He scanned the layout of the garage and house. Nice place. He'd noticed this old blue Victorian before, but never really looked at it. It did need work. The construction mind of his saw the warped gutters, the wood that was starting to separate on the siding, and single paned windows that leaked any heat as fast as an old furnace could produce it.

Yet, despite all that, Merry wanted this old, run-down house, and he wondered once again if Willie G. could be encouraged to sell it to her. After all, the old coot had no real interest in it, and he had known what he was doing when he'd rented it to her and moved into another house that was in closer proximity to the restaurant he owned and ran near Santa Fe.

The front door swung back and Merry re-emerged. She was wearing the same clothes, but her hair had been neatly tugged back from her face, and she now wore heavy boots that went partway up her calves. She hurried sure footedly down the steps, around the front of the truck, and the door opened to let in a gust of wind and snow. She quickly climbed in, shut the door on the weather and glanced at Gage.

"Thanks so much for offering to take me to the center. I'm carless for now, I guess."

He backed slowly out onto the road, headed toward the main street and stopped at the corner to let the heavy skiing traffic crawl past at a snail's pace. He sat back, his hands resting on the bottom of the steering wheel. "Skiing here just before Valentine's Day is crazy."

"I guess so," she said softly.

He glanced at her, and saw color in her cheeks along with the touch of a smile at her lips. "Are you going to share?"

She blinked. "Excuse me?"

"You look as if you just heard you won the lottery."

She chuckled softly. "No lottery, but I'm going to see the kids. That's winning on every level."

He saw the gleam in her eyes, the smile growing a bit. She looked happy, and on some level he was jealous that he seldom felt that way anymore. Not that he was depressed, or a negative person, but the highs in his life just didn't draw that much pleasure for him, at least not lately.

"I guess it is," he said. The traffic parted and he pulled onto the road, heading toward the hospital and the family center adjacent to it. "Mind if I ask a question?"

"Sure."

"What happens to the kids when the grant's gone?"

She sighed softly. "I intend to be around here, in one form or another, and I think that if I work it right, I can still be in the kids' lives, and maybe kids that show up later on, too."

"What about the rest of your life? The life beyond your work at the center?"

"What about it?"

He maneuvered around some cars that were double parked in the snowy street. "What is it going to be like?"

"The million dollar question," she murmured, and when he had the chance he glanced at her again.

She looked out the window ahead to the street, her hands once again clasped in her lap. Her teeth worried her bottom lip, a trait he recognized she did when she was thinking hard. "That's pricey," he said.

"I just…I'm not sure. I know I want that house, and I want it to be my family house. Maybe when my stepfather retires, they could come and live there, at least now and then."

"And what about you?"

"I think that maybe, by then, I'll have my own family, and make this town our home. A place they'll leave when they grow up, but a place they'll always come back to."

"Like you did?"

"Yes, exactly."

He had to ask the next question, something he'd wondered about, something she'd never hinted at during their time together. "Do you have someone in mind to build that life with?"

"Oh, no," she said quickly. "There might be someone, but even if there isn't, there are lots of kids out there that need someone to love them, like Erin, and adoption is a real alternative for them."

Kids, maybe a husband, maybe not, a long life in Wolf Lake. Again, he felt some envy at her situation. She knew what she wanted, and she was on that path. Just as he knew what he wanted and was on his own path. Maybe he wasn't as passionate as she was about her plans, but he still had his plans and they were every bit as firm as hers were. Build the business, keep moving, don't be bored, and maybe he'd meet someone who shared that vision and maybe he wouldn't. As far as kids went, he'd never even thought about them. He wouldn't start now.

He felt Merry sit forward a bit, and excitement filled her voice. "Oh, finally, it seems like a lifetime since I left here!"

He saw the center, by the glass and steel visage of the hospital with a sprawling parking lot that was slowly being hidden by the steadily falling snow. The center was as theme-oriented in structure as the hospital was clearly functional. The center had been designed to touch the past, with adobe appearing walls, two stories with a line of windows on each that were framed by rough timber, a flat roof, and a huge side yard with every imaginable playground toy that the money an anonymous donor had supplied.

The massive letters that looked carved into the adobe front above the second line of windows, spelled out, "Wolf Lake Family Center." Gage drove toward the partially covered semi-circular drive that swept past the massive wooden entry doors, one with a carved eagle in flight and the second door with a wolf, head lifted, baying at the moon.

"Oh, wow," Merry breathed, opening the truck door before Gage had brought it to a full stop. "Thanks," she called back over her shoulder as she sprinted away from him as quickly as she could in the ankle-deep snow.

He watched her for a moment, transfixed by her spirit and enthusiasm. "Hey," he called after her, realizing she hadn't taken her things with her, but she kept going. Quickly, he turned off the truck, left it by the entry and headed after her. By the time he pushed back the doors to go inside, she was nowhere in sight, but he knew where she was going. The second floor, suite B, the same place he'd gone earlier in the day. He passed through the reception area, by walls displaying wonderful murals of children playing, backdropped by the suggestion of the low desert.

He got to the bank of elevators, spotted Merry's name on the register, "Dr. Merry Brenner, Therapy & Counseling, #2B" and passed it as he stepped onto the car that had just arrived. In a few seconds, he was on the floor obviously dedicated to her kids, from the brilliant primary colors, to picture after picture of kids that lined the walls. He headed to the door marked 2B, a few feet from where he'd stepped off the elevator.

Before he could push it open, he heard squeals and laughter. He then stepped into a massive room obviously decorated for children. More primary colors, interactive games and activities were everywhere, and scattered in a space off to one side that had what looked like sleeping mats. But the main focus of Gage's attention was in the middle of the room.

Merry.

Surrounded on a round carpet that was probably twenty feet across, fashioned in deep green pile, was Merry with the six or seven kids he'd seen that morning. Then he saw Merry reaching out to the little girl, Erin, a tiny thing pushing her way into Merry's arms. And Merry was smiling. That sight almost took his breath away.

Earlier he'd thought Merry's pleasure at thinking about seeing the kids was stunning on her face, but the smile right then eclipsed that by a mile.

He almost backed out, but she saw him, and motioned him to come over to her. The kids parted to let him near, but they kept very close to the woman on the floor. The boy he'd been introduced to as Brandon Sage sat by Marsala, and he got up, limping over to Gage. He was about ten, skinny with a flushed face and a walking cast on his left leg.

Cocking his head a bit to look up at Gage, he said, "So, you came back?"

"Yes, I came back," Gage said, trying to

get his bearings before actually speaking to Merry.

"My uncle, Big Mike, from the Rez, says he knows you, that you're some bigwig that crashed in an airplane. Is that right?"

He saw Merry blanch slightly, before he nodded to the kid. "That's me, but *crashed* is a bit strong. The storm was bad and I had trouble landing." He spread his arms at his sides. "As you can see, I survived just fine."

"He says you used to live here, but now you live in some big city and make tons of money. Where do you live?"

"Where do I live?" he echoed.

"Yeah, where? Big Mike couldn't remember."

The kid was persistent and Gage could feel Merry watching him carefully. Where *did* he live? In the small single room apartment he'd had in the same building as his head offices, or did he live in his plane? Or at least, the next plane he'd buy? Or did he live here in Wolf Lake? Nothing fit, so he just said, "A long way away."

That actually seemed to satisfy the boy, who turned and limped back over to Merry to ask her a question. "How come he knew you were back when he came here this morning?"

Merry stood, but each hand of hers held the hand of a child. There were two girls and four boys, ranging in age from what he'd guess was about six years old to ten or eleven. He knew Brandon Sage. Joseph, the one obsessed with red vans, held Merry by one hand, and Erin hung on her left hand.

"He met me, and said he'd let you kids know I'd call you or come by this afternoon," Merry explained. "I wanted to see you, not call, so he gave me a ride to come and see all of you." Her green eyes met his. "Let me introduce you to my friends." One by one she introduced the kids, ending with Erin.

She'd mentioned adoption with Erin, and he thought he could see why. The little girl held tightly to Merry, her eyes huge and watching him warily. She looked a bit like a scared fawn. Maybe she was afraid of Merry leaving again. Or maybe the fear came from some new person walking into this world uninvited.

"I left my things in your truck, didn't I?" she asked.

Along with a black hole of emptiness, he thought with a very uncomfortable poetic bent that didn't make it any the less true. But when he spoke, he said, "Yes, but since you're without a car, I thought I could run you back to your house on my way home when you're finished here." He glanced at the snow still coming down. "It's no day to walk."

She nibbled on her bottom lip for a long moment, then said, "An hour or so. I need to do a few things with the kids, catch up on a couple of—" She shrugged. "Just a few things, and I would appreciate a ride. Thank you, again."

He didn't know why he felt so relieved that she'd accepted his offer, but he knew it was a lot better than heading away from here alone. "Good, that's good."

She looked around. "First I need to figure out how to put together a table a donor gave to us, but it's in pieces, and I don't like puzzles." She frowned. "The table could take a while to get right."

"Lady, you're looking at a construction master," he said, smiling broadly at her. "I'll do that while you do whatever else you have to do."

"You can't do that."

"Watch me," he said, and then turned to Brandon. "Can you build stuff?"

"Me and Joseph do Legos a lot," the boy offered.

"Perfect. You two lead the way to the pieces."

Erin suddenly pulled free of Merry's hand and came across to Gage. Without any warning, she caught his hand in hers and held tightly to him. Gage glanced at Merry, lifting an eyebrow questioningly.

"Erin loves to watch," she said.

Gage nodded down at her. "Want to help?"

She shrugged.

"Good enough," he stated, then looked at the boys. "You two ready to do this?"

"Can you really put stuff together?" Brandon asked.

"Actually, I usually build things from scratch. In fact, Miss Brenner hired me to make you kids a bulletin board to go by the door." That's when he looked back at the entry door to the space and saw the paper sign Merry had told him she'd put up about her leaving and coming back. "Then Miss Brenner can use it to make announcements when she needs to."

"Okay," Brandon said seriously. "Come on."

The boy started across the space, moving quickly for having a cast on his leg. Gage gazed beyond him at a pile of red wooden pieces and a scattering of hardware along with a hammer and some screwdrivers. He got to the materials for the table, and Brandon and the other boy started to sort through them. "Put pieces that go together, together," Gage said. "Legs, supports, screws."

The boys did exactly what he said, but Erin never let go of his hand. "Don't you want to help?" he said, crouching down in front of her. She shook her red curls. "I thought you could sort the screws and things?" She shook her head again. He wasn't even getting a one word answer out of her. "Do you know where the screws are?" he asked, hopeful that she'd talk then, but she simply pointed to a neat pile of different length wood screws off to one side on a single sheet of white paper. "Oh, okay," Gage said and stood, the little hand still gripping his.

After almost an hour, Merry walked up to where Gage was sitting on the floor with Erin at his side. The child's grip on his hand had changed to her holding a clump of his shirt sleeve, giving him a bit of freedom to manipulate the screwdriver and screws. "I'm about ready," she said to him, then gasped. "Oh, my gosh, you really did it!"

The boys were sitting near Gage, and the red table stood proudly in front of all of them.

"They did a great job," Gage said as he pushed to get to his feet. As soon as he was standing, Erin captured his hand with hers again.

He looked down at her. "Miss Merry and I have to leave, Erin. I'm sorry."

She seemed stricken, but didn't utter a word as she simply let go of him, turned and walked over to where Joseph sat watching them. "We need to get a red van," the little boy with a pinched face said very seriously. "Red, like the table."

"Yes, yes we do, Joseph," Merry said and crossed to crouch in front of him and Erin. "I'll be back in the morning, and we will hunt around for some chairs to put with the table."

Marsala kneeled by Erin and held out her hand. "Let's go look for those chairs for Miss Merry." She spoke to the other kids. "Actually, let's all go and find the chairs."

The kids nodded and gathered around Marsala, then headed off with her to another part of the huge room.

Gage thought he saw some reluctance in Merry to go. "I understand a bit better why you took your promise so seriously," he admitted as they headed down the hallway to the elevator.

She stopped and gazed up at him, her head

cocked slightly to one side as she considered him for a moment. "You do, don't you?" She looked surprised, but pleased on some level. "You were terrific with Erin."

"You said both her parents are gone?" he asked.

As they rode down in the elevator and crossed the reception area to the front doors, Merry told him that Erin had been abandoned by a drug addicted mother, who later died, then was taken away from her father because of his incarceration. The foster home she lived in was good, but not her family, and she ached for a real place to call home. He shook his head. "She's so young."

"Too young, and too vulnerable," Merry agreed. "She's special, very special, and very alone. The center has been a real help to her. While she's here during the day, she's got a type of family with the other kids that all the children understand on some level."

They walked to the truck and got in. As soon as Gage had it going and the heater turned on, he let it idle while he rested his left arm on the steering wheel and his other hand on the back of Merry's seat. "You're right in the middle of all of it, aren't you?"

"I want to be."

"It can't be easy." He fought the urge to reach out and gently stroke her flushed cheek. "I'm not sure someone should be around sadness like that on a regular basis."

She closed her eyes for a moment, before looking back at him, and he could see the few snowflakes that clung to her auburn streaked hair, slowly melting. "The way I look at it, those kids are having a bad life, but me? I can do whatever I want. They don't have that option. I want them to have that option," she said simply.

He gave in to his need and touched her cheek. Her warmth on his fingertips seemed to be seeping into him. "Those kids are so lucky to have you," he rasped and moved closer. His hand cupped her chin, lifting it ever so slightly until he bent forward and found her lips. The kiss was a light connection, but it added to the heat unfurling inside him.

He tasted her, felt her hand touching the spot over his heart, and then slipping up around his neck, pulling him closer. The kiss deepened. A world he'd never even known existed, opened to him in that moment, and he drew back, literally fighting for air.

He looked at Merry, watched her eyes flutter, then open, and the connection intensified. "Oh, Gage, you understand," she said, her voice a choked whisper. "I'm so…so…" She took a shuddering breath. "That's so wonderful."

She was wonderful, no, more than that, and she was changing his world. He stroked her cheek, brushed at her silky hair, and could almost catch the taste of her on his lips. He didn't want to lose whatever was happening right then, and he measured his words carefully. "I need to ask you something."

MERRY WAS STUNNED. The kiss had shattered some barrier she knew she'd been trying to put up, to stop whatever had been happening to her since meeting Gage. But it was gone now, and she realized that she was so very close to loving him. The way he'd responded to Erin's neediness had surprised her, and warmed her heart. His patience with Brandon and Joseph added to her growing hope for something. She hadn't defined that "something," but right then, with his taste still on her lips and his hand on her face, the definition fell into place with remarkable ease.

Hope. She finally had some hope. Maybe hope for a miracle that was gradually being revealed to her. Slowly, she lifted her hand

and covered his where it touched her face. "A question?" she managed to ask, staring into his eyes that seemed to echo the intensity of her feelings. Hope. It grew slowly but persistently, but this time she didn't fight it, she didn't fear it. She embraced it.

She saw him take a deep breath. "I have to leave in a day or so. The snow's blocking the area now, so there's no way to do the work I came to do, and I have meetings already set up in Florida and Houston." She waited, not thinking about him leaving right now. He continued in a low voice. "I'm leasing a plane."

He actually smiled then, the dimple appearing and she moved her hand to touch the tip of her forefinger to it. "You're going to fly?" she asked, her voice sounding very unsteady to her ears.

"Certainly." The smile faded a bit and she drew back as his hands left her face. "It's like the old adage about horses—when you fall off, you get right back on."

She could feel her chest throbbing, and the overwhelming feelings from moments ago, were being overlaid by a growing fear. "Sure, but if you fall off a horse, you don't drop twenty thousand feet into trees and snow and cold and..." She heard the hysteria explode in her voice and she cut off her own words.

Gage watched her, his dark eyes narrowing, then he reached for her and held her to him. She ignored the way the side of her seat pressed into her hip, but just held tightly to him, burying her face in his chest. The idea that she could love him was eclipsed when she knew without a doubt, right then, that she already loved him and probably had for forever.

"Hey, it's okay. I'll be fine." His hand made circles on her back, but barely touched the fear that filled her.

"No, it's not okay. It's not okay..." she mumbled against his chest.

"It will be. I'm getting a good plane, maybe a bit bigger." He said the words as if they should make all the difference in the world. "I need to get to the meetings, and it will take me to them."

She squeezed her eyes shut, and asked something that she had to know before she let things go any further. "When will you come home?"

His hand stilled on her back, then he eased away from her, but kept his hands on her shoulders. Before he said the words, she knew what they would be. Speaking slowly, as if forming the words carefully, he said, "You mean home, as in here?"

"I don't know. Where is your home, or the place you call home? You never answered Brandon."

He let go of her shoulders and shrugged. "I guess home is wherever I am."

She bit her lip hard before speaking again. "Do you know how sad that is?"

He frowned, the withdrawal growing even greater. "Sad? No, I don't see that as sad at all. I was born here, and I can come back here off and on, whenever I like." He ran a hand roughly over his face, then blew out air before continuing. "I *want* to come back, and I will come back here more than I have before, if the firm wins the bid." He turned away from her, gripping the steering wheel with both hands. "I just have to figure out about this…"

He motioned with his right hand, from her to him and back to her again before letting his hand fall on the console between them. "Whatever this is. Maybe it's just from the survival thing, or maybe it's more. But I want to know."

"How do you do that?" she asked, flatness tingeing her voice as that spark of hope began to dim a bit.

"I'd kind of hoped you might meet me in Florida or Houston for a day or two."

"I just got back here." She didn't bother repeating that that was one of her miracles, and she wasn't sure there would be any more in her life, at least not any that Gage would be involved in. "I'm not leaving again."

"Then I'll have to try to get back when it's possible, and, as I said, if we win the bid, I'll be around more than normal for a while."

"And then what?" Merry asked, hating herself when she added, "Will you just do the damage here, then take off and not stick around to see what happens?"

He frowned deeply. "You can't let that go, can you?"

"Sorry," she said, looking around, feeling almost claustrophobic in the truck with Gage so close. "Can we leave now?"

"You bet we can," he said under his breath and put the truck into gear to pull away from the center.

CHAPTER SIXTEEN

NO ONE SPOKE on the slow drive back to her house. That silence lasted until Gage drove over the pile of snow that a plow had deposited earlier, almost blocking the driveway. He'd stopped by the side entry, but left the truck idling as he turned to her. "Answer me this. Why am I the bad guy for doing what I do, for what I'm being asked to? And why am I a bad guy for not wanting to be stuck in one place forever?"

Merry's eyes burned as she stared straight ahead, back at the garage that had snow drifts halfway up the door. He wasn't a bad guy. He was Gage Carson, pure and simple. And she was who she was, part of her ready to admit that she was almost afraid to leave Wolf Lake again. Abnormal attachment? Probably, but now that she'd found what she wanted and needed, she couldn't let go.

The simple truth was, she thought with growing awareness, opposites might attract, but that didn't mean there was any chance of being compatible.

"I'm sorry," she said. "I'm so sorry. Of course you'll leave. That's your choice."

"What did you think I'd do?" he asked bluntly.

Be here forever, she thought sadly. The old impossible, happily-ever-after fantasy. But instead she said, "That you'd leave. You have a job to do and when it's done, you'll be gone."

"I told you, I can come back. I understand you don't want to fly." His expression eased, the frown shifting to something less harsh. "And this is where I'd like to come when that happens."

"Then what?" she asked.

"Then...whatever happens, happens," he said simply.

"Oh," she whispered.

"And if you can figure out how to get over your fear of flying, you could meet me somewhere if I can't get here."

"And what about the kids? I can't be a temporary thing in their lives. I won't be temporary in anyone's life," she added without realizing she was going to say it before the words slipped out.

He shook his head. "That's the way you see what we could have—something temporary?"

Not until right then. "I don't know," she admitted, suddenly tired and wanting to just go inside and close the door on everything and everyone.

"Merry, it's not like that. I want to come back and see you. I'm not talking being just a friend, either. I want to be with you, and find out more about you." He moved toward her, hesitated, then framed her face with both of his hands. "I want to really know Merry Brenner," he said in a low, rough voice.

She closed her eyes tightly. "You know who I am, what I am," she whispered, then turned from his touch and reached for the door handle. But before she could get out and run, Gage had her by the hand.

"Can you really just let this go? Hide in your house, and in your work, and pretend this all never happened?" he demanded.

She didn't move, but kept her face averted from him. "There is nothing to let go of," she managed, her words almost choking her. "This isn't real. It's about emotions out of control, some strange survivor syndrome." She bit her lip hard, then said, "If I hadn't pushed you to bring me back here, you would have never given me a second thought—if we ever crossed paths around here. Now, please, let me go," she said with stark finality.

"I don't care about your professional assessment, I don't want to just file it all under 'a crazy reaction,' and keep going without a second thought. I don't want to just let you go," he said, never releasing her hand.

She didn't move. Her heart was breaking and she'd never felt that before. Odd that she knew exactly what was happening. She waited calmly for him to finally let go of her hand. But when she was free, she couldn't make herself move.

"Merry?" Gage said, barely above a whisper. "If you can just walk away, do it. Don't ask me to be the one to do it."

She sighed and turned back to look at him. The image of the man who was so close to her was almost her undoing. Why couldn't she agree to whatever it would take to keep him in her world? Yet…why would she? Was this really love? She wanted to know him better, to know him completely, but she wanted a home and stability and to be in Wolf Lake forever. There was no middle ground, no compromise, no forever, and that tore at her.

"I don't understand why you won't let go of

what you think you need. Why can't you take a chance and see how things are?" His voice held a hard intensity. "Can't you for once stop being so uptight about everything, and—"

"Go with the flow?" she supplied past clenched lips. "Been there, done that all of my life, and I won't do it again."

She felt nauseated and wished on some level that she didn't care so much about her kids, or want a family so much, or maybe wished that she'd never met Gage. "I hated it for the past twenty years while I was living it," she said with raw emotion. "I'm here now, and I have a home and my work with the kids. This is my life and what I want and need." It was the truth and she wouldn't hide it away.

His jaw tensed, but he didn't speak.

"And I will do whatever it takes to protect this town and the kids in it." Merry hitched in a breath, then blurted out, "And you're not part of this place anymore. You don't want to be, but I do."

"Okay, you've made that very clear." She thought he was leaving, that she had her freedom to go inside and map out how to make her life work, without a man who had become so much to her that she couldn't even form the words to fight him any longer.

"I hate this," he said. "I hate what's happened to us." Then he leaned toward her and stunned her when he planted a fierce kiss on her lips. Just as quickly, he pulled back. "Goodbye." Turning from her he gripped the gearshift in one hand and the steering wheel in the other. He obviously wanted to get out of there as much as she did now.

She fumbled for the door handle, jerked hard on it to get it open, then hustled out and into a foot of snow that covered the drive. Making her way as fast as she could around the front of the truck, she never looked back. She kept going, up the steps, to the door, and took far too long to get the key in the lock. Finally she was inside, the door closed with a thud, and she threw the dead bolt into place.

The sound of metal against metal when the lock caught, echoed in the total silence of the old house, starkly underlining the end of everything with Gage. She turned her back to the door, leaning against the barrier for support as the truck roared to life. As the sound gradually faded into the distance, she hugged herself tightly. Then the sound of the engine was gone completely.

She didn't move, waiting, harboring a weird notion that he'd be back, even if it was to argue again, to defend his choice and position. But he didn't come back. He was gone and her fingertips touched her lips. Gone.

But she was home. And her life would go on, one way or the other.

The first day of April was a big day at the center. The kids went crazy with April Fools jokes. By noon, Merry knew she'd lost control of the place, and gave up any thoughts of counseling sessions going anywhere. Brandon kept up his joke about, "I just heard you won the lottery," and everyone acted duly surprised and excited, then were caught with, "April Fools!"

When three o'clock came and the kids were due to be picked up, she said goodbye to them, then let Marsala escort them downstairs. She went into her office and started to document the few things that she had finished that day. Next she heard footsteps behind her on the hardwood floor.

She turned, expecting to see either Marsala or one of the kids back to collect something they left behind, or with one last April Fools joke. But it wasn't any of them. "Hey there, Moses," Merry said with a smile. She liked the doctor and was enjoying watching him and Mallory become a full-fledged couple. Although both of them acted as if nothing was happening. That made her smile grow a bit more. "First, let me tell you there is no April Fools joke that I have not endured today."

He looked puzzled, then said, "Oh, April Fools. That one passed me right by without me noticing. All day surgery."

She motioned for him to have the empty chair nearby. "You must be exhausted."

"I am wiped out," he said as he sank down in the seat.

"I bet. Did you need something from me?" she asked.

"Just some information." He looked a bit hesitant before he went on. "I wanted to ask you what your biggest concerns are about the entertainment complex coming to town."

She felt her whole being tense. She'd heard that Gage's company had won the bid, and felt the division in town that the information brought with it. Almost half wanted it done, and the other half didn't want any part of it. "What difference does it make?" she asked a bit flatly.

"I'd like more details from your perspective, that's all. It's pretty much a done deal, but that doesn't mean that there can't be changes, compromises in the process."

He was right, and for the next twenty minutes she laid out her main concerns. The lure of gambling and other possible addictions that might increase in the area and stretch their resources even further, the negative effect it would have on adults and kids alike. And then her last complaint. "The kids in this community won't directly benefit from any of the new money that will flow into Wolf Lake. Not a penny, unless they drop out of school and go to work there, or sneak into the casino to try their chances."

Moses nodded and didn't argue. It seemed as if he was making a mental list for himself. "All good points," he stated.

"And it's in the wrong spot. If it is going to be done, it needs to be between the main road and the town, not between the Rez and the town."

He just nodded.

She'd never asked him point blank about where he stood, but she did then. "None of this bothers you?"

"It does," he said as he stood and rotated his neck to loosen up the muscles. "A great deal, actually."

"Then you're opposed to it?"

He shook his head. "No, not really. I think it's doable and manageable, that there is no right or wrong in the mix, just degrees of adjustment."

She looked up at him. "And Gage is your best friend?"

She didn't know why she said that and wished she could take it back, but Moses didn't look angry. "Yes, he is, but we've had our differences over the years, from girls to the right way to climb the rock face up near the lake." He chuckled. "Sure wish I'd won more of the arguments, but Gage can be pretty persuasive when he wants to be."

"I guess he can be," she agreed, not wanting to talk about Gage or think about him. Things went better that way for her. Out of sight, out of mind. Not that that was actually true, not when she kept thinking she saw him on the street, or stepping into a shop or restaurant, or even pulling up to the center in the large black truck. She'd been wrong every time, and she supposed she was thankful.

"Let me know if you think of anything else," Moses said. "I need to get home and get ready to head out for dinner." He paused. "If you aren't doing anything tonight, how about coming to dinner with me and Mallory? Nothing fancy, just good food and good company." She'd almost thought about taking him up on his offer until he mentioned, "Gage is always interesting. Lots of stuff going on with him these days."

Merry was glad she was sitting down. This wasn't an April Fools joke, and she knew it. For some reason, she'd always thought if Gage were around, she'd feel it intuitively, but obviously she was wrong. She'd been wrong the other three times he'd been back in Wolf Lake, too. There was no connection between them, she decided, and stayed in her chair, afraid her legs might not totally support her if she stood up just then.

"No, thanks. Not this time, but I appreciate your asking."

"Okay, maybe next time," he said, then started to leave, but turned back to her. "The reception lady downstairs, Elisa Hammer, said to tell you that there's some delivery for you in the main office, and she wants you to stop in on your way out."

"Thanks," Merry said, still trying to deal with Gage being in town.

When Moses was gone, she grabbed her jacket and headed off to check with reception in the main office. Luckily, Merry found Elisa at her desk. "Moses said you had a delivery for me?"

"Oh, yes," Elisa said, getting up and crossing to a cubby space where they kept the mail and any packages. She came out dragging a large parcel on the soft carpeting. "It's darn heavy," she said, getting it to the table legs where she propped it against the polished wood. "It came about half an hour ago and I was going to open it, but it's addressed to you."

Merry went closer. The package was at least four feet long and probably that high, along with a depth of about six inches. She crouched down in front of it, and her heart almost stopped when she saw the company logo. Carson Construction and Architecture.

"Who brought it?" she managed to get out.

"Mr. Carson," she said matter of factly.

Merry stared at it, unable to move. Gage? He'd been here? Another April Fools joke? No, Elisa wasn't kidding at all, merely anxious for Merry to open the package. "Gage Carson?"

"Yes. Last week he'd said he would be back with something, but I totally forgot about it."

"What?" Merry exclaimed, then realized

she'd reacted too dramatically to some news that shouldn't have meant anything to her. "Sorry, I didn't…uh." She swallowed hard. "He was here last week?"

"He came in on your day off, and he saw the kids. Erin really does take to him," she said. "He's so good with them. Joseph was pestering him about the red van."

"Just a minute, he was with the kids and no one told me?"

Elisa frowned. "He didn't ask for you, and he didn't tell me he wanted to speak to you or anything. Besides he was only here for maybe half an hour. Then he said he'd be back with something in a week or so."

"He didn't ask for me at all?" She tried to hide her disappointment.

Color touched Elisa's face. "All he asked about you was when you had your days off, and I told him today, because it was supposed to be your day off." Her tone was getting defensive and Merry knew she'd handled this all wrong. "Maybe he didn't want to see you or something."

That hit home for Merry. "Probably so," she conceded.

The receptionist pointed at the parcel.

"Well? Are you going to open it?"

Merry reached for the paper wrapping to tear it back. The minute the front sheet was pulled away, she sank to her knees on the floor, unable to go farther. Obviously impatient with Merry, Elisa reached around her and tore at the rest of the paper.

"How amazing," she said as the large bulletin board was exposed. Red, yellow and blue ran riot, the frame had balloons, along with silhouettes of children dancing and playing. At the top of the board, *KIDS ARE COOL* had been carved beautifully in cartoon lettering. "It's gorgeous," Elisa breathed

It was beautiful. Special. Merry wanted to touch it, then stopped herself. "Can you have Harry take it up to the main room and put it up near the entry so the kids can see it when they come and go?"

"Sure," Elisa said and took off to find the maintenance man. Merry studied the board. It was everything she'd told Gage she wanted, and more. Oddly, she'd forgotten all about it, but he hadn't. Running a hand over her face, she was shocked to find her cheeks were damp. No tears, no tears. But how could she possibly keep her emotions in check?

Gage had kept his word.

Merry left before Harry arrived in Elisa's office. She needed some air. On foot she headed down Main Street. Was she looking for Gage? She shouldn't be, her mind warned her. She stopped at the Mexican restaurant to get takeout, and then, feeling a bit foolish and a bit sad, went directly home.

MERRY KEPT LOOKING over her shoulder all the next day, and as soon as she started to breathe a little easier, accepting the fact that Gage was gone again, she was almost felled by something else he had delivered to the center.

A call came near closing time, when the kids were soon to be picked up to go home. Elisa had spoken in a rush. "You won't believe what is down here right in front of the place."

Merry wasn't up to a guessing game. "What?"

"You have to see it."

Merry hung up, a bit annoyed, but went downstairs and crossed the entry space. Elisa was there with some other staff members looking out the open doors. Approaching them, she looked outside and stopped in her tracks. A bright red van was parked right out front. A man in a brown work suit, stood by it, looking around impatiently.

"What's going on?" she asked.

Harry, the maintenance man, turned to her. Tall, thin and with dark, weathered skin, he grinned at her. "Nice wheels."

She made her way past the small crowd and went out into the chilly April afternoon. In a thin cotton shirt and dark slacks, she felt the cold through to her bones. Approaching the uniformed delivery man, she said, "I'm Merry Brenner. What is this about?"

"As soon as you sign for it, it's yours."

"Oh, no, you're very much mistaken about that."

"Well, lady, these papers say it's yours for use at..." He looked down at the papers in his hand. "The Family Center at Wolf Lake."

"That can't be right," she insisted, but knew if that van really was hers for the center, she'd take it in a heartbeat.

"It's right. Just gotta get your signature, and you've got it, whether you want it or not." He held out the papers he'd snapped into a clip board. "Bottom of page one, center of page three."

She took the papers and quickly read them. She didn't understand. It had been paid for in full, an exorbitant sum for all the glittering chrome, deep red paint and tinted windows, perched above a huge set of tires. It didn't make sense. Then she heard a scream and Joseph came running. "It's here! It's here!" he shouted and all but flung himself at Merry. "He did it! He promised and he did it!"

"Who did it?"

As he answered her, she felt as if she might faint. "Mr. Carson. He said he'd get me one that the center could use for trips and hiking expeditions and getting to the ranch for riding and even rescues! He said to call him Gage, but my mom says I can't, that that is disrespectful. But I don't think so."

She willed herself to stay relaxed and figure out what was happening, then she turned to the man who still held the clip board. "Please, sign this so I can get going," he pleaded.

Joseph, not usually demonstrative, hugged Merry around the middle and begged her, "Please, please, we need a red van."

CHAPTER SEVENTEEN

"HEY, MERRY?" SOMEONE called out to her from behind the small group of people oohing and aahing over the van.

Merry spied Moses stopping beyond the group, and he motioned her to come over to him. He was grinning. "Nice van, huh?"

"Very nice," she managed to say, though she felt breathless and caught off guard by the gift. "I don't understand why Gage did this."

That made the doctor sober completely. "You don't? He did it for the kids. It's that simple."

"No, I mean, I get that, but..." She stammered.

"But what? Take it, say thank you, then move on with your life. Now you can do it in a new van."

"I need Gage's phone number, please."

"To call and thank him?"

She ignored that question and asked hers

again. "His number, do you have one I can use to contact him?"

"Of course I do."

"Thanks," she said as he took out one of his business cards and quickly scrawled a number on the back. Handing the card to her, he said, "He's trying, and I do think that sooner or later, things will change."

She had no idea what that meant, and jumped when Moses touched her on the shoulder.

"Take it for what it's worth, if for no other reason. The kids really need it, right?"

She cringed at his reminder. It wasn't all about her, nor should it be. He was on point with that, and she wished desperately that he wasn't. "I need to talk to the delivery man," she said and moved quickly to catch him before Moses could say anything else.

She signed the papers, asked the delivery man to drive the van to the staff parking lot behind the center and leave the keys at the front desk. As soon as the van pulled away, she walked with Joseph over to his mother's beat up car, promising he could check out the van the next day.

Waving goodbye to Joseph, she went back to her office. Merry toyed with the card Moses had given her and sat for several minutes, trying to decide what to say to Gage. Finally, she got up her nerve and punched in the number. It rang and rang, then went to voice mail.

She hung up without leaving a message. Then thinking better of it, realized it would be easier to tell him what she needed to tell him via a message than having him on the other end of the line. Before she could dial again, her phone rang. She looked at the caller ID. It was the same number she'd just called. Hesitating at first, she then gathered her courage and said, "Yes?"

"Merry?"

Just hearing him say her name made her sink back and use the high support of her chair to settle against. "Yes."

"You called me?"

"Moses gave me your number. The van, it came today," she said.

"Good."

"Why did you do that?"

"Do what?"

"Just drop a van here that costs more than I'll make in two years, just like that without any warning. You never even asked me about it, let alone let me know what you were thinking."

When she stopped talking, the line sounded almost dead, then he spoke again. "How did Joseph like it?"

"That boy loves it, and you knew he would."

"That's why I got it," he said evenly. "Do you want me to take it back?"

"Oh, so you're going to make me the bad guy?"

He actually chuckled at that. "You're not the bad guy, far from it," he said. "And if you don't want the van, let me change the title to make the center the full beneficiary of it, then your conscience or your pride, or whatever is making you upset, will be placated. And the kids still have a van that was meant for them in the first place."

She held the phone tightly to her ear, her lips clamped together just as tightly. "Why did you do it, Gage?"

"I wanted to."

"Why?"

"For Joseph and the rest of the kids. I'm sorry, Merry, I have to go." With that, he hung up.

She scrunched her eyes shut, clamping down her rising anger. Of course the kids needed that van; it didn't matter why he did it. Joseph loved it, and the others would be in heaven riding around in it. They could even start doing pickups of the students so the parents wouldn't have to get them to the center. It was perfect, and she almost hated Gage for doing it. But a part of her could admit that hate wasn't even in the picture. *Hate* Gage Carson? She had to be joking.

THE GENERAL MEETING for the review of the final version of the contract for the entertainment complex, was set for the first day of May at two in the afternoon. In the notice that Merry received, it listed the speakers, including people from the town council, the gaming commission and included representatives of the contract's recipient, Carson Construction and Architecture. However, on that long list, the only name she really saw was Gage Carson.

Obviously, he'd be there, stupid to think the head of it all wouldn't be. She wasn't sure about going to the meeting at all. Gage had been back in town twice since the van fiasco, and she'd made no attempt to contact him. She didn't ask anyone about him, either, not Moses or the kids or his family. The red van was in full use, and, if the circumstances of its donation had been different, Merry would be thrilled. She was happy, but there was an edge to all of it because of Gage.

On the day before the scheduled town meeting Mary was sitting in her office after everyone had left and stared out the windows. In her sights were the majestic mountains far off in the distance. Marsala had been with her earlier and pointed out the mountain where Merry and Gage had crash landed. A prominent rise, so far off and so high in the heavens. A place out of time.

She abruptly pushed those thoughts out of her mind, and was shocked to find Erin silently standing in the doorway. Merry got up and went over to the tiny girl to welcome her. "What are you still doing here? Aren't you supposed to be on the van by now?" Merry didn't see anyone coming up behind Erin, looking for her.

Erin shrugged. She stared at the floor.

"What is it?" Merry asked softly.

The child glanced up at her. "Mr. Gage," was all she said.

"What about Mr. Gage?"

Erin turned to walk away.

Merry caught her by her arm and felt a trembling in the girl. "Erin, please, what about Mr. Gage?"

The girl's blue eyes met hers and she didn't miss the glimmer of unshed tears in them. "He's…" she started in a whisper. "He's gone."

"What?"

"Gone."

"No, he's in town." Merry was totally confused by this. "Was he here today? Did you see him?"

A shake of the child's head sent her loose hair tumbling around her shoulders.

"If he did leave, he'll be back. He's got work to do here. I promise, he'll be back."

Words meant to comfort the child did the opposite. Erin's face screwed up with misery and she threw herself into Merry's arms. She hugged the child tightly, desperate to comfort her. "Honey, please, it's okay."

Without warning, Erin shoved back. Her delicate hands were balled into fists, and when she spoke, she said more than she'd spoken in the six months since Merry had met her at the center.

"No," she persisted. "No, he won't. Mr. Gage won't come back. You went away and you didn't come back, and you promised, too!"

"But I did come back," Merry said, trying

to speak in a soothing tone. "I did. I'm here, and I'm never going away again."

"Mr. Gage said he would come and see us, but he won't!"

Merry moved closer to the child, tentatively touched her shoulder. "If Mr. Gage said he'd be here, he will be. He always keeps his promises."

Erin studied Merry intently, and then as suddenly as the emotional storm had come, it faded. Merry could feel the tension leaving the child's body. "Okay, Miss Merry."

"Sweetie, he will be back." She gently pulled Erin into a hug, wishing she could protect the child from every kind of sadness and fear and disappointment.

No one could do that, though. All Merry and the staff could do was to just be there for her when she needed them.

Merry stood with the girl still in her arms. "Come on, Erin. I'll carry you down to the van."

Erin buried her face in Merry's neck, and never saw the woman's tears, for which Merry was thankful. The last thing she wanted to do was upset the young girl all over again.

Merry opted to call it a day after first making sure Erin was off home safely.

As she opened the front door of her Victorian, her cell rang. She glanced at the caller ID and instantly recognized the number. She swung the door shut with a cracking thud, looked back at the cell phone ringing in her hand, then laid it on the kitchen counter.

She started dinner and was checking through her mail when the phone rang for the fifth time. Finally, she lifted the cell from the counter and hit the talk button. "Yes?"

A throaty female voice asked, "May I speak to Miss Merry Brenner, please?"

"Speaking."

"Hello, I'm Myra Lane, executive assistant to Mr. Carson. He asked me to contact you to let you know we have sent an overnight packet to you with the final agreement for the project in Wolf Lake and that you should have it today."

"Why did he ask you to do that?"

"I don't know. Mr. Carson simply asked me to," the woman said evenly. Merry thanked her and hung up. After Erin's outburst, she wasn't capable of dealing with anything else this evening. She poked through the rest of the stack of mail she'd been looking at and found the large brown envelope amidst her bills and circulars.

She stared at the envelope, and then ignored it. She wouldn't read it. She didn't want to see it all down in black and white. Willie G. and the others in opposition would be at the scheduled town meeting, intent on being heard; they could fight it out with the others. She was too weary to even think about it.

That night, Merry's sleep was torn apart by strange, random dreams. Dreams of Erin, the kids, the crash landing, the fear, the hope, and Gage woven through them all. She came abruptly awake just before dawn, shaking and feeling so alone that she could barely breathe.

She clasped her knees to her chest, pressed her forehead to them and closed her eyes tightly. Erin's accusation about her not keeping her promise, not coming back when she'd said she would, mixed in with Gage making the bulletin board and giving the center the van.

He always keeps his promises.

She threw back the covers, went downstairs and found the envelope still sitting by the stack of mail she hadn't opened. She held it for a long moment, then went back upstairs and got into bed, leaning back against the headboard as she ripped the seal.

A packet of papers fell out, three bound

bundles of neatly typed pages. She started to read, flipping past a lot of legal jargon, all about costs, overrides, estimates, an agreement with all the concerned parties. It appeared to be just like any other sort of standard business agreement. Then she picked up the last bundle, reading that it was an addendum to the original agreement, to "be executed in full, with all good faith, before the product could be deemed complete and final payments were made."

As she went farther, she felt as if she had been thrust into a surreal place where word for word, her world was being straightened after it had been tilted on its axis for far too long. *Her world.* And she knew what she had to do.

MERRY LEFT THE center promptly at noon the next day. She went home, dressed in a blue silk shirt, black slacks and walking shoes, and showed up at the meeting in the high school multipurpose room a half hour early. Still, she almost didn't get a seat. The place was packed with townspeople, and a stage had been set up at the front of the room with a long table and seven chairs. Name signs fronted each chair. Gage Carson's card was at the far end of the table, which seemed off to Merry. She'd thought he'd be at the center of the dignitaries who were going to speak.

Sitting by Willie G., she waited, her nerves getting worse with each passing minute. Sleep had been impossible after she'd read the contract, and she was impatient to get on with this meeting.

As if on cue, six men and one woman arrived together and took their places at the table. Her gaze went directly to Gage. In casual clothes, a chambray shirt, jeans and boots, he looked nothing like the power behind the pending multimillion dollar deal. She admired that, in fact, there was a lot about him that she admired.

The mayor stood first and introduced everyone to the crowd with a smattering of applause, until it came to Gage. The boos started softly, and then rose as he stood and went to the podium.

Someone stood up and hollered, "Traitor!" Another man shot to his feet and yelled, "Turncoat!" Merry never took her eyes off of Gage. He didn't flinch, didn't blink, just stood there until the voices tapered off. "Now, you here all know me, for better or worse, and you know this is my home. I wouldn't do anything to harm it."

The boos roared to a crescendo, and Gage waited again, seemingly unmoved by the outburst, but Merry held on to that one word—home. Gage motioned to a man near him, a blond-haired fellow with a weightlifter's body under a well-cut gray suit. "Mr. Tarkington Davis, my job manager and architect, will go over the plan with all of you," he explained, and then said, "Please, do him the decency of listening to the entire agreement and the latest amendments before you challenge him."

To another chorus of jeers, Merry watched Gage take his chair and sit back as casually as if he was sitting on a front porch watching the river go by. His eyes stayed on the speaker while Merry was staring at him. Without warning, his eyes met her gaze. With a faint nod, he looked away from her, and back to his assistant.

Tark Davis, aka Boom Boom, started to go into the details that Merry had read the previous night. She forced herself to listen, to make sure she'd understood the documents correctly, but her gaze slipped back to Gage, whose eyes never left Tark. After the outline of the main part of the agreement, Tark ended with, "making it work for all residents of the town." The big man paused to make eye contact with the crowd. "We have high hopes that the final amendments will ease some people's concerns. Let me reiterate, our company will do everything it can to make this important project amenable to all and we will endeavor to listen to any concerns you might have. Our legal counsel, Moss, Moss and Creighton, can be reached at any time about concerns and solutions.

"The most important amendment is that the gambling will be self-contained within yet still separate from the rest of the complex that is to be relocated to a parcel of ground between Wolf Lake and the highway. The hotels will be farther from the heart of town, impeding less of the local industries. All and any designs for the complex will fit in with the land and nature of the heritage around it, honoring the feel and core of Wolf Lake and the dream of the founding fathers."

Someone called out, "How do we know you're going to do all of that? Changing the location has to be expensive!"

Tark looked in the direction of the voice. "We have a clause included in the contract for full restitution, no matter how far along the project is, if it does not comply with every provision by the strictest interpretation. The contract for the land is in place as a straight exchange for the past location." He glanced around the quiet crowd and kept going.

"Upon awarding our company the project, our firm and its architectural division, accepted the input from all parties—what they wanted, what they didn't want and what could be done. Then we wrote those worthy provisions into the contract by means of the amendments." He paused then said, "We require that a percentage of the money for the project that would have been used for a more elaborate complex, be put in a special fund that will support the addition of education and medical research resources.

"That will expand the children's wing of the hospital, and the schools. There will also be a special grant for the support of children with developmental problems, namely an expansion of the Family Care Center."

Merry must have stirred or said something because Willie G. looked at her. "Are you okay?"

"Yes, yes," she said quickly, not wanting to miss any of what Tark was saying.

"Another provision is that a local resident

and staff person of the Family Care Center, Ms Merry Brenner, be asked to set up an advisory committee to oversee that expansion to protect the interests of the community and the children."

She could barely breathe as she realized she had read everything correctly—*everything*. Tark went on, "There has been a pledge from the Carson family to match any and all donations made to a fund being set up for special education, art development and on-site housing for native children. Merry didn't move.

It was true.

The plan, as it was now laid out, would make the pluses from the development far outweigh any potential losses. And Gage did it. All of it. She knew that without having to ask anyone.

She looked toward him, but he was gone. His chair was empty. Someone called out, "And we should believe all this because...?"

Before Tark could answer, Merry was on her feet, "Because Gage Carson gave his word, and his word is gold."

People murmured, shifting in their seats to see her as she spoke. She took a breath and continued. Well, she'd come this far.

"This is his doing, his modifications, his

example of how much he cares about his home." Tears threatened and she knew she had to get out of there. "We're lucky to have him at the helm of this project," she told them and turned to leave.

Willie G. stood, his face a mask of shock. "Are you serious?"

"Life and death serious," she replied and moved past him, ignoring people patting her arm and congratulating her. When she did get outside, there was no one there, only lines and lines of parked vehicles. The large black truck she was particularly looking for was nowhere in sight.

She tried to think where Gage might have gone.

Lark Carson came up beside her. "Merry, I just wanted to tell you how pleased we are to have you on board, and thank you for defending Gage like that."

"Where is he?" she asked, not meaning to be rude, but she had to know, now.

Lark smiled before answering. "He was heading back to the ranch to get ready for his flight later. He has to be going shortly, and actually, he wasn't sure how this would go. He's never been one to sit by."

She had to get to him. She'd walked to the

meeting and she had to get her car. Lark must have figured out what she was thinking because she touched Merry's arm and held out a set of car keys. "Take mine." She pointed out a black SUV.

Merry didn't argue. "Thank you so much," she said. Claiming the keys, she ran.

GAGE TOOK HIS time checking out the new plane, the exact model of the one that he'd flown in with Merry, down to the color. He'd done all he could do about the business in Wolf Lake, and everything he could think to do about Merry. She was lost to him; he knew that by what had happened in the past few weeks, or better yet, what hadn't happened. She didn't want to be around him, or hear from him, and now that the deal was structured to be what he thought was best for both sides, he just wanted to get out of here. But at least, he knew her life would be good. He'd make sure it was, for her and her kids.

He'd concentrate on this project, and his brother. Jack had flat out refused to be legal counsel for the project, and hadn't even shown up at the meeting. Gage wasn't sure what to do for Jack, but he knew he'd do whatever was

necessary to have the "old Jack" back for all
their sakes.

"Hi, there," a female voice said from behind
him. Gage turned to find Merry less than ten
feet from him on the ranch's airstrip.

It was as if time had gone backward and
she was there to beg him for a ride home to
Wolf Lake. He quietly watched her, noticing
the tension in how she stood, and how her
hands were clasped so tightly. And she had
a paleness that he could have sworn wasn't
there before. Her presence was overwhelming for him.

When she didn't say anything else, he
asked, "What are you doing here? I thought
you'd be celebrating with Willie G. and the
others, or demanding more concessions."

She slowly approached him and he saw her
tongue touch her lips before she spoke. "Why
didn't you tell me what you were going to do?"

"I assumed, when I didn't hear from you
after you'd read it, that you still weren't happy
with it. With me."

"I'm sorry. That makes sense."

"So you read it?"

"Yes, I did." She took another step forward.
"I want to thank you for everything, the way
I should have thanked you for the new van. I

know it's all your doing, that you heard what I said about the kids, and changed things to help them as much as possible. And I know that the money wouldn't be there for the new plans without what the complex can take in." She was talking fast, just like that first time she'd asked him for the ride. "I want to, no, I *need* to thank you for caring so much, for listening, for doing what you're doing."

"Moses was in on the changes, too," he admitted, but wouldn't tell her about the arguments.

"I'll have to thank him."

"You're going to lead the advisory panel?"

"Yes, I will, but I need to apologize for what I said to you. I was so wrong."

"How so?" he asked, a bit edgy about what she might say.

"You belong here. You always have."

"Thank you for that," he said. "It means a lot, especially coming from you."

"And you're not the bad guy, either. I probably implied that. I was just so centered on what I thought was right, on what I wanted, that I couldn't see any other alternative. Silly of me."

She looked behind him and her eyes widened. "They fixed the plane?"

"No, it's a new one. The one we had doesn't exist anymore, except for a bit of useless debris, I guess."

"And you're going to fly in this one?"

"I already have. Four flights total." He could see the fear in her eyes, the fear that came from all they'd been through. He reached out to her, and gently pulled her into his arms. She almost sank against him. "It's okay. We made it. We had our miracle," he whispered, wondering if he'd ever have another miracle in his life.

He closed his eyes, fighting to burn the moment into his memory when she said, "I owe you so much."

"No you don't," he said.

Her arms around him tensed and she pressed even closer. "Oh, yes I do. Everything you managed with the complex. You listened to all sides and figured out a solution."

"Hey, that's just good business," he murmured, brushing off her praise. He tried to tell himself her words really didn't mean much to him. As he would have with anyone else. But then another thought formed and the raw truth in it stunned him.

All he wanted was her. She was his everything. And the clarity of his next thought settled into his being.

He loved her. He'd loved her from the first. And the restlessness he'd had since leaving her the last time hadn't come from boredom. It was because she wasn't with him. The sleeplessness was because she wasn't beside him. So, he'd kept moving. But now that wouldn't work. Not when he knew exactly what could cure him.

He needed to tell her all of that, but the words wouldn't come. They stuck in his throat. And he knew a fear that was unlike any fear he'd known before. If he said the words, what if they were all wrong? What if was too late? What if she didn't want any part of him?

An ache built in his stomach, made worse when she drew back and said softly, "I'm so proud of you, really proud. You're making a difference, and even if you can't stay here, you've done so much to protect your home."

Her words demolished whatever wall he'd managed to keep in place. "No, I'm not that altruistic or that much of a civic minded person," he said, hating the way she began moving out of his arms until there was only emptiness. "I did all of that for a purely selfish reason that I didn't even recognize until now."

She looked confused, much the way he'd felt until a moment ago. "Selfish reasons?"

"I wanted to make things right with you, but I didn't know how to do that. The next best thing I could think of was trying to make life easier and better for you."

She placed her hand over his heart. "Gage, all my life I've been so afraid of not belonging, of never having a real home, and that dominated who I was and the choices I made. Then I came back here, and it's wonderful, and the kids are fantastic. I've found a place to be, but since I met you, gradually I've realized that it's not the place, it's really the people. A place is nothing without being with someone you love, someone you truly care about."

He didn't understand. "You've got your kids. Little Erin, especially. And when you meet someone, I know you'll have kids of your own."

She looked pleased. "Yes, I probably will. I've been thinking that I might move forward with my plans to adopt a child."

"Oh?" He wasn't surprised.

"Yes, I've thought about Erin. She has no one, just a foster family that sooner or later will decide that she needs a lot more love and attention than they can give her."

He beamed at her. "Of course you'd adopt her. She's a sweetheart who doesn't think she has anyone, or any place to be. A bit like you used to be."

A sad smile touched her lips. "Maybe I do see a bit of me in her, with no place to be, until I got here, that is. And no one to really love me."

A single tear escaped from the corner of her eye and he acted instinctively, pulling her back to him. "That's not true," he said with a fierceness that he couldn't control. "It's not true."

She pushed away and looked up him. "Why not?"

He met her green eyes and said what he should have said a long time ago. "I love you, Merry Brenner. I love you so much that I just want you with me forever."

Her face brightened. "You're going to stay?"

Gage considered her question, and knew he had only one answer. "I just want to be with you, wherever that is."

Her arms went around his neck and he bent

to meet her lips. The connection was real and complete.

As he drew back from the embrace, he said, "I've been thinking about bringing my office to the area around here, maybe Albuquerque, or Santa Fe? I can work from anywhere because the jobs aren't where my business is based. They're all over the country."

She seemed hesitant to believe him. "Do you mean it?"

"More than anything, but…no matter where I go, this will definitely always be home."

A smile came to her lips, the tear long gone. "You know, I'm not sure about flying again, but sometimes I could go with you, you know, just the short trips. Maybe, I can sort that out after my lesson."

"So you're still going through with that?"

"A deal's a deal. But the most important thing is, I always thought that home had to be *somewhere,* but now I know it's right here, in your arms."

"One last thing?" he asked roughly, his lips close to hers.

"Anything."

"I told you I loved you, but you never once said—"

"I love you, Gage Wolf Carson, with all my heart, and you're my home. Forever."

Gage had lived in Wolf Lake for most of his young life, and always had it to come back to when he needed to. But now it was home to him, really home, and the spot in the world that was his and Merry's.

And he'd been wrong. He did have one more miracle in his life, and he was holding her in his arms.

As if she read his mind, Merry whispered against his lips, "Welcome home."

EPILOGUE

Two months later

GAGE'S HEART LEAPT as he and Erin both ran for Merry as she disembarked from the small plane that had just landed safely on the Carsons' airstrip.

Merry thanked her instructor then turned to them with a brilliant smile. "I did it!" she called out, both arms held straight up in victory.

She'd done it. She'd actually done it.

He and Erin hugged her tightly. So, how did it go?" he asked, loving Merry's radiant face.

The instructor, a friend of Gage's, walked past the group. "A born flyer," he quipped, and kept moving.

Gage kissed her, and scooped up Erin in his arms.

Merry looked at Gage. "Thank you," she said. "I know you have a lot going on with Jack and—"

"Hey, I'm just glad I'm here for him." He brushed at a stray lock of hair that had curled at her chin. "What about you? You said you had a surprise for me, beyond this flying lesson."

"It's going to happen, the adoption," she announced, her green eyes suddenly bright with tears. "Being single and all won't be much of a problem, I don't think, but..."

He winked at Erin and set her down on the ground. He gave Merry another quick kiss. "It won't be a problem," he said. "Believe me."

"I hope you're right," Merry said a bit doubtfully.

"Merry, I love you, and I want you to adopt Erin, but I don't want you to do it alone."

She was suddenly still and focused on him. Waiting.

"I want to be part of it. I want you to marry me." As the words left his mouth he knew he'd never been more honest, more committed in his life.

Merry gazed at him as Erin pressed against his leg, her freckled face turned up, her large eyes going from him to Merry and back to him again. It was as if she knew the importance of that moment for all of them.

"Did you hear me?" he asked, afraid he'd gone too fast.

"Yes," Merry breathed. "Yes."

But she didn't move. "Yes, you heard me or yes, you'll marry me?"

"Yes and yes," she replied, and threw her arms wide open.

He lifted Erin up and drew Merry in with both of them, kissing the little girl, then the woman who would be her mother and his wife.

"Yes, yes, yes," Merry said over and over again between kisses for him and for Erin. "Yes."

Gage hugged them both, never wanting to let them go.

"Another miracle," Merry spoke into his ear.

He felt the tiny girl's arms around his neck, and Merry so close he could almost feel her heartbeat. "Yes, indeed."

Along with so many others…

The construction and planning of the entertainment complex was generating a lot of jobs for the locals of Wolf Lake and in turn was helping a lot of other people as well. There was also Willie G. agreeing, after some persuasion from Gage, to sell the old blue Victorian so Merry would have the place she wanted to make a family. And his brother Jack was verging on a recovery from his grief. He was going to take over their grandfather's ranch and make it live again, just like him.

And all that started here for Gage, with Merry and Erin, his world, his home.

* * * * *

*Don't miss the compelling
conclusion to Mary Anne Wilson's*
THE CARSONS OF WOLF LAKE
*miniseries coming in the fall of
2014 from Harlequin Heartwarming!*

REQUEST YOUR FREE BOOKS!

2 FREE INSPIRATIONAL NOVELS
PLUS 2
FREE
MYSTERY GIFTS

Love Inspired

REQUEST YOUR FREE BOOKS!

2 FREE INSPIRATIONAL NOVELS
PLUS 2
FREE
MYSTERY GIFTS

Love Inspired

HISTORICAL
INSPIRATIONAL HISTORICAL ROMANCE

YES! Please send me 2 FREE Love Inspired® Historical novels and my 2 FREE mystery gifts (gifts are worth about $10). After receiving them, if I don't wish to receive any more books, I can return the shipping statement marked "cancel." If I don't cancel, I will receive 4 brand-new novels every month and be billed just $4.74 per book in the U.S. or $5.24 per book in Canada. That's a savings of at least 21% off the cover price. It's quite a bargain! Shipping and handling is just 50¢ per book in the U.S. and 75¢ per book in Canada.* I understand that accepting the 2 free books and gifts places me under no obligation to buy anything. I can always return a shipment and cancel at any time. Even if I never buy another book, the two free books and gifts are mine to keep forever.

102/302 IDN F5CY

Name	(PLEASE PRINT)	
Address		Apt. #
City	State/Prov.	Zip/Postal Code

Signature (if under 18, a parent or guardian must sign)

Mail to the **Harlequin® Reader Service:**
IN U.S.A.: P.O. Box 1867, Buffalo, NY 14240-1867
IN CANADA: P.O. Box 609, Fort Erie, Ontario L2A 5X3

Want to try two free books from another series?
Call 1-800-873-8635 or visit www.ReaderService.com.

* Terms and prices subject to change without notice. Prices do not include applicable taxes. Sales tax applicable in N.Y. Canadian residents will be charged applicable taxes. Offer not valid in Quebec. This offer is limited to one order per household. Not valid for current subscribers to Love Inspired Historical books. All orders subject to credit approval. Credit or debit balances in a customer's account(s) may be offset by any other outstanding balance owed by or to the customer. Please allow 4 to 6 weeks for delivery. Offer available while quantities last.

Your Privacy—The Harlequin® Reader Service is committed to protecting your privacy. Our Privacy Policy is available online at www.ReaderService.com or upon request from the Harlequin Reader Service.

We make a portion of our mailing list available to reputable third parties that offer products we believe may interest you. If you prefer that we not exchange your name with third parties, or if you wish to clarify or modify your communication preferences, please visit us at www.ReaderService.com/consumerschoice or write to us at Harlequin Reader Service Preference Service, P.O. Box 9062, Buffalo, NY 14269. Include your complete name and address.

ReaderService.com

Manage your account online!

- Review your order history
- Manage your payments
- Update your address

*We've designed
the Harlequin® Reader Service
website just for you.*

Enjoy all the features!

- Reader excerpts from any series
- Respond to mailings and
  special monthly offers
- Discover new series available to you
- Browse the Bonus Bucks catalog
- Share your feedback

Visit us at:
ReaderService.com